STRANGE BODIES ON A STRANGER SHORE

Other books by Ann Copeland

The Golden Thread (1989)
Earthen Vessels (1984)
The Back Room (1979)
At Peace (1978)

STRANGE BODIES ON A STRANGER SHORE

ANN COPELAND

GOOSE LANE

Published by Goose Lane Editions with the assistance of the New Brunswick Department of Municipalities, Culture and Housing and the Canada Council, 1994.

These stories have been published in the following journals or anthologies: "Strange Bodies on a Stranger Shore" and "Rupture" in *Canadian Fiction Magazine*; "Leaving the World" in *American Fiction*; "Find the Story" in *Casements*; "Another Christmas" in *The Fiddlehead*; "Speaking Bodies" and "Seducing Piety" in *Matrix*; "Inheriting" in *Oxford Magazine*; "Lifeline" in *Quarry*; "The Magic Monastery" in *Snapdragon*.

Cover painting "Clothesline" by Gillian Saward, 1977-78. Oil over egg tempera on masonite, 43.2 x 53.4 cm. Reproduced with the permission of Frances Saward, courtesy of the Mendel Art Gallery, Saskatoon.
Book design by Julie Scriver.
Printed and bound in Canada by Imprimerie Gagné.
10 9 8 7 6 5 4 3 2

Canadian Cataloguing in Publication Data

Copeland, Ann. 1932-
    Strange bodies on a stranger shore
    ISBN 0-86492-143-8

I. Title

PS8555.05925S77 1994   C813'.54   C94-950192-1
PR9199.3.C647S77 1994

Goose Lane Editions
469 King Street
Fredericton, NB
CANADA E3B 1E5

CONTENTS

These stories are for Andrew Edward Furtwangler

STRANGE BODIES
ON A STRANGER SHORE

"Who am I," he said, "to deny a dying woman her last wish?"

It was one of those opaque statements he excels at, one that could mean several things: I'll humor her, you. What do I, a mere nineteen, know about such things? This is your baby, not mine. And so on. How did he manage to sound patronizing, arch, ironic, all at once?

My son is hard to read.

I took him at his word.

"I'll wait in the car," he said. Clear unambiguous statement.

The car sat beneath a spreading elm outside the convent door. After the steaming asphalt and thronging sidewalks of Manhattan, the broad shade swallowing our gleaming car came like wet cloth to hot flesh. At last a breeze had come up. A cooling down. We'd barely spoken since we pulled out of Manhattan an hour earlier, not sorry for once to leave that gritty glamour. Mid-July. Ninety-eight degrees Fahrenheit in the shade. Who needs it? When I extracted myself from the driver's seat, my back and thighs stuck to the upholstery.

At last, after a year of hearing about her, I'd met Peter's girlfriend, tromped with them both down to the Village, found a chic outdoor restaurant with sophisticated waiters in black and white. This was a Meet My Mother visit, but he was too quiet.

We sat beneath a green and white striped awning nibbling and chatting. She, a vegetarian, daintily consumed her cold pasta salad while I, unenlightened, shamelessly savored my beef tips and lemon-asparagus. Our fine china plates and heavy silver cutlery sat on a thick white tablecloth. A tiny bouquet of fresh daisies and some small purple flower decorated the center of our table. We ordered wine. Peter watched me observe her, contributed little, smoked constantly. He'd taken the train down from upstate New York where he had a summer job waiting on tables. They hadn't seen each other since the end of freshman year, eight weeks ago.

Afterward, I bailed out and hiked alone back up to the New York Public Library, found myself an abandoned metal chair, dragged it to a quiet spot on the outside level facing Fifth Avenue where I could sit, sun burning the back of my neck, and play at reading someone's cast-off Sunday *Times*, all the while trying to ignore ragpickers browsing through nearby trashbins. One of them, a girl of about sixteen with a drained expression and lank dark hair, disturbed me. She wore a pale pink T- shirt that hung almost to her knees. One sleeve had been ripped out at the shoulder. Beneath the shirt, her pale scabby legs were bare and dirty. Around one wrist what looked like strands of colored cord were coiled. I watched her extract a bashed-in carton of something (apple juice? — juice of some kind), carefully press it into shape, tip back her head, and pour the contents down her throat. Finished, she walked over to the trash bin nearest me and threw in the carton, passing within inches but never looking at me. Her feet, caked with dirt, were in what we called flip-flops. As she brushed by me, I felt I didn't exist.

Now Peter and I were at last on our way back to Connecticut to visit my mother. First, we had this slight detour to navigate.

I pressed the convent doorbell. Almost instantly, I heard steps inside. The door opened on the smiling face of a small middleaged woman in light blue.

I introduced myself.

"Yes, yes, of course." She opened the door wider and I stepped into the cool light hallway.

Did I know her? No more black and white. No more veil. Sister Marion, she told me, was her name. She didn't seem to know me. Or perhaps she was just discreet. She had a round, pink, overly powdered face, and a touch of pink lipstick brightened her small round mouth. Tiny pearl earrings adorned her pierced ear lobes. Her hair looked freshly done, soft waves of white framing that unlined forehead. She looked too cool, too tidy for such a blazingly hot evening.

"I'm sorry to bother you at seven in the evening, but Mother Theodore wanted to see me," I apologized. "I know she's very ill. This morning I spent a couple of hours at the college reunion. Sister Gertrude happened to see me there and brought me a message that Mother Theodore was . . . dying. Someone had told her I might be at the reunion and she asked if there was any way she could see me. Something was bothering her and — " *Was I betraying a confidence?*

"Yes, yes, of course. " A plain pewter cross on a silver chain rested on the gentle valley between her breasts. "If you'd just wait here a moment," she motioned me to the right, through a doorway and into a small parlor, "I'll see."

What mysterious cubbyhole in the brain center secretes a sense of place, stashes it away to resurrect it alive and well, thank you, decades and lives later? Over thirty years later! No madeleine for me, no sweet taste to elicit memories of sweetness past; instead, the familiar bland austerity of an updated convent parlor to elicit, even now, something timeless, lost, lived. How could this blank faceless room, so blatantly tidy, work so powerfully to shut down a part of me deep inside — a part I couldn't ever name but always knew if it was dead or alive, a part I'd felt to be so throbbingly alive just two hours before in the raging wilderness of a hot New York City.

An icon of Mary hung on one wall. It looked like something they'd burn holy candles in front of in Ukraine. Mary's skin, olive-golden, her eyes dark and fathomless, her expression exotic, luminous and opaque. How did art manage to illumine such contradictions, I wondered? No overfed complacent Madonna here. No barebottomed cherubs. Above the small telephone table (pale pink touchtone phone) hung the familiar homely face of Pope John XXIII. Opposite the small couch, which was upholstered in peach tweed, sat one easy chair done in a color my mother might have called eggshell. A handsome hammered crucifix of an ascetic but definitely triumphant Christ dominated the wall above the couch. No pastel sappy art here. Nothing garish. No gentle Jesus in burnished light, his smooth face offering comfort, solace, peace. None of that knocking on the door, a lamp in his hand. Even in my day, the Order had prided itself on good taste. The days, years, centuries of heavy dark furniture, mitred cardinals, solemn-eyed bishops, transfixed stigmatic saints staring down from heavy gold frames: gone. The decor had become if not all sweetness, at least lighter.

I peeked out through sheer curtains at Peter, not twenty-five feet away, slouched in the car. It reassured me to see him, somehow. The lug. Sun glasses off. Eyes shut. A small mottled cat leapt onto the hood of the car as I watched, and I restrained the urge to bang on the parlor window, wave at Peter to shoo those claws off my metal.

"Mother Theodore will see you now. Please come this way."

This way meant down a short linoleumed hallway past the large pastel parlor with its mammoth oriental rug and closed grand piano to the elevator. Where was everybody? The hallway, the parlor, the whole place felt cool and empty. They should be somewhere talking. Recreating. It was about that time of night, if they still kept to the old schedule at all.

Sister Marion's hair must be naturally curly, I thought, as I followed that head, those broad blue shoulders, then stood beside her for the elevator. The forehead appeared so untroubled. I knew better. She might have witnessed horrors. She might have tended elderly cancer-ridden nuns, praying by them to their last strangled gasp. She might have mopped up dribbled egg from the bibs of idiots. She might have taught Sunday school, sowing the seed on good ground only to watch its fruits carelessly tossed away. She might be in love with the confessor. She wasn't telling.

The elevator arrived, she pushed back the door, followed me in, and we ascended in silence to the second floor.

"Mother Theodore is very glad you came," she murmured as she opened the gate.

I never lived in this particular convent. Friends did, including one I see now, all these years later, as we howl our way through raising teenagers, and pick our soul-conditioned paths through the mine fields of this last decade of the century. Attached to this convent is a still flourishing girls' academy, no mean feat in years of pressure toward co-ed everything. Most of the students go on to good colleges. Many will marry rich men. The principal, of my vintage and a classicist by training, offers elementary Greek for students motivated to arrive at school by seven o'clock in the morning. Last year she had twenty takers. I learned this just yesterday during my few hours at my thirty-fifth reunion, in the Order's one college, across town.

Sister Marion motioned me off the elevator. "If you'll just wait here a moment, I'll make sure she's ready," she whispered, and disappeared down the hallway, around a bend.

Into Manhattan I had worn a pink and purple sundress with a halter top, and sandals. Peter had travelled light, bringing only the clothes on his back for this visit to his grandmother, so recently sprung from a convalescent home for the second time and now back in her own house waiting for the knee to mend. We'll spend the night there together. Tomorrow he'll take the train back to work, while I stay on for a few more days.

It had been a day for bared flesh, a day to leave off whatever you could. Standing in the second floor corridor now, I felt grit between my toes. Perspiration had dried on my bare shoulders and arms and left the skin clammy. It felt as if something alive were moving gently over me, half caress, half threat. I thought of an odd fact spouted at the dinner table long ago when Peter was enthraled with ninth grade science. "Worms, Mom, do you know how they breathe?" I was probably worrying through a white sauce. "No, how?" "They breathe all over their skin." That's it, I thought. Something's breathing all over my skin. An hour ago I'd felt too covered. Now, alone, in the silent white corridor on the silent second floor of this convent in White Plains, New York, I felt unacceptably bare.

Why did she want to see me? What, after all these years, could possibly still be bothering her?

Over thirty years had passed since I stood outside her door, hot and awkward in my long black serge and celluloid collar and cuffs, holding a ratty postulant's veil in my nervous fingers from which I'd scrupulously removed all trace of nail polish just the night before. I knocked as I'd been instructed by the earnest novice, Sister Thomas, who had met us at the novitiate door half an hour earlier, shown my parents into the parlor with other anxious parents, ushered me upstairs, whisked away my secular dress in a brown paper bag, helped me into my long black postulant's habit, and directed me, in a tone I would later know as the silence tone, to the novice mistress's office door with the instructions: "We call her Our Mother. And kneel when you talk to her, Sister."

Who was this "Sister" she was addressing?

A folding screen had been opened out across Our Mother's doorway. As soon as I knocked against the screen, I heard that throaty voice that always sounded as if she were about to choke.

Awkward in my long sleeves, long skirt, stiff black Oxfords — ("We have to wear THESE?" screamed my friend Genevieve as we convent-shopped in Manhattan that hot June after graduation) — I pushed back the screen a bit and stepped into the office. A figure in a black habit sat at a desk wedged in sideways at the end of the narrow booklined room. "Sister Claire?" How did she know? We'd never met.

As I knelt, I tangled my big feet in the hem of my long skirt. Almost falling over, I managed to extend one arm and thrust the black veil toward her as I went down, landing on my knees, my free arm reaching for the floor to brace myself. She'd turned sideways in her chair to face me and, once I righted myself, she fluffed out the ugly net veil with its ruffled elastic headband, reached over and set it on my head. During this procedure I kept my eyes down as I'd been instructed. I felt her having a little difficulty stabilizing the veil's elastic band in back, beneath my cut-short hair. ("Do they shave your head?" friends had asked. "Surely they're too civilized," I'd said, hoping it was true. "This isn't the Middle Ages." It turned out I was right.) As I reached up a tentative hand to help her, my celluloid cuff caught on the net of the veil, then broke free. I glanced up quickly. Mother Theodore remained unsmiling.

Then, my veil securely in place, she leaned forward, raised one hand and made the sign of the cross on my brow, her fingers light and cool against my hot forehead.

"You may go join your family now, Sister. Matins will be at

five o'clock. No picture-taking is allowed today. Be sure to tell your family that."

She turned back to whatever she was doing at her desk. What on earth was Matins?

I stumbled out — awkward, embarrassed and disappointed. Was nothing more to be made of this life-altering moment?

I carried from that office a sense of Mother Theodore, Our Mother, engraved on my heart, an impression later incidents would confirm and deepen: A woman of few words. A woman of mystery about whose background we knew nothing. A woman whose extraordinary self-possession made you feel verbose, awkward, vaguely suspect, incurably frivolous. A woman, it would turn out, of refined intellect. Surprisingly, a woman of wit. To a nervous postulant who confessed she had not dusted the library chairs that morning, Mother Theodore replied drily, "I believe they've been dusted notwithstanding, Sister." A woman of imagination who remarked casually one evening on a recreation walk down the path toward the farm gate, "How do we know God didn't become incarnate another way on another planet? Maybe the Holy Ghost did." In those days that member of the Trinity was still a ghost. A woman who could betray remarkable depths of feeling. On bitterly cold winter mornings she carried a tub of water into the chapel sacristy to bathe the frostbitten feet of the sandalled Capuchin who walked through snow to offer our morning Mass. At Christmas she took simple delight in a resplendently decorated Christmas tree and the singing of carols, the wonder of postulants experiencing their first convent Christmas. During Lent she sometimes made us lesser beings feel uncomfortable by taking her breakfast kneeling. Through it all, those two and a half years of learning how to be a religious, while your own knees were aching and you dozed at prayer, you had the sense that her thoroughly chastised flesh enclosed a spirit soaring free. Surely she was in touch with God.

Still, a woman of no frills. No refreshments on that tormentingly hot day for parents who had driven hours to deliver their virginal daughters to the welcoming arms of Holy Mother Church. No cup of water in His name, or any other. No words of encouragement. Clothes of the Old Man returned to heavy-hearted parents in a plain paper bag. Picture-taking strictly forbidden. Nothing sentimental. A straightforward no-nonsense initiation of daughters into the highest vocation to which a Catholic young woman — these were the fifties, remember — could aspire. The message was clear: Casting off the Old Man and putting on the New meant business.

What infantile sense of poetic justice makes me carry in my wallet today a picture of myself and another postulant, the same who laughs with me through motherhood now, as we stood stripped of color, swathed in pre-synthetic black, smiling valiantly at her father who sneaked the photo of his eldest, donated daughter, and thus put one over on Mother Church. And Mother Theodore.

Why did the first superior I'd ever had, my old novice mistress, want to see me after all these years? She was dying. If anyone should be ready, she should.

Sister Marion reappeared.

"Mother Theodore will see you now." The silence tone.

Acutely conscious of my fuchsia toe nails, I followed her thick ankles and low sensible black shoes down the gleaming hallway. Doors on our left and right were open. As we passed, I could see neatly made beds with white spreads, clean windows with white shades. Once, I would not have been allowed up here. I would have been kept downstairs in the parlor, the proper distance for seculars, permitted only to send up a greeting. "Unless you hate brother and sister and mother and father in my name, you are not worthy of the Kingdom of Heaven." Harsh words. "Who are my mother, my brothers, my sister?" We tried to lose our past. It was good for nothing, so much chaff. "He who putting his hand to the plow looketh back is not fit for the kingdom of God." How earnestly we sought to forget. . . .

The door to her room was open.

She was sitting on her bed, legs hanging over the side. A black bathrobe covered her long white nightgown. A small white veil — nightveil, we called them — covered much of her brown hair. It was tied over her ears and looped around to the back of her neck, peasant style.

Nightveil: a heavily symbolic item for me, that simple piece of white seersucker with its tie strings. As the bell was ringing for a midnight fire drill at the secular university where the Order reluctantly sent me, I stood in my graduate dorm room, considering. Others pounded by in the corridor outside. I held the nightveil in my hand. Wear it? Leave it off? The rest of me was properly covered with the type of white nightgown, black bathrobe and slippers Mother Theodore was wearing now. Standard issue. What suddenly made the nightveil a question? That evening, for some reason, I decided to leave it off, decided to expose to the world hair unevenly cut and already turning gray. On the fire escape I met the slim graduate student whom Peter would one day call Dad. Beneath a crescent moon and winking stars we stood there talking as the others filed past us back into the dorm. As we talked I grew acutely conscious of a breeze ruffling my hair, lifting it from the back of my neck, a sensation until then quite forgotten, conscious also of mere seersucker separating my entire body from the touch of warm night wind. It seemed, as we stood there, that the flimsiest partition, tissue thin, separated me from some other life, a life I already yearned inchoately to touch.

Mother Theodore's hands, those long, slim fingers I had always thought artistic, rested on her lap. Even near death, she had that composure, that self control. Black slippers covered her pale feet. Did Sister Marion get her put together?

She might die tomorrow.

"I'm glad to see you," she half whispered in that strangled voice.

Could she have had cancer of the throat all those years? Suffering it nobly, without complaint, as she gave us memorable conferences on the spiritual life, notes written on the back of used envelopes in the name of religious poverty?

I kissed her cool smooth cheek. Unthinkable act. This was the time for unthinkable acts. As I bent over her, I glimpsed a black rosary folded inside one hand. She made no sign of the cross on my brow.

"You look wonderful," she said, eyeing my brashly bare sundress. I found no hint of irony in her words. "It's very hot outside?"

"Yes, Mother."

Was she in excruciating pain? Suppressing agonies? There was no sign. She sat very still, hands clasped over the rosary. I wanted her to tell me what it was like, now on the verge. Did she see beyond? Could she give me a glimpse?

"I've been disturbed," she said.

Don't speak, it's too much, you're in pain, I longed to say.

"Because I owe you an apology," she went on. "You remember when you came back years ago to visit once at the college?" I nodded. Years ago, over fifteen years. The boulder in my throat choked me. "I was there that summer and you had made an appointment to see me." I nodded. "I was eager to see you after all those years. I hadn't seen you since you'd left the novitiate, though I'd heard about your studies, your teaching. I knew, too, that you had some . . . difficulties. I waited and waited over in the convent. And . . . you never came at all that day." I nodded, remembering an afternoon long since forgotten. Shouldn't her mind be on other things? Not the past. The *future.* "I was furious," she said, her voice suddenly cracking.

"Should I get you some water?" My own voice sounding like a stranger's. A pitcher of ice water stood on the small table by her bed.

"No, I'll be fine." She paused. Not a muscle moved. Over her bed hung a black crucifix, the white plaster body on it tortured into a familiar position, almost graceful, head down as if resting on the collar bone. "I was so angry," she continued. "And then you wrote to me after you went home. You wrote and apologized." She took a deep breath, lifted one hand slightly, let the black beads slip into the other like a string of precious black pearls. Then she folded her hands again, hiding the beads.

"I felt very bad," I murmured. I wanted out, down the highway, radio blaring, Peter making his ironic cracks. Anything, anything. I wanted fresh air, hot or not. "I knew I'd broken an appointment, Mother. I wouldn't usually do that. But — "

"You wrote and explained," she said again.

The details came back as through a moving mist.

"And . . . and you apologized. You asked my forgiveness. I never answered you."

This is it? This the absurd speck in her own eye she wishes to cast out? Against the beam in mine?

"I want to ask your forgiveness now," she said.

Oh pain. Oh life. The woman was about to push through

the veil, pass over to the other side. She was making her peace. If at the altar you remember you have anything against a brother (something like that), first make your peace . . .

She should be spared this absurd pain.

I rose from the small hard chair someone had set by the side of the bed. I leaned forward, wrapped my arms around this woman of my past. This holy unreachable woman. I hugged her. It wasn't easy.

"There's no problem," I said. How could I reassure her? "I felt terrible afterward, Mother. I just saw the organ there that day, and . . . it had been so long . . . and I wanted to touch it . . . I just wanted to make that music again in that place. I wanted to feel the instrument beneath my hands . . . I can't explain it."

I felt her bones as I spoke. Fragile mortified bones. Strong chastised bones.

Touch — the forbidden word. Forbidden act. Did she realize there was a piano in the novitiate parlor I lusted to touch for two and a half years? That as I dusted its keys daily, I could taste desire, the urge to let go, to belt out in that quiet cloister of earnest virginity a dynamite boogie woogie, a jazzy "Tea for Two," or a passionate Chopin scherzo? Instead, day after day, I dusted the ivories and left them silent, closed the lid, and moved on to the rungs of the heavy mahogany chairs, the sills of the leaded casement windows.

Yet it was she who said one day, after I'd survived three months, "You know how to play the piano, Sister. You could learn how to play the organ. Practise it every day for twenty minutes. You could play it at Christmas." Gradually I learned how to make my feet find the pedals as my fingers again touched familiar keys. My organ playing would serve the community, enhance the liturgy. It was justified, no mere indulgence.

As I put my arms around Mother Theodore now, I felt her

flesh beneath my fingers, a surprising amount of it wrapped around those cancerous bones.

In three days she would be dead.

I held her a moment, then turned to leave.

"Pray for me, Sister," she whispered.

I nodded blindly.

Nothing more was required.

A woman of no frills.

Sister Marion and I took the elevator back downstairs.

"Where is everyone?" I asked her.

"They're showing a movie tonight, over in the school," she said.

"There's a TV with a good screen over there and that's where the VCR is. I'm over here because it was my night for portress duty."

Portress duty. Some of the vocabulary had remained unchanged.

The elevator door opened. Laughter.

We turned left, followed the sound.

There he was — black pony tail, half-grown moustache, tie-dyed T shirt, khaki shorts, hairy legs, sandals: the whole nineteen-year-old body, flesh of my flesh. Drinking Coke and laughing with a nun. Solitary male in the convent refectory, surrounded by spotless formica, he sat at a table, his legs crossed, one leg swinging jauntily as he talked. Not smoking, thank God.

We paused in the doorway. "That's your son?" said Sister Marion.

How did she know? Any resemblance is purely coincidental.

"Hi, Mom." He was on his feet, one last swig of Coke, then loping over to us.

"You're Peter's Mom?" said the young nun, a bright eyed redhead, thirtyish, in a navy cotton sailor dress. Instead of a pewter cross she wore a discreet symbolic pin high over her left breast.

We shook hands. Firm grip. "I'm Sister Barbara. I thought your son must be hot out there so I invited him in for a cold drink."

She laughed. "I was attracted by his earring."

A small silver peace symbol dangled from his left ear.

"How was it?" he says, as we pull away from the shade of the tree, he at the wheel, evidently refreshed.

"Fine."

We decide to take the Merritt Parkway back to Connecticut, an old road that in my college days had a certain charm: flowering trees and shrubs, lots of dogwood in spring, blazing maples in fall, handsome curved stone overpasses. All this still remains, but the Merritt is less efficient now than Route 84, which we're avoiding since neither of us feels like coping with transports.

"She's really dying?"

"So they say. But she's remarkable."

"She knew you?"

"Yes."

He never met her, and on that fact hinges the whole story which, once we're safely on the parkway, I decide to tell him.

Peter was almost three. I wanted to show him off. He could walk, he could talk, say bright things even, he could still be tucked into a cute little navy blue outfit with a red and white fire truck appliqued on its bib. He wore blue and white striped baby sneakers and white socks. He had a summer cap with a small peak. He was a knockout.

I try to be judicious, selective, as we drive along. I leave out the cornier details, the appliqued sunsuit for example. He lights another cigarette. I keep the window open. Air rushing past and around us is still hot, though it's already past eight-thirty and the evening has mellowed to a golden gray-blue. My skin is no longer crawling. My throat is no longer clogged.

"It was my first trip back," I say to that inscrutable profile as I watch smoke go down, deep deep down, blackening his youthful lungs. "For a long time I didn't want to go back. The whole idea repelled me. I'd moved so far away, in every sense. I — "

I could tell him, oh I could tell him, but what's the point? Could tell him how I wanted to return whole, intact, fashionable and fertile, dammit. Yes, fertile. Loved. Alive in the flesh as well as the spirit. In good shape, with a tan. Making visible progress through my new — distanced, married, mothering — life. Certified by an Ivy League institution to have an ample supply of brains.

"So I brought you," I tell him now, "the only grandson — and a late one at that — to visit your grandmother for four brief days. Going back home was difficult for me."

He eyes me with great understanding.

"On our third day there, Granny proposed a trip back to the college to see old friends and show you off. I welcomed it."

These are the details I leave out:

I considered carefully what to wear. I settled on a brightly flowered cotton skirt. Color was essential for return to that black and white world, no longer black and white, of course, but still in my imagination colorless, bland, virginal. A shocking pink tank top. Bare legs. Sandals. "You're going to wear that?" my mother asked, donning her own new teal blue linen summer suit. "Are you wearing stockings?"

"It's 1972, Mother," I answered. "And it's over ninety out-side." Then, to distract, "Doesn't Peter look cute?"

"I hope he never changes," said Mother, picking out a bone-colored purse to match her shoes. "He's such a dear little boy."

Second detail I leave out: Part of her motivation for want-ing to go back and visit the nuns at my college was the need to conquer shame. Her shame. I knew it and resented it. A few months after I'd walked out of that convent, she called me at the university to tell me she'd almost met some old nun friends of mine when she was in New York City. "I saw them coming toward me," she said, "and I didn't know what to do." I was coping with my own transition, newly returned to my campus in technicolor. "There was a small church right there," she said, "so I ducked inside to avoid them."

As I listened, furious, I wondered: Why hadn't she run right up to them and shouted, "I'm proud of her, glad she did it. She's made a wise choice. I'm behind her all the way."

Why did *she* feel betrayed?

I said none of that. We'd been trained in restraint, and it took.

"We had about three hours on campus," I continue to that dear little boy behind the wheel. "Does this bore you?"

"Not at all."

Opaqueness again. Is he simply humoring me? Is he here in body only, but still in his imagination pounding the streets of Manhattan with Laurie? She was attractive, his girlfriend, a long drink of water, full-bosomed in a spandex body suit (no bra), covered (sort of) by a transparent pastel skirt. I stood at the top of the main steps inside Grand Central looking down at harried and hot commuters, prowling panhandlers. Peter stopped to give one of them something. "I can't resist," he said later. "I'm a pushover." When the slim tanned girl came loping in from her train, looked around, spotted Peter over at the Information Booth, waved and went toward him, when I saw how comfortably he kissed her, threw an arm across her shoulders and turned to look up and around for his discreetly distanced, subsidizing mother, I envied that comfortable easy relationship, that bodily freedom.

"Want to hear the rest?"

"Of course I want to hear the rest, Mom. Why do you keep asking? After all, it's MY history." He cuts in close to the fence on the left side of the parkway as he negotiates past a sleek navy blue Cadillac. Windows closed. Airtight. The driver has heavy glasses, a bald head, a chin that slopes down into his neck. Beside him a white-haired woman is opening and shutting her mouth.

"I'd called ahead," I go on. "We drove down to campus in the morning. We were to meet an old friend, one of my college teachers, in the small house she and a few other nuns lived in at the edge of campus. The old convent had been condemned. I was eager for you to see that old building, though. It had been an inn in the nineteenth century, Charles Dickens stopped there, it was built like a castle, replete with turrets. I thought you'd be fascinated."

"Was I?"

"You were bored silly. But you did like the attention you got from the nuns. Lots of it. We sat in the yard outside a house called St. Cecilia's."

In the twenties and thirties, slowly buying up property around the Ladies School soon to become a college, the Order had also bought some of the small frame houses. Now, with the old convent condemned and the new post-sixties push toward having nuns live in smaller, "more human" groups, many able-bodied nuns opted to live at the edge of campus in small houses. A new convent had been built on campus and it housed many of the elderly.

He doesn't need to know all this.

"We sat out on lawn chairs, Granny, I, and Sister Clarence. She'd taught me philosophy in college. When the Order sent me back to teach there, she became a good friend.

"Granny was worried. 'Do you think he'll be all right over there, Sister?' she kept asking Sister Clarence. You'd begun to dig with a small yellow plastic shovel in the dirt near the lilac bush.

"You know what Granny's like. Sister Clarence told her not to worry. You were just to enjoy yourself.

"It was funny, Peter," I venture. "There in the garden outside that small house, listening to Sister Clarence, I felt it all over again, the ordered life. Up at five, prayers till eight, breakfast, work. . . . Time with community. Time to study. Time to garden . . . "

Peter looks over at me, flicking his cigarette in the ash tray.

"What happened with Mother Theodore?"

The facts, just the facts.

"She'd been in charge of me when I entered the novitiate."

He nods, savvy about such esoterica connected with his mother. "She was austere. I'd never met a nun like her. She spoke not one more word than was necessary. When she knelt in her stall at the rear of chapel with her eyes closed, you had the feeling the building could tumble down around her and she'd still have unbroken contact with God."

"Um."

This bit may interest him. He's tried meditating, Buddhist style, in the manner of his generation. He gave me a book on the subject which I dutifully take down from time to time, then instantly put back as I begin to taste a dryness in my mouth. Some part of Peter seeks the disciplined life. On the other hand, he racks up library fines, his room is a catastrophe, he smokes a pack of godknowswhat a day, and last year he was arrested for speeding through a red light.

"I was terrified of her. She seemed to represent something, oh, I don't know . . . so far beyond, above me . . . "

He puts the car back on cruise control.

"I didn't know Mother Theodore was on campus in the new big convent when Granny and I brought you down that day. I hadn't thought about her in years. After we arrived, Sister Clarence asked if I'd like to see her. What could I say? Of course. The woman had been important in my life. So Sister called over to the convent and made an appointment for two o'clock. That meant we had lunch to get through. They would have given us something to eat there, but Granny and I decided to take you out."

"That Sister Barbara offered me supper," says Peter. "I said no. She was cool."

"You were restless at lunch. A real pain."

"I don't believe it. *Me?*"

"You. We ate at a restaurant down near Long Island Sound. Out back they had a large garden and a wading pool. After we'd eaten, Mother said to me, 'Why don't you go back alone. I'll watch Peter here. He's got that long ride ahead.'"

"But he'll sleep," I said, thinking it mattered that Mother Theodore see you. We'd brought a stroller.

"Your Granny was adamant. She probably wanted time alone with you. She insisted. 'I think it would be better to keep him here.'

"She was worried you'd be cranky, misbehave. So she kept you there."

"Smart Granny."

"I drove back to the college alone. I was just as glad. I hadn't enjoyed the morning one bit. Even showing you off wasn't what I'd thought it would be."

"Thanks."

"Nuns kept coming by and cooing over you, chatting with Granny, then asking me how I was doing. I was ready to leave, but I had this damned appointment with Mother Theodore. At least I was alone.

"I parked the car outside chapel and went in the side door, walked up the stone steps I'd climbed hundreds of times, as an undergraduate and later as a young nun. At the head of the stairs, right in front of me, was a small wooden door. I knew where that led but I wasn't taking it.

"Instead, I went through the large door on my left that led into chapel proper, up front near the altar rail on St. Joseph's side. I looked around. Empty, except for one old lady — a nun? — kneeling up straight in the last pew. She held her bowed head in her hands.

"All of a sudden, I knew what I wanted to do. As I remember now, I barely thought about it. This was simply too good a chance to pass up. Mother Theodore could wait. You can do only so much rummaging around in the past. What had I to say to her? Or she to me? I certainly couldn't imagine that it mattered that much to her. She'd trained hundreds of novices over the years and she'd always seemed to inhabit some other planet, anyhow.

"So I left chapel by the door I'd come in, went out to the small vestibule at the head of the stairs near the holy water font, opened the heavy wooden door into the small transept. It was a dark room where you could sit and watch Mass with a side view of the altar. There were about five pews in there, plus a pipe organ angled so the organist could see into the sanctuary."

"I didn't know you played the organ, Mom. I thought it was only piano."

"I didn't get near a piano for over ten years. It drove me nuts. But if you really love to play, you'll touch whatever keyboard you can get your hands on. In the novitiate Mother Theodore let me play the organ. Later, in the house of studies, the Order gave me a few lessons. After that I was assigned to play the organ in every house."

"So you stayed there and played that day?"

"Yes. I dug into the organ bench, found a few pieces I could sight-read, fake through. I had only about an hour."

I don't tell him how deliberately I ignored ripples of guilt, how cool and reckless delight fanned through my marrow, my bones, my whole body as I threw caution, obligation, responsibility, courtesy to the winds. In the vast emptiness of that familiar chapel I again made music. I longed to play and play. What must that old lady down in back have made of the sudden burst of sound from nowhere? I took air and transformed it. The chapel resounded with Bach, Buxtehude, Purcell, Stanley, Vierne. . . . "Jesu, Joy of Man's Desiring." My feet, tentative at first, then more sure, located the pedals. I'd been away from the organ for over seven years. It felt like a century. Yet it was all there to be tapped, a reservoir of glorious sound I could touch into being, I, a mere visitor stopping by, technicolor wizard of the keyboard, a wand'ring minstrel I, with no community to serve, no liturgy to enhance except the private liturgy of my own spirit. This was more important than showing my child through the convent castle, more important than healing my mother's shame, more important, certainly, than a visit with an old novice mistress who had nothing to say to me. And to whom I had nothing to say.

"Why did you play?" he asks.

It strikes me as an odd question. The answer seems so self-evident. But then, he plays no musical instrument.

I look out at green and yellow branches fluttering in the soft evening wind. It all sounds so simple now. Almost idiotic. It wasn't simple.

"I played because I wanted to."

That was it. I see it with the clarity of revelation — the sureness that guided my feet out of chapel, into the transept, made me roll back the cover of the organ, turn on the switch, set the stops, play. There had been no hesitation. Quite simply, nothing else mattered.

I played for my own pleasure.

I touched the keys, found the pedals, lifted sound from that instrument simply because it pleased me — deeply, thrillingly. Pleasure: immediate, recovered, transcendent, unforgettable.

Peter nods.

"Afterward, when I looked at my watch and saw I'd been at it an hour, I had to go back and get you and Granny. Take you both home. No way I could see Mother Theodore. Somehow, I didn't even want to send her a message. Whatever I'd gone there for, it was over. I left campus that day without seeing anyone else. I waited until I got home and then I wrote her a note, trying to explain. That wasn't easy. And I apologized."

"Were you sorry?"

"I was sorry to hurt her feelings, if I had. I was sorry to be discourteous. I wasn't sorry to have had that hour at the organ."

He looks satisfied.

Two hours later, we are back at my mother's house in New Britain: the same house from which we set out to show off a darling toddler seventeen years ago; the same house from which my parents and I set out to deliver me to another world, another Mother, thirty-five years ago; the same house from which they carried her husband twenty-two years ago, stricken with a stroke from which, mercifully, there was no return.

"How was the reunion?" she asks. The healing hip is cushioned, the slippered foot resting on a needlepoint footstool she must have created — when? Perhaps as a young bride. She has arranged herself with care in her favorite floral chair.

Peter, reading *TV Guide*, has tuned out.

Behind Mother's white hair a cluster of carefully arranged family pictures adorns the top of her dresser. The house is dustless and tidy. She cannot tolerate clutter.

We were later than she'd expected. She'd already put on her nightgown and pink velour bathrobe, taken her pills and settled in her chair when I peeked through the window, about to turn the key in the lock. How had she done it? I'd come from a thousand miles away to help her do such things, ease her for the second time through the transition from convalescent home to real home.

"I was so worried about you," she said. "I said my rosary. After ten o'clock I thought of calling the police."

Echo of my life, theme and sub-theme: Mother's relentless worry. Her anxiety. *You may get sick. You may fall off your bike. You may fall out of the tree. You may get in with the wrong crowd.* As I grew up it hung around my body, my heart, invaded my nervous system like a debilitating virus I could never break through, never shake.

Where does this come from? I used to wonder, resolved not to catch it.

The world was a minefield, traps galore. A jungle, vines stretching to strangle. A faceless threat, masked, armed. *Anything can happen.*

Did she never hear that He hath given angels charge over us to keep us in all our ways? Does she not know the hairs of her head — white and soon to be permed — are all numbered? Does she not believe He marks the sparrow's fall?

"I thought you'd had an accident," she says again, now that we're settled. "I listened to the news to see if they reported an accident on the Merritt."

She eyes Peter. "And did you and Mom have a good day in the City?"

She imagines us strolling up Fifth Avenue, window shopping in her favorite stores — Lord and Taylor, Saks, Bergdoffs — or enjoying tea and ice cream at Schraffts. "I used to love to get into the City."

"It was hot," he says, stretching out bare feet and wriggling his toes. "We stopped at White Plains on the way back."

He eyes me.

I briefly recapitulate my time with Mother Theodore who on that day long ago sent Mother home with a paper bag containing a cast-off periwinkle dress with fake daisies at the waist.

"The reunion," I say, "was okay. Hot. I saw classmates" — I run by her a few names she may remember — "and nuns."

"I was alone almost all day," she says.

"Did Nellie come in to fix your lunch?"

"Nellie came but couldn't stay. Her husband is in the hospital."

"What did you do?"

"I dozed, said my rosary, talked to Loraine and your cousin Stella on the phone, did my exercises. I was worried about you driving into the City alone."

Peter keeps his eyes down.

Worry. What's that?

As we were about to turn off the highway at New Haven, he said to me, "Want a coffee?"

He never drinks coffee.

He pulled off. We went into the Three Judges, a diner that has been there forever.

We slipped into a booth and he ordered a large Pepsi, hamburger and fries. Wolfed them down.

Still in the aftermath of Mother Theodore, I nibbled my Danish. Was she dead already?

"We broke up," he said.

I continued to nibble.

"I saw it coming . . . Laurie's going to Europe next year, I'll be back at school. . ."

How blooming and radiant she'd looked. Not upset. Not worried. Bent to impress me under our green and white awning, telling me how well she'd done in high school. How her English teacher thought she'd be a writer.

She had enormous blue eyes, the kind a romance writer might call limpid, a full-lipped sensuous mouth. Her tanned shoulders were smooth and broad as you might expect of an athletic eighteen year old, a swimmer. But it was the breasts that mesmerized. Nothing athletic about them. No pint-sized additions. Full, perfectly formed, slightly drooping, hanging lusciously there beneath electric blue spandex, nipples clearly outlined. Satisfying simply to behold. You had to work not to stare. This was the girlfriend Peter had characterized as "lovely." I could see what he meant. It didn't matter that she was an airhead. She knew exactly what she had to offer. That was clear. She had a body that made you want to touch it, skin that breathed invitation, asked to be fondled and stroked. The waiter, a slim oily-faced man with a careful smile, stripped her with his eyes. Peter took that in.

"When I saw what she wore to meet you, I . . . " Peter stopped.

Did he actually care what she wore to meet me? I found it hard to believe, though there had been something naked, daring, inviting — bold, even — to my eye. But my eye is not to be trusted in 1989. My eye has been too conditioned. So I tend to hold back, wait to hear, distrust my own feelings about such things. I had thought her dress inappropriate. I recognize this as a thought my mother might have had.

"She was falling out all over," he said. "And . . . "

I tasted the last of the cherry filling, its sweetness coated the tip of my tongue. I washed away the traces with cool coffee. We'd walked together down The Avenue of the Americas. We couldn't decide where to eat. Inside? Outside? Intimate? Splashy? They really didn't care, I saw that. I was supposed to decide. Peter was oddly silent. I felt he probably wanted to touch her, that was all. Who wouldn't? What a drag to have a mother around. I imagined lust raging through him as we made stupid light talk beneath the green and white striped awning. What was I doing there? Paying the bill, that's what.

I'd bailed out as soon as I could, hoping he'd find his chance.

Now he tells me they've broken up. Just like that.

"And . . . you couldn't even get near her?" I dared.

He looked surprised. "Well . . . you might say that."

"And now it's over? Kaput?"

"Right. It's over."

"Our whole trip to the city was a waste?"

"I wouldn't say that," he said. "Depends on how you read waste."

Ah, there was nothing to say. Nothing at all. How does one read waste?

He'd wanted the wildness, the release, the escape, the coming home to flesh he knew. He'd wanted the touch of flesh he might claim, however fleetingly.

"Remember your camping trip last summer? The fried porcupine?"

He smiled. He was reaching into his pocket.

"I'll pay for this one," he said.

"Remember the little cast iron frying pan you used?"

"Yeah, I remember. Didn't we bring it back?"

"You brought it back okay," I said. "I still use it all the time. But all summer, for weeks on end, every time I heated something up in that frying pan it gave off a wild smell, really strong. People coming into the house would ask, 'What's that smell?' It was like having a wild animal in the house. Something alien. I loved it."

I spare him more details. He'd had a fantastic few days out there.

"It was a blessing I didn't know about it until afterwards," I'd tell guests, explaining the smell. Because the scorn of an eighteen year old adventurer can wither the hearts of those who would worry for him.

So it was a blessing.

Because it could have killed him. Poisoned him. They could have lain there, Peter and his buddy John, slowly dying beneath the starry June sky, eyes half opened toward those heavens so close and yet so vast, so extravagant in their nightly display above the soft lap lap of fathomless bay waters. The fire the boys had nurtured on the shore would have flickered down to ashes beside their bodies . . . just a short distance from their tent pitched safely, wisely, above the line of those treacherous tides, the highest in the world. They would have lain there side by side, weakened, slowly destroyed by what they had devoured . . . so alone, cut off, dying, far from family, telephone,

car, cut off from contact with civilization. Away from the
world. It was, after all, what they'd sought. Perhaps the hungry
tides would have swallowed them, erased them, cast them up
weeks, months later, strange bodies on a stranger shore, faces
reduced to blobs for others to stare at, puzzle over, then turn
away from — grateful for family intact, however flawed.

And it would all have been of their own choosing. So to
speak.

"But it tasted good," he'd said, grinning, smacking lips surrounded by five days' growth of stubble and carrying still, on
his flesh, in his clothes, the smell of salt and sea and wilderness
and brush fire and maybe even — who could tell? — killed,
skinned, disembowelled and fried porcupine. "I put some peanut butter on mine," he added.

When does a comic sense turn cruel?

"And we had escargot soup. Bay of Fundy Special. Big ones,
Mom. We cooked them over the fire and put them in our to-
mato soup."

And so it ended.

He'd never known of the red tide on the other coast poi-
soning the northern part of Northumberland Strait, warnings
daily over the radio which I'd half heard as I peeled potatoes,
scraped carrots and thought vaguely of Peter and his friend
spared this domesticity and revelling in the discovered tracks of
a coyote. Imagined them rising in the morning fog, damp and
chilled to the bone, drying out, scrounging for berries, wolfing
down bread and peanut butter, sunbathing, swimming naked,
cavorting in the surf. . . . Part of me longed to be there. Only
part.

The smell remained.

And all that summer — as pansies bloomed and were gathered, as tuberous begonias were nursed into radiance, as
geranium baskets swung heavily on the porch in the evening

wind from the bay, and strawberries, then blueberries, at last came into season — all summer long, when I put anything into that small iron skillet he and John had taken into the wilderness at the edge of the bay, there came that invading smell, a wild smell, a reminder: kitchens, houses, gardens do not contain the earth. Pungent, like a smoking wood fire, alien and titillating, it met the nostrils and seemed to fill the lungs, proclaiming the days of the captured porcupine, the few days when Peter had succeeded in finding another world.

He can be maddeningly matter-of-fact. And private.

He looked at me as I downed the last drop of my cool coffee and we prepared to drive the rest of the way home.

"It's okay, Mom," he said quietly.

I saw that he was looking much older these days, a certain depth in the eyes, a thinning in the cheeks. A way of picking up the check that said, I'll manage.

"We'd better go," he said. "Granny'll start to worry. That's all we need." He slid from the booth, then stood by the side of the table for a moment, stretching, lifting his long tanned arms above his head. The T-shirt rode up, exposing for a few seconds a ridge of dark hair beneath his navel. Then it disappeared.

"It's nothing to worry about, really," he said. "We had a good year. It's over. But . . . " I could barely hear him now, for he'd turned away to head for the cash register, "it'll be a hell of a long time before I forget her."

LEAVING THE WORLD

And at once they left their nets and followed Him.

For years those words had rung for Claire Delaney with the seductive power of the absolute. In early childhood they had been simply words, part of a story as familiar as the furniture in her home, the contents of her closet. As she grew older in the Church, however, she began to hear echoes. *And the Lord said to Abram: "Go forth out of thy country, and from thy kindred, and out of thy father's house, and come into the land which I shall shew thee." And the Lord said to Moses: "I will send thee to Pharoah, that thou mayst bring forth my people, the children of Israel out of Egypt."* So often the command was to go into another country. *"Take the child and go into Egypt."* To leave. *"Arise and go into the city, and it will be told thee what thou must do."* To venture forth into the dark, the unknown. *"Go ye forth . . . "*

And so, as years passed and she became what they called educated, worked her summer jobs, matured as a Catholic young woman did in those days, she knew all along that there was more to life than this. The gospels said so. Saints proved it. The very nuns before her dramatized it, albeit imperfectly. Leaving the familiar everyday world was the greatest adventure. Every explorer knew that. And what greater path to embark upon than the path to holiness? What greater world to discover than the world of God Himself?

He who loses his life will find it.

I

When the novice mistress, Mother Theodore, spoke to her twenty novices and postulants gathered away from the world to learn a new way of life, she put before them the response of those hardy fishermen, Simon and his brother Andrew, to the Lord's invitation, "Come follow me." *And immediately they left their nets and followed Him.* Magnetic words to Sister Claire Delaney, encased now in her trappings of adventure, starch and black serge.

Occasionally, as she dusted them in the morning, Sister Claire would look through the mullioned windows of the novitiate library, a room that housed books to dust, not read. She might glimpse a cardinal or bluejay swooping toward the apple tree, a squirrel nibbling away at acorns, or simply the shaded patch of clover and wild daisies at the far end of the sloping mowed lawn. Sometimes, on summer mornings when the novices sat outside making their meditation from five-thirty to six-thirty, a deer would emerge from the forest surrounding the novitiate house. Alert and wary, it would stand poised, stare at the odd spectacle of fifteen white-veiled figures dotting the lawn on camp stools, eyes shut, hands folded, books balanced on their black laps. Then, with a turn and a flick of the tail as if to say Phooey, it would bound back into the woods.

The novitiate was well situated for those who would put hand to plow. Its only approach — an unmarked dirt road plunging through dense woods — wound past scrub brush, alders, wild berry bushes, an immense corn field, cow pastures, an apple orchard, and a small mountain before it finally reached the large half-timbered house with its attached chapel.

Yet even here, so far removed from the world, Claire Delaney soon learned that will has limits. Desire does not so easily die. Kneeling to dust chair rungs, window sills, she yearned to see the tail flick of a fleeing deer — something unbidden, unexpected, a vision to cherish, gift unsought.

Novitiate days are outwardly simple: hours of prayer, manual labor, strain to learn this other way, care about the letter of the law in hopes of someday moving into that freer realm where one lives by the spirit. How many worlds are there to leave? Too many to number. The journey to leave, to begin, grows endless, like rings on a tree, waves in the sea. One longs to be done with the purgative way. But to hope for the higher way — the illuminative, the unitive — might be pride. When does aspiration become ambition? The last shall be first. Jesus wasted no sympathy on one mother ambitious for her sons.

Nonetheless, these were the enlightened late fifties and everyone, even nuns, knew that educators must keep up.

So it was that, two and a half years later, on a January morning aglitter with diamond-crusted snow, the novice mistress gathered her black-veiled, newly professed sisters on the freshly dusted library chairs for their last conference before leaving the novitiate womb.

"The Order has built a new house of studies in Washington, D.C.," she told them. "To this house all of you who have already completed college will be sent. You will undertake graduate training for a master's degree in whatever field the Order deems suitable."

Another departure.

Would Sister Hillary be sent with her? They'd been together from the beginning. And what academic field would the Order "deem suitable" for Sister Claire? Departures were part of God's plan. What country would open out before her, now that she had crossed the threshold of her first vows?

"We must live each day as if it were our last, Sisters," said their new superior two days later, by way of welcome to Washington.

A woman esteemed for remaining humble even with a Ph.D., Reverend Mother Dominic projected pain through a resolutely joyful face. "I know you have been well trained in the novitiate. This is a time of further testing. We must live, Sisters, in the world but not of it. You will be pursuing studies on a university campus. You must carry with you everywhere the presence of God. And to help you in this you will have all that the Order can give you, including the monthly retreat Sunday required by rule."

This was the day they lived eschatologically, as if each breath would be their last, a day of intense preparation for the final departure.

Claire anticipated higher studies with apprehension. Novitiate efforts to erase secular knowledge, to wipe out what sixteen years of Catholic education plus tuition and fees had so deeply imprinted, had left her newly minted religious mind a *tabula rasa* suspended above a pit of exhaustion. Names and dates were Back There, back in the world of Martha, ah Martha, so busy about many things that she missed the One Thing That Mattered. For where your treasure is, there will your heart be.

Now, with her sisters, Claire Delaney had reentered the world of moths and corruption. New person, new garb, new place. Returned. She must cross the bridge of sighs, ascend Mount Snowden, suffer Bosworth field, head for Canterbury, sail once more into the heart of darkness. For they had decided, thank God, that she'd study English literature. Surveying anew those literary texts she'd struggled to forget, she must test how completely the scales had fallen from her consecrated eyes.

But first they were set to painting. It was early February. University classes would not start for the latest group of arrivals until the following September.

"I will mix the paint for you, Sisters," said Reverend Mother Dominic.

They understood it as an exercise in humility.

The house, newly completed, smelled still of plaster and paint and Gyproc and sweet wood shavings. Their task was to transform the small square room on the first floor into a rosy-pink chapel.

"If our building progresses according to plan, we will use this room for only one more year. Nonetheless, it is the house of God."

Each morning Mother Dominic gathered her five new charges in the basement laundry room for paint-mixing. Nothing is insignificant in the eyes of God. The shade must be just right. She pinned back her veil and her large outer sleeves, donned a bibbed gingham apron and hungrily eyed the cans through her bifocals. Then, with muscle one would not have expected, she took a long flat stick and stirred. "Just a little more white, Sister." Stir. Stir. "And now some yellow, please." Stir. Stir. "Now, just a bit of red." All these directions given in the silence tone. Thick ribbons of color swirled and blended into a uniform rosy-pink.

The grim intensity of her superior's stirring depressed Sister Claire. Despite the smiling face, the unflagging energy, the brisk walk and expert enthusiasm, she made you feel like such a slob. You knew you were sandpaper to her soul. She suffered you nobly.

Her inner life, Claire would think years later and a life away, must have been riddled with pain, one raw wound, for throughout the house she cast a pervasive gloom, a soul-eroding anxiety that even after twenty years those who'd survived her formation flinched to recall. Too long a sacrifice can make a stone of the heart.

During the weeks of chapel painting she left them alone, morning after morning, once the paint had been perfectly mixed. In the presence of the God to Whom they were vowed they worked silently, transforming His dwelling-place to a rosy-pink.

What, they wondered, had this to do with becoming educated? They rolled on the paint, prayed for perfection, and perspired in silence. God's ways are not our ways.

After two months, their painting done and the chairs in the chapel all refinished, Reverend Mother set them to learn how to bind and patch the library books they were not yet permitted to look at. That would come in the fall when they were formally admitted to Catholic University.

These things bear telling because leaving the world, one discovers, is immensely complicated. An act never completed.

Gone the woods and orchards and pastoral simplicities of novitiate days. Gone the simple earnest hopefulness of beginning. The tree of knowledge had begun to cast its shade.

Every morning, as sizzling summer melted into burning September, they went out now to the university, a stream of black-veiled young nuns walking silently toward the groves of academe, readying themselves for the challenge by meditating or saying their rosary as they walked.

The world seeps in.

"You are to keep the rule of silence at all times, Sisters. Especially when you are on campus. You are not to speak to men. You are to report any lapses to me."

"What's your name, Sister?" he asked, as he bent to pick up

the pencil she'd clumsily dropped that first day in Romantic Poetry.

"Sister Claire." The hair on the back of his hand was red. He bit his nails.

How could she refuse to give her name? Besides, he reminded her of her brother Paul, now off somewhere in uniform. Surely, such occasional contact surely did not merit reporting to Reverend Mother.

Except for time in the university library, they were to study in common in the convent, never alone in their cells. Eventually, when the new chapel was completed, they would have a large study hall beneath it.

For now, they must study each evening after supper in the small library, crammed around one long table. Claire writhed as pages turned noisily on either side of her. She couldn't concentrate. The breathing of others sounded so steady, so untroubled, compared to the addled workings of her own print-fogged brain. Sister Jude, a student of American history, was permitted to look at the daily *New York Times*. Who would have thought the rustle of news could so shatter Wordsworthian solemnities, so dilute the epistolary anguish of Keats? Staring at her poetry anthology, Claire fought the urge to make marginal notes. She could not own the book. It would be returned to their library shelves at the end of the course. In the name of poverty, she was permitted only its use. She longed to write a note, cast her bottled message onto the unknown sea of the future. "I sat here in December 1958. I survived. I was discouraged, too. Hang in there." Or maybe, beside "Preface to the Lyrical Ballads," one simple word: *Nuts*.

"You must pursue your studies with purity of heart, Sisters," admonished Reverend Mother. "There is a variety of gifts."

Nonetheless, everyone knew she expected A's. As if veil and beads conferred on newly sanctified grey matter the capacity for excellence. As if brain power thrived on privation. *Amor vincit omnia*.

The world seeps in.

It lies within you, along with the kingdom of God. Discovering the two so deeply intermixed brought Sister Claire Delaney up short with a start, almost pain. It was her second summer in the house of studies. The chapel had just been completed.

Throughout that spring they'd suffered the pounding, drilling, sawing and sanding with resignation. Each evening in June, at the end of recreation, Mother Dominic had brought her junior nuns to the threshold of the chapel to see what progress had been made.

One had to admit that the sunken flagstone nave, the oak choir stalls, the stone sanctuary with its austere lines, its plain marble table, had about it a simplicity that appealed. It avoided clutter, bespoke a sensibility aimed out and up. Transcendence. Aspiration. Leaving. Climbing. Departing. Sister Claire liked it. She could hardly wait to leave the rosy-pink room where they'd knelt for a year and a half, shoulder to damp shoulder, breathing air that grew fetid in Washington heat as twenty-two nuns meditated for an hour each morning or chanted their blurred way through Divine Office. Gone the long sloping lawn of the novitiate. No fleeting glance here from a wayward deer. One longed instead, futilely, for Reverend Mother to turn on the fan.

At Saturday chapter the day before July Visiting Sunday, Reverend Mother spoke to them about the meaning of the new chapel. She took as her text, "I will go unto the altar of God, to God Who gives joy to my youth." She spoke, rather grimly, of joy. The crucifix, she told them with something that bordered on exultation, would represent the risen Christ. And then she announced that tomorrow some would be having parents for a visit.

Sister Claire's heart leapt. She had not seen her parents for a year and a half, not since Profession Day in the novitiate when she'd emerged from the vow ceremony radiant beneath her new black veil, proudly conscious of heavy beads rattling against her knee, the large crucifix tucked into her leather cincture. She kissed her father and the lingering smell of his shaving lotion smote her heart. She decided then not to mention the advantages of martyrdom. If she were to die that very day she'd go straight to heaven. They wanted her to go on living.

And so, in truth, did she.

Now they would see her over halfway toward her final vows, the day she would say "forever" and receive the ring.

"I have prepared descriptions, Sisters," Reverend Mother was going on, "of the two statues and the crucifix that are available for donation, should any of your parents wish to be remembered in our chapel. It is a rare opportunity."

Claire stifled a tremor.

Next morning, after breakfast, she surreptitiously picked up from the table outside Reverend Mother's office the small folders describing the new chapel and available memorials: a statue of Mary, of Joseph, a crucifix of the risen Christ, a small pipe organ, choir stalls. In the interests of economy Reverend Mother had decided against stained glass.

When her bell rang, Claire slipped the folder into her pocket, left chapel, and went to meet them.

He looked sallow somehow, and smaller. Not the man she remembered from a year and a half ago. He'd been ill. Gallbladder operation, persistent trouble with blood pressure. The shoulders inside his blue and white striped cotton jacket stooped ever so slightly. The small hands that once had commanded attention by their quietly graceful gestures, their magic on a keyboard, looked unsteady as he took out a pack of cigarettes and then, at her look, put them away.

Hugs accomplished, they took their places in the three-seat parlor not far from Reverend Mother's office. Clackety clack, clackety clack. A speed typist, Mother Dominic was at it all day, her door wide open in case a sister needed to see her. Clackety clack. No escaping this insistent background to their visit. In the novitiate, even on the coldest Visiting Sundays, Claire had always taken her parents outside. They'd walk up toward the barn or apple orchard. Her father would smoke, observing her, while her mother rattled on.

"So, how's the scholar doing?" he asked now, somewhat formally.

"Surviving." Was he hinting about her grades? "This summer we're all taking two courses at the university — one in kerygmatic theology from a wonderful German theologian and the other in the sacraments from a Benedictine monk."

Her father's eyes glazed over.

What then to tell them?

"Now, Claire, I've brought you something," chortled her mother, rummaging through a bulging straw purse. "I've been saving them for months."

"You know your mother," said Burt Delaney. He shifted his weight on the straight chair, stretched out one leg.

Claire remembered well the overstuffed quality of her enthusiasms. He hid his worries, let them slide over into angers often hard to decode. She, on the other hand, defeated introspection, broadcast her anxieties. Beneath a surface cheerfulness, her fears ran deep. Happy now to be again with her only daughter, Vivien Delaney pulled from her purse a bundle of folded newspaper clippings. "I saved what I thought you'd be interested in."

With pudgy ringed fingers she began to straighten out the clippings, laying them on the small glass-topped table between her and Claire, her daughter, so recently of this world.

"But, Mom — "

"Now, there's one about Lucie Barnes. She got married — when was it, Burt? October, I think. To Billy Meehan. Remember him? His youngest brother went to school with you at St. Jerome's. And yes, that's right . . . I brought the whole account of the Fiftieth Anniversary at St. Jerome's. Father Hurley put on a buffet with the help of the ladies of the parish, and . . . "

Claire saw them, the nuns of her youth — pleated bibs, starched headdresses, marshalling segregated recess lines, drilling on *The Baltimore Catechism*. Why did God make you? God made me to know, love, and serve Him in this world and to be happy with Him forever in the next.

"But Mom — "

"Remember Sister Damien?"

"Vivien, maybe Claire has some things she'd like to tell us."

"Mom, we're not allowed to read the papers."

"Good God, Claire!" His anger blasted her like hot air, scorching her soul. "You're in graduate school!"

She eyed him staunchly. He always made a kind of sense. At least with him she could argue. "But we require permission, Dad. We're still in formation. And my field isn't history, anyway. I'm busy reading poetry."

"Now, here's one for you," trilled Vivien. "Remember Jackie, dear? Well, he finally got married. And who would you guess was the lucky girl?"

Lucky girl! . . . Jackie of the heavy breath, sweaty hands, big feet on the dance floor . . . Jackie Halloran whose mother thought it would be so lovely if only . . .

"Katie. Oh, here it is — "

She handed Claire the picture. Katie Ryan. June bride. Frozen smile. Satin princess. Bouquet held loosely, just so. *Come to me all you who labor and are heavily burdened and I will refresh you.* They'd been close friends.

Suddenly, at the door, Mother Dominic.

Anxiety gripped Claire as she stood, but Reverend Mother seemed not to notice the worldly clippings. She greeted them, invited them to see the new chapel, offered to show them the inside way toward it.

"After next Sunday's dedication I wouldn't be able to take you this way," she said as they hurried down the corridor beside her. "Papal enclosure, you know. The entrance for seculars will then be from the outside only."

At the back door of chapel she stopped. "I'll leave you here. I'm going into chapel, Sister. You can take your parents to the visitors' gallery." She shook hands and disappeared.

Claire led her parents up a few steps and into the small visitors' gallery. She pulled down the kneeler in the second row. They knelt together, looking down at the heads of five or six meditating nuns in the chapel below. Although it had not been dedicated yet, the nuns were permitted to pray here. Most elected the rosy-pink room, where the Blessed Sacrament remained. This chapel was cooler, however, and today the mercury was pushing a hundred degrees Fahrenheit.

For a few moments they were quiet.

Vivien stirred, leaning her rose linen against the back of the pew. "It's so . . . bare," she whispered.

"It's new, Mother. Monastic. This is not a parish church."

No garish Stations of the Cross, no rouged plaster statues. Claire felt inside her deep pocket for the folder. Quietly she handed this to Burt.

"Claire," whispered her mother again, louder. "I've never seen a crucifix like that. Why is it like that?"

Reverend Mother was kneeling in her stall at the rear of chapel, her head just a few feet away from them.

"Look at this," said Burt to his wife. "We could make a contribution, Viv. Though one might argue we already have."

Claire's heart beat faster. Had Reverend Mother heard? They sat back in the pew and together looked at the brochure.

Why should this matter to her? He was not rich.

"Oh, Burt, wouldn't that be nice." Vivien took the brochure to study it.

"Let's get out of here," said Burt, standing up suddenly, jarring the kneeler.

Claire quickly pushed it back.

They left the gallery and this time, instead of heading back through the convent, she opened the door to the outside. Ten concrete steps would lead them out of the cloister, down to the street.

Burt pulled out his cigarettes. Lighting up, he seemed to relax.

"Well, Claire, what do you think?"

They began to walk in front of the long cinderblock building. Sister Anthony had cut the grass just yesterday. The small lawn looked trim, cared for. A few weeks of this heat would leave it parched and yellow.

"About what?"

"Shall we donate something . . . more? What do you think?"

"Oh, Burt, wouldn't it be nice to know something was here that we'd put here?"

"It already is."

"Oh, not that. You know what I mean. A part of our daughter's life has been here, after all."

"Exactly my point."

"And then, even after she's gone . . . wherever they send her" — her mother had in mind perhaps Rome, the first female pope — "there'd always be something here. I like that idea, don't you, Claire?"

"Your mother excels in looking forward to looking back," he said, sprinkling ashes in the freshly swept gutter. "What about you, Claire?" His eyes bored into her. "Does it matter to you?"

How to answer? *She wanted to knock at Mother Dominic's door later today, enter her office, kneel by the tidy desk and announce quietly, modestly: "Reverend Mother, my parents wish to donate . . . " She wanted to see the light of surprise erase pain in those blue eyes. She wanted the secret pleasure, when she knelt in the new chapel, of knowing that her parents had contributed . . . that she, Sister Claire Delaney was needed . . . that but for her . . .*

Her father was watching.

She reddened

"Well, maybe, Dad. If you and Mom really want to, you might" — it came out in one tremulous daring breath — "consider the crucifix."

Except for the organ, the most expensive item on the list.

The afterbirth brought pain.

Because it entailed looking up at the resplendent carved crucifix with its priestly robed Christus, that patient face, that strong noble figure suspended before her above the main altar, and knowing, with a tinge of sadness, that the world was still definitely within. She'd known that before, of course. But this knowing was new and sharp. Outsides and insides, the simple squares of her eschatological bookkeeping, had deceived, would deceive. Leaving the world — strange phrase — meant confronting it. In oneself. And the possibilities of discovery, confrontation, were endless.

She prayed for detachment, for a spirit of poverty, for purity of heart. She prayed to recognize the truth when she saw it, whatever its guise.

And several months later, courses over, dissertation completed, she rejoiced to learn that she would rejoin Sister Hillary, already in the community of Holy Name, a flourishing girls' high school in southern Massachusetts.

Sister Claire Delaney prepared her soul to reenter the world.

II

"It's a fantastic story how we got this place," says Sister Dorothy, settling down to darn the heel of a stocking.

Three summers later now, seventeen nuns of various ages and dispositions are easing into a rhythm Sister Claire thought she'd forsaken forever. Vacation.

After prodding freshmen through Latin I, walking sophomores and juniors through *The Thomas More Anthology of Prose and Poetry,* and threading the labyrinthine intricacies of community life, she isn't protesting.

Late June sun, locust buzz, shimmering humidity, the heavy dampness of black serge against human skin remind one, even a resolutely mortified one, that some skins can be shed, that people do, in some worlds, shed layers in summer, shed in fact as much as possible. They might leave their skins, if they could. Though that, of course, is in the world. That other world, the one left behind.

So here, at Lake St. Mary, high up in New York State, a narrow lake one mile long, half a mile wide, surrounded by dense pine woods and bordered by clots of lazy wildflowers, here the nuns from Holy Name vacation.

There is a spacious central house with cathedral ceilings, a large kitchen, a dining area and a large living room, and five small bedrooms off the upstairs walkway. This main house also boasts a broad verandah with wicker chairs. But the best part, Sister Claire thinks, is the smaller cottages with one or two bedrooms, some four or five of them stretched in among the trees along this side of the lake.

To one of them she has been assigned with Sister Hillary. A kind fate put both their names on the same vacation list. And Sister Edwin, a sympathetic woman assigned as this week's vacation superior, has arranged for the two of them to share the same cabin, St. Catherine's.

Sister Hillary will be working this summer on an M.A. in Greek. Sister Claire is ready for anything. Anything, in this case, will be reading through the *Oresteia* in translation with Sister Hillary.

For a couple of hours each day, revelling in the coolness of the students' blue gym suits which they wear at all times except for meals and hours of prayer, they will set chairs by the side of the lake and muse on the rashness of Orestes. They will explore the mystery of *hubris*. And they will have a chance to talk.

With minimal exceptions, the rule of vacation is To Each Her Own. Prayers remain, of course. Otherwise, days are pretty open.

Every morning Sister Luke goes off in gum boots with her fishing rod and pail. Sister Josephine disappears with her flute. Sister Stella sits beneath the huge ash tree near the main house composing a learned article on "Lycidas." Some knit. Some crochet. Some stare at the lake. Some cook.

Hours of prayer in the specially built chapel, a square building with a screened side facing the lake, constitute a special pleasure. Morning birdsong and a cool lake breeze against one's back confer a gentle edge on the gospel. Divine Office is said in private, perhaps as one walks around the lake.

If this is spiritual childhood, it's okay.

At evening recreation on the second night, reclothed in habits, they sit in a large circle on lawn chairs between the main house and the lake. Some laps hold piles of stockings to be darned. Faces are already red or brown, freckled, peeling. Bodies seem to have loosened. There is a quiet tolerance here that Claire never feels in the convent at home.

"So how did we get the place?" asks Sister Hillary. She resists the very thought of darning.

Sister Dorothy smiles, eager to tell. "She got the whole place — lake, cottages, main house, everything except the chapel, which we built — lock, stock, and barrel . . . free."

"Providential," murmurs Sister Beatrice. She is hooked on Divine Providence.

Sister Eleanor, a square-jawed nun with a rugged athletic look, stretches a measuring tape across the width of a small crocheted baby blanket lying on her lap. "Tax break," she murmurs.

"One day, inspired by the Holy Spirit perhaps, who knows . . . " Sister Dorothy sets down her darning egg, "Reverend Mother just went upstairs without saying a word and got the big statue of the Infant of Prague. You know the one just outside the upstairs chapel?"

Claire knows it to the motes of dust on His crown, for which she is responsible.

"Reverend Mother had great devotion to the Infant," says Sister Beatrice. "A blessing."

Once again, Claire feels her disadvantage. She never knew the legendary Reverend Mother William.

"So she carried Him down to the portress booth," continues Sister Dorothy, "set Him on the table in front of her, and asked the portress to dial a number for her."

"None of us knew until later," chimes in Sister Eleanor,

folding her pink blanket. "Not even Mother Gerard, who was sub-mistress then. Only Mrs. Borgia, the portress. She's the one that told the story."

"Anyhow." Sister Dorothy sends abroad a shushing look. "When Mrs. Borgia had made the connection she handed the phone to Reverend Mother, who identified herself as from this convent. She explained her mission. She had a houseful of nuns, eighty of them. They were tired. They worked hard all year in a large girls' high school and two parochial schools. They taught, they studied, they prayed. They needed a vacation, some arrangement that would make getting away for a few days each year possible. Until the past year they'd shared a summer house on Long Island with another convent in the province, but that could no longer be. It was a case of overcrowding. And she'd heard — who knows how, maybe she'd seen it advertised in the real estate section of the *Times* — that this lake in upper New York State was for sale. She understood he'd built the houses for his family, a regular compound, and it was no longer used."

"Here she touched the Infant," breaks in Sister Beatrice.

"And she asked how would Mr. So-and-So like to donate the whole thing to a worthy cause."

Lake water laps nearby. Behind chapel, the setting sun fires leafy green tips. Somewhere out in the lake a loon laughs.

I shall never forget this moment, thinks Claire.

Although she'd never known Reverend Mother William, she can see it all — the polished oak top of the portress booth table, the discreet portress, Mrs. Borgia, being helpful, moving aside, tactful. And Mother William, daring. Taking them all on. Was she wise as a serpent, simple as a dove? Perhaps that's what the passage meant. As Claire and Hillary once agreed, Christ's words, "The children of this world are wiser in their generation than the children of light," were a colossal putdown if ever there was one.

Tax break or not, charity or greed, whatever his motive, bless him, thinks Claire, in these days of water and sun and talk and something indefinable she would call "community." Bless the rich donor. Thank God for Reverend Mother William's nerve. There's a word for that, isn't there? she dredges it up: *Chutzpah.* That's it. *Bless Mother William for her chutzpah.*

She says it to herself dreamily, floating on her back in the middle of the lake, or rolling over into a dead man's float. *Chutzpah . . . chutzpah . . . chutzpah. . . .* Water fills her ears. Hanging onto the far side of the raft she looks over at the opposite, deserted shoreline with its waving fireweed, its clumps of strange yellow and purple flowers, its darkly clustered cat tails. *So many things in nature I cannot name,* she thinks with something like regret. Then dives deep, parting the black waters, seeking the depths until her ears hurt and her head feels funny. With a panicky frog kick, she pushes herself back to the top and breaks the surface, gasping for air. *Chutzpah . . . chutzpah . . . chutzpah.* Any deep dive takes nerve. *Chutzpah.*

For languid hours she lies in the rowboat, letting it drift among lily pads as she stares straight up at the sky of soft white and blue. The book she's brought along out of a vague sense of duty lies unread. *Giles Goat Boy.* The mother of a student lent it to her. But time for drifting is too precious to waste. The book is tedious, far more tedious than Aeschylus.

Whether or not others join her, she forces herself into the water every day, letting numbness steal her toes, her feet, her shins, her thighs, nerving herself up for the cold finger against her stomach, her breasts. It has been so many years.

One day, when she is swimming alone, a sudden idea grips her. She is careful to stay on the far side of the float, out of sight of the house. Sister Anthony is tatting down near the water's edge. Several figures sit on the verandah, reading.

Claire loosens the buttons of her water-logged gym suit, no easy task, and eases it down from her shoulders. Back and forth she swims, half naked fish streaking through the lake underworld. The cold water icing her breasts, her nipples, her back, feels strange and wonderful. Her skin becomes satin, or is it the water against her skin? The heavy gym suit drags about her waist like a deflated tube. If she could, she'd shuck off the whole thing, swim about immersed in this alien thrilling embrace. Too complicated. It would be just her luck to lose it. She sees it happening . . . the blue cloth slowly sinking out of sight, away, her desperate plunge to retrieve it as it moves toward the other side of the raft, her waiting, hopeless, growing cold, skin going pruney, shivery, until at last she can wait no longer, twilight is coming, the peepers have started, the sun has sunk behind the trees . . . and she swims to shore, bursting forth in pink embarrassed splendor, an accidental Venus, shaking all over, oh so naked. The sisters run for towels, averting eyes . . .

Giggling, she blots out the picture with a quick underwater duck and swims forward. Through the clear water she sees her pale breasts following, swinging mysteriously in bubbles created by her own breath. She remembers now nights at the Connecticut shore when she and her friends would sneak out from their cottages after dark. Modest, as young Catholic girls would be, they'd slip into the black water quickly, ducking out of the cold night air, dive into a mouthful of salt, then strip off their suits and stash them atop a barnacled rock. Swimming about in total liquid joy — screaming, teasing, giggling — they'd float down watery moonlit paths, dive to the slimy touch of seaweed ribbons, shrewdly gauge their strength against the undertow and seek out elusive warm spots.

So many years later, so far away, in this cloistered lake, out of her sisters' sight, half naked, she swims about in an unknown donor's gift, swims to joyous release, surprised to feel so little guilt.

It feels almost natural.

Directly opposite the raft, on the uncloistered side, a huge willow tree hugs the edge of the lake. Its elegant filmy branches hang out over the water, weeping downward, creating another tree below, a water tree, on the dimpled surface. From her spot beside the raft, Claire can see the water tree. It moves slowly, almost dances, as a soft breeze stirs the yellowish green above. Yet it holds its shape, a large uneven darkness on the lake's surface.

Praying no one will come and discover her, she swims toward the shade. Bit by bit, as she approaches, she loses the outline, but the cool darkness tells her she has arrived. She turns over and floats, looking up into the pale green canopy that blocks the sun. Then she turns again and dives, down, down, leaving far behind on the surface the dancing shadow tree. Near the bottom, white pebbles glisten in murk, and tiny quick silver fish dart about like slim silver coins, avoiding her pale feet, racing away from this intruder.

Now she is above again, inside the water tree, swimming along its branches, scissor-kicking its trunk, diving through its leaves, playing discreetly amid the rippling foliage. Limp lance-shaped leaves above become flat dancing shadows all around her. Exhilarated, she swims about in them, joyous, almost content. Revelling to frolic half naked in the watery shade, gift unsought, hers alone to explore, to dive beneath, to embrace, hers alone to swim through, to leave behind, to remember.

She cannot see the future, cannot dream the world of time ahead, prepare for new wildernesses, new shades. Nor is it required.

Enough to be here . . . floating . . . diving . . . swimming . . .

in the secret water tree she has found, a tree she can never possess, never encompass, that from time to time she can only see and swim to meet, divining its shadow against a distant shore, aware that in the moment of her arriving it will already have disappeared.

FINDING THE STORY

"Not a room," says the creative writing instructor. "It's inert. The heart of all narrative is change."

"But I can't get that room out of my head. You want a story that comes from a real source in us. My story is about a room."

"Very well." He sighs. "If you must. But for God's sake give your room character."

"It already has character. Had one. I haven't seen the room for years."

"What about dialogue? Rooms don't speak."

"Certainly rooms speak. Any room with character carries on a silent dialogue with you from the moment you enter until you leave. My room speaks."

"What does it say?"

"It used to say: '*In this house I am the room with distinction. I am the room that has refused to be modernized. I hate* aggiornamento. *Come on inside and feel what it once was like around here.*'"

"It says that to everyone?"

"Of course not. He who has ears to hear, let him hear."

"Say more." He lights his cigarette and sips coffee from styrofoam.

Coke machines are being punched in the background. Somewhere outside tennis balls pong, back and forth, back and forth. I must find my story. He humors me with the look of one who has heard it all before, a hundred searches for the significant. When will this tiresome woman shut up?

I ignore his cynicism, his boredom.

"My room says: *I'm static. I don't change.* Therefore, it is a deluded room. Its wallpaper presents the legend of the unicorn. It's not really wallpaper but finely grained cloth and carries a repeated pattern in dark colors. To make that out, you must stand up close and study. Then you see it: the circle, the unicorn there in the center."

"So this is a deluded room. You're not making sense, you know."

He has a habit of glancing away, shifting weight on his plastic chair. He wants to get home to his wife. Or lover.

"My room thinks that by keeping the same wallpaper it can stay unchanged. Its molding remains dark. On the front side of the room a mullioned casement window with perfectly leaded panes faces the street. To open this you must stand in the little alcove and lean forward, pushing . . . "

"And does this room keep its windows open or shut?"

"I've never seen them open. Perhaps they are now. But that would make it another kind of room."

"Okay, so the unicorn grazes on the walls, the windows keep out air. What else? I'm still not getting a *story*.

"Corpses are laid out in there."

"Corpses!" He gulps on his coffee.

"Corpses. Dead bodies. They lay them out in a simple pine box in the center of the room. Beneath the chandelier. Inside the simple box, the corpse's hands are hidden in long black sleeves. A tall beeswax taper burns at either end of the box."

"Okay. More please. I'm beginning to get interested. Perhaps there is a possibility . . . "

"For those occasions, a *prie dieu* is carried into the room and set at one end of the box, the head end. On that a sister kneels, praying, for two days."

"Two days?"

"Well, I mean they take shifts. But for two days, until the

funeral, there's always some nun keeping watch. Family is allowed into this room."

"How come? I thought you said the place was cloistered?"

He has set down his emptied coffee and begun picking at the styrofoam rim, tearing it. Perhaps he wants to be out playing tennis.

"It is cloistered. But some rooms are open to outsiders. They have to be. The body has to be laid out here so family can come, students, people who knew the body before. So, into my room they come."

"Does the room, your room, have a name?"

He's interested.

"Yes. The Blue Parlor."

"So . . . bodies are laid out in the Blue Parlor. Family comes. Nuns kneel and pray. What else?"

"Other times, you'd never know."

"Never know what?"

"Never know a dead body's been laid out in there. You interview students there, on occasion."

"What kind of occasion?"

"Like this."

Someone, somewhere, is shouting "Hey, H-a-r-r-y! Goin' to the game this Saturday?"

"Well, on second thought, not quite like this. It's an all girls' school. You know the scene. Suppose a student has work overdue, a term paper, for example. Her teacher has left the school part of campus and is back in the convent. Say the student needs to see her. She has to brave the lion's mouth."

"Lion's mouth?"

"The front door of the convent. Students hate it. The doorbell is inside the lion's mouth. It's a campus joke. The building was put up in the early 1900s when they went in for such details. It's an intricately carved lion."

"Okay. So I'm a student, I gotta see my teacher, she's no-where around, my paper's overdue, I gather up my nerve and stick my finger in the lion's mouth. Does she come to the door?"

"She probably meets you in the parlor. You sit there and stew while her bell is rung by the lady called a portress who answers the door. Then the teacher hears her bell and comes swishing into the Blue Parlor."

"Are drinks allowed?"

"No drinks. You sit there stiffly, wishing you could be inter-viewed in some normal place. The room has already begun to speak to you. It says things like: 'Control yourself, don't get excited, remember your manners, be a lady.' You've stared at the unicorn in his circular pen. You feel helpless about the damned term paper."

"So you plead? Make excuses?"

"Depends on what she's like. In this case there's no plead-ing. No give."

"So you leave?"

"You leave discouraged because you thought you had a great idea. It won't do, at least that's the way you feel now. The room and the figure worked together. You might have stood a chance if your interview had taken place in the cafeteria, the student union, the library even. Not *here*."

"So the room is an ally, it worked for the teacher?"

"Exactly."

"Brother, I wish I could find such a place!"

When he smiles, his eyes grow lighter. He seems to be con-sidering.

"Wait a minute, though. I thought you said the room changed."

"It does."

"How?"

"First of all, think 'parlor.' The very word speaks of white gloves, ladies in hats, tea from china cups, manners, courtesies, stuffiness perhaps. Who today entertains in a parlor?"

"Who ever said anything about entertaining? I thought this was a room for corpses."

"It is. But when there are no dead to serve, the alumnae come and are served tea and fancy sandwiches in here at the long heavy trestle table."

"Where the coffin is set at other times?"

"How did you guess? They draw up the heavy dark carved chairs for the alumnae, serve them, the college gets its money, the alumna gets her satisfaction. At last, in a world where everything is going to smash, there's one place that hasn't changed, that stays the same. The Blue Parlor."

"So then it *doesn't* change. What are you saying?"

"You can look out its windows late on a Saturday night and see across the street the girls coming in from dates and kissing their boyfriends good-night."

"You're kidding. Even now?"

"What do I know about now? This is what the alumnae remember, sitting in the room with the unicorns. There was the standard joke about a girl who was about to kiss her boyfriend goodnight when suddenly a voice boomed out from a window overhead: 'Child of Mary, you owe him nothing.'"

He is about to light a cigarette, tapping it on the back of his hand. He is preparing to leave. I must find my story fast.

"Look," he says, "let's finish. Here in the Blue Parlor you might find a corpse, a nervous student, a well-bred alumna, but . . ."

"There's a huge ornate mirror over the unused fireplace, magnificent andirons, a whole carved wall above the fireplace. There is also a hidden panel on the front side of the room, in the corner."

"Hiding what?"

"A bathroom."

"You're kidding."

"No. Even nuns pee. It has carvings on the front panel, I forget of what. You slide this panel open and slip sideways into a small triangular bathroom hidden in the corner."

"Modern plumbing?"

"Of course. One last thing — "

"Wait a minute. You said this was the room in the house with distinction. Why?"

"Because all the other outside rooms, those outside the cloister I mean, have been toned down. They've put new upholstery on all the furniture. They've hung soft scenic pictures. Only a few grumpy- looking bishops remain in dark corners. They've watered down the out-of-dateness. This room alone remains colossally anachronistic. It's dated. It proclaims it."

"Okay. I get you. It's truthful."

"Sort of. Only then a funny thing happens. The world shifts. Enrolments drop. People leave. The house empties. It's condemned anyway."

"By the fire department?"

"Among others."

"Never mind elaborating. You've got to have something left to put in your story. What you're telling me now is all exposition."

"I suppose. The Blue Parlor remains unchanged. There is no longer anyone for it to speak to. Meetings are held to discuss, What can we do with these empty rooms? Offices? Conference rooms? Adult education seminars?"

"And your room? I'm awfully sorry, but I've got to leave in about three minutes and I can see finding this story matters to you."

"The other rooms change. The nuns' mailroom downstairs

becomes the faculty mailroom. Male and female. The old underground passageway called the catacombs which used to be the cloistered route from one part of the house to the other, now it's open to anyone. The chapel is deserted. The rood beam proclaims GREATER LOVE THAN THIS NO MAN HATH to no one. There's a new convent now, for old ladies who move about after ten in slippers and nightveils."

"But the room?"

"That's the strange thing. You go to revisit it after ten years or so. You've changed. No more slippers, no more nightveil, no more veil, period. No more kneeling by corpses watching the taper throw shadows on motionless sleeves. No more interviewing nervous students in the chair by the casement window. You're on the hegira of memory. You're dragging your three year old, though he resists."

"This is a nostalgia story, then? Sprung nun revisits scene of crime?"

"*You* might see it that way. Motives are hard to analyze. . . . Anyhow, you go to the Blue Parlor. Everything outside that room is new, updated, functional. Filing cabinets line the hallway, color coordinated couches and chairs abound. Yet, here it is, a parlor still, and still perfectly . . . *functionless*. You take your son by the hand and try to interest him in the unicorn. Boring. The andirons. Boring. What does he know about corpses? Besides, that evidence has disappeared. Then you bring him over to the carved panel of the sliding door. It captivates him. He has the sudden urgency to pee. He slides inside. You wait. Hear the toilet flush. He slides back out looking pleased. He is totally fascinated. Doesn't want to leave. Wants to keep sliding that panel back and forth, back and forth, discovering all over again the secret place."

"I understand."

"To him, the rest of it is dead."

He is rising now, pushing back the plastic chair, snapping shut his briefcase.

"So what do you think?"

"Do you have the ending?"

"Not yet . . . "

"I think it has possibilities. Work on it."

ANOTHER CHRISTMAS

Silence.

All Advent, an absence of noise and talk, a silence deepening and enfolding, weaving an expectant cocoon about us as we moved through daily tasks domestic and unnoteworthy: cleaning the house, memorizing the vow catechism, learning church history, studying the Ignatian way of prayer, trying to practise it. We were postulants — knocking, as the word itself suggests, at the door of the Order we'd chosen, asking for admission. The initial trial period of six months was almost over. In less than a month, if all went well, we'd be admitted to become novices, to wear the habit and white veil. For now, we had the sense — the seven of us left — that trial time, our first trial, was coming to an end.

For me the Advent silence had held one notable interruption. Each day, for half an hour, while others were busy with extra Christmas preparation, I'd been permitted to enter the small novitiate chapel and practise on the pipe organ. It was a permission not easily given, but in view of the important feast coming, I, as the one keyboard person then at the novitiate, was permitted to prepare.

Every afternoon I'd slip into chapel, remove my white celluloid postulant cuffs, set them on the bench beside me, lift the rolltop cover of the organ, click on the motor, touch again the smooth ivory keys. Sometimes Sister Henry, the sacristan, would be working in the sanctuary at the far end of chapel. Black skirt hooked up beneath a special white sacristan's apron, white veil pinned back, she'd glide about her privileged domain with feline efficiency, dusting the pale green marble sanctuary steps, polishing to full lustre the gold and sapphire mosaic lamb on the altar front, draping spotless white across the sacrificial table. A short three years later, before she ever stepped into the classroom, she would die of leukemia, mourned by parents bewildered that God should take so early a daughter they'd already given him. In her memory they donated a bronze virgin to a new chapel in Delaware.

Flipping through the hymnal I would consider possible pieces, play them softly, tentatively, experimenting with stops — the mellow flutes, the throatier reeds — seeking sounds suitable for what I imagined Christmas Eve would be. Trumpet? Too brash. Celeste? Too schmaltzy. I was flying blind, choosing by ear and by instinct. I'd never spent a Christmas here. Nor had I ever been at an organ, responsible for Christmas music. For twenty-one years I'd spent Christmas Eve at home, immersed in the domestic tensions of family Yuletide. I didn't miss that.

I chose my hymns with care. I knew it was taboo to enjoy Christmas carols ahead of time. That the whole point of Advent was penance (three Sundays purple, one rose), that it was a time of preparing, hollowing out, making crooked ways straight. That to burst into "Hark the Herald Angels Sing" when, so to speak, the child was still on his way to our hearts, would hardly be appropriate. Nonetheless, I did have to practise them. I hadn't practised seriously on a keyboard in over four years. Now I discovered how totally I must give myself to this demanding instrument — feet, ankles, heels, trunk, arms, wrists, fingers, mind always focussed, ears open, listening. "You play the piano," our novice mistress had told me. "Surely you could learn the organ." Frustrated by slack ankles, I drilled my wayward feet to gain a sense of intervals, retrained my fingers to precision as they released air so magically turned to music. Closing the swell box, I barely whispered the forbidden carols in the empty chapel, Mary and Joseph sculptured and impervious in their distant niches. Some selections seemed less objectionable, more properly liturgical. For those I luxuriated in the organ's full palette, boldly displaying the sensuous harmonies of Palestrina, urging aloft with a single one foot principal the ancient cry: "O come, O come, Emmanuel." "Drop down dew, ye heavens, from above, and let the clouds rain the just one," sang mellow flutes in limpid legato, as afternoon sun slanted gold and purple through the high stained glass and the single red sanctuary lamp continued to flicker. Unashamedly, I boomed the mighty O Antiphons we began to sing on December 17, each with its final stirring plea: *Veni ad docendum nos . . . veni ad liberandum nos . . . veni et illumina sedentes in tenebris mortis.* A single golden harp sang "The First Noel," jubilant silver trumpets "Joy to the World," the *Gloria in Excelsis Deo* became a revolving prism of bells splintering into shards of opalescent joy, praise transparent as crystal.

As Christmas drew nearer, buoyed up by the possibilities my fingers were uncovering, I decided to risk a simplified version of "Jesu, Joy of Man's Desiring" I'd found in the organ bench.

Aside from those few hours at the keyboard, the weeks before Christmas grew stark. Bleak. Rations diminished. I hated the dry toast put out for collation each afternoon beside our required glass of milk. Scrubbing intensified. The sweet astringent smell of lemon oil pervaded the visitors' parlor; ammonia gassed us as we rubbed imaginary spots from already gleaming windows. We were to wax and polish the entire old rambling two-storey timbered country house, once the home of Margaret Sanger. By what process it had become the nest where consecrated virgins were hatched I never did learn.

Years later, beset by the need to link my own offspring with that harbor of my spirit, would bring them to visit the noviate, only to discover loosestrife blossoming among the rubble, buttercups and violets winking where once I'd tackled arsis and thesis, daisies rampant in the sacristy. The whole building had been gutted by fire. Only the stone frame of the chapel remained.

We picked our way over debris, stepped through the hint of a doorway. Inside — nothing. No altar. No windows. No communion railing. No choir stalls. No organ. Had the chapel died on a grander scale, had there been time for moss to grow and sparrows to nest, had my children been more attuned to invisible angelic hosts — we might have stood within that transformed temple and imagined monks chanting, our spirits refreshed by the echoes of their strenuous piety. Bare ruined choirs. But no. Nothing like that. No sweet birds sang. A bat swooped. The iron sun beat upon our uncovered heads. Weary from hours of travel in a hot car, the children were thirsty and irritable.

Farther down the road we came upon a large square concrete building. Sterile. We pulled up to the front door. I got out and rang the bell.

A grim-faced modernized nun with whiskers answered, opening the door suspiciously. Feeling grimy and vaguely suspect (how had this woman and her children found their way to this spot so carefully hidden from the world?) I asked politely if we might have a glass of water.

"Wait here," she said and disappeared, closing the door behind her.

A few moments later she returned with one styrofoam cup full of tepid water.

I could have quoted her chapter and verse: "Whatsoever you do unto the least of these . . . " Instead, we drove away.

That abortive trip begot in me only the urge to get on with life, leave the past where it belonged, to the bats in that particular belfry.

Afternoons, after Vespers, we gathered for an hour of choir practise, twenty postulants and novices sitting erect on straight chairs in the room we called the library. Sister Dolores, choir mistress that year, drilled, persuaded, cajoled, entreated.

"Follow the line of the notation, make your voices soar, then dip. Listen!" Behind her round hornrimmed glasses, her soft brown eyes shone as her sweet soprano voice caressed those Latin vowels, belling forth pure desire. Twelve years later she would be carted away to a mental hospital, fed to the electric shock system, transformed into a frightened husk of tremulous docility.

We tried to imitate her, holding our backs ramrod straight, eager to miss no chance for bodily mortification even as we aspired to the condition of angels.

"Now, Sister. The Introit for Midnight Mass on Christmas Eve. *Dominus dixit ad me, filius meus es tu, ego hodie genui te.* Imagine you are singing from the bosom of the Trinity. Put into your voices the quiet, the hush, the mystery. This is a song from the other side, from eternity."

Day after day, as pale sun fingered frost on the casement windows, we drilled, vowelling our way toward the empyrean. Staring intently at the square notations on the tissue-thin pages of our libers (held high above our knees) we fought aching bones, tin ears, raised our voices in hope, linked in a communal fugue of the spirit. Everything was an opportunity.

For Matins on Christmas Eve, the two senior novices with the best voices, Sister Thomas and Sister Dolores, would intone the great invitatory. Though it would be sung in Latin that night, each of us was set to translate it ahead of time. " . . . in the year, from the creation of the world, when in the beginning God created heaven and earth, five thousand one hundred and ninety-nine; from the flood, two thousand nine hundred and fifty-seven; from the birth of Abraham, two thousand and fifteen; from Moses . . . " All history divided into Before and After. We rejoiced to live in the After.

The week before Christmas, at odd moments, you might come upon the two choristers practising in the most unlikely places. One afternoon, on my way to a starching session in the laundry, I met them out back near the garbage pails, their white veils fluttering in wind, blue and white gingham aprons covering their black skirts, thin shawls about their shoulders, their voices calling out across the bluelighted landscape of dead alders and denuded oaks. " . . . from Moses and the coming of the Israelites out of Egypt, one thousand five hundred and ten; from the anointing of King David, one thousand and thirty-two; in the sixty-fifth week, according to the prophecy of Daniel . . . " It might have been a clip from Ingmar Bergman.

Another day, as I carried slop to the pigs who rooted in their hardened mud enclosure at the far side of our immense vegetable garden, I came upon the choristers standing at the entrance to that snowcovered wasteland. Sister Thomas eyed me, then looked quickly down at her liber. She was my angel, an earnest, oppressively conscientious soul, charged with encouraging me through the first difficult six months of learning a new life. Those humorless eyes, that ruddy face. Later, she would leave, run off with the chaplain in her convent, a tall gaunt Jesuit with ancient-mariner eyes and a greying beard. We would not be told for days. First — her empty place in chapel, refectory. Her classes discreetly covered. Then the square typed notice on the community room bulletin board. Surrounding it all, ominous silence, the kind of silence one dreaded. In those days we all prayed daily for perseverance.

As I approached our rambunctious piglets and leaden sow that December afternoon, emptied the two heavy pails and watched the animals wriggle and snort, I heard behind me the two voices again calling across the dead landscape. " . . . in the year seven hundred and fifty-two from the founding of the city of Rome; in the forty-second year of the empire of Octavian Augustus, when the whole world was at peace . . . "

Pigs notwithstanding, it seemed to me eerily beautiful.

Peace. And starkness.

Our Advent meditations focussed on John the Baptist, on deep and simple virtues — penance, contrition, poverty, purity, humility — old fashioned words, almost an embarrassment to utter now without a tinge of irony. We avoided exuberance. We had no touch with the outside world. Advent mail would be held until Christmas Day. The house felt emptier and emptier. There was, of course, no Christmas tree, though we were surrounded by acres of evergreens. No wreaths. No presents. No candles. No tinsel.

The world outside bleached cold and grey. Snow came early that year, intensifying the sense of isolation. Isolation, separation: these were necessary. These were the sword. He had come to bring the sword. His promised peace would follow. For one half-hour a day I turned air into silver and gold, lute and reed, charmed from pipe and bellows the promise of a savior. Ah, sweet alchemy of music, strange liturgy of air. What more did I want, expect, of Christmas? Surely not the boredom of watching a lonely uncle open yet another gift-wrapped tie. Not the tedium of vacuuming styrofoam, refolding wrapping paper, organizing thank you notes. Not the catatonic post-turkey doze of geriatric relatives. No, not that.

What, then?

A week before Christmas, Sister Thomas, looking secretive and smug, surprised us postulants.

"You are permitted to make cards for your families," she said, smiling as if we'd been offered the moon. "Meet me in the novitiate room at four o'clock."

I could practise until four fifteen and did not intend to sacrifice one minute of it. By the time I got to the novitiate room, the others were already busy.

A square room on the second floor above the refectory, the novitiate room had windows along two sides, blackboards along the inside wall, and two long pine tables with chairs stretching the length of the room. Here we survived the weekly chapter of faults, absorbed conferences from Mother Theodore, and here only were we permitted, in rare moments, to study. On Visiting Sundays, whatever goodies our families brought us were set out on the long pine table to be collected by the senior novice and put away for sharing or distribution, when needed. In this room, also, each of us had a cubbyhole in the corner, a shelf which held our reading book, a notebook, pencils, various small items like that.

Now, spread out in colorful disarray along the table, were strips of colored construction paper, pencils, colored ink, brand new crayons, a calligraphy set, shiny silver foil, stars — the kind the nuns stuck to our papers in grammar school. Even a pile of cotton wads and varied pieces of colored felt. In six months I had not seen such litter, such color — except in my musical imagination.

When I entered the room Sheila glanced up with a wink that said *imagine this,* then bent quickly over her work.

Still in the afterglow of "Jesu, Joy of Man's Desiring," I

found a place, tried to think what would mean anything to my parents after the long drive up on Christmas Day to see me. I leafed through my liber, my office book, came to the three Masses of Christmas, then the Vespers. The *Magnificat* Antiphon. *Hodie Christus natus est; hodie Salvator apparuit; hodie in terra canunt Angeli, laetantur Archangeli; hodie exsultant justi, dicentes Gloria in excelsis Deo, alleluia.*

That was it. I would make a card that said simply: *Hodie Christus natus est.* Like an ancient monk, I would illuminate it. Something in gold and silver, with touches of red. First I'd outline the whole thing in black.

I began to work.

By Christmas Eve we'd finished our cards. The house shone. My back ached. I'd done what I could at the organ. Sister Angelica went over the whole service with me, checking cues. I was nervous.

After choir rehearsal we went, as usual, to the novitiate room. Here our superior wrote on the blackboard what we were to do next, setting the hours out before us like jugs. Into them we poured what we could, turning the water of time into the wine of eternity. Every minute counted.

On the blackboard in her perfect Palmer Method, she'd written: *Postulants, with Sister Thomas, go to Our Lady's Garden at 2:30.*

Our Lady's Garden? In December?

Too well trained to indulge in questioning glances, we turned and headed downstairs to the cupboards near the laundry where we kept aprons, shawls, boots. It was bitter cold, below zero. In winter we wore only a narrow crocheted shawl when we went outside, a balance to the opposite perversity that required us in ninety-degree heat to be swathed from head to toe in ten pounds of serge and plastic. In any case, that day, without a word, we gathered shawls, donned boots and aprons, and followed Sister Thomas. She carried a pail in one hand, several small knives in the other.

She headed with us out across the long front lawn, covered then with several inches of snow, toward the overgrown garden at the end of the lawn. Our Lady's Garden. Here, in summer, surrounded by nodding delphinium and iris, a wilderness of sprightly daisies and robust wild pea, I'd sit for afternoon meditation in a pool of sun watching ants, bees, mosquitos, frogs — life moving and jumping around me as I tried to still my spirit to attention. Now, in late December, the garden was a frozen tangle of choked bushes and dead roots, presided over by a glazed virgin with chipped hands and a stare as blankly cold as the pale eye of sun above us.

"We need moss," said Sister Thomas. Her full cheeks were already raw from the wind that bit at us as we crossed the long lawn. Her eyes, sharp blue, had begun to water. She pointed to the pail. "I've got a few knives. Once you've loosened the moss with a knife, it'll just pull up in strips. We need all you can get and we have only about an hour."

We didn't look at each other. This was modesty of the eyes. We didn't ask questions. This was restraint of curiosity. We separated and tried to imagine where, when no snow covered it, we could remember seeing moss. We knelt in the snow, felt wet go through out habits, our stockings, striking our callused knees. No matter. We found moss.

I pulled and yanked, got my quota. Kneeling low behind a mess of what would again be forsythia, come spring, I was somewhat protected from the wind. Nonetheless, cold fingered my bones, coated my lungs, dried my throat. My face burned, or was it numb? After a while pain began to pound at my temples. I remembered Dante's hell, a frozen pit. Judas there. Frozen. I couldn't feel my feet.

I tried not to focus on my misery. It was only body. Sister Sheila, kneeling near me, sat back on her heels and looked at me. She let out a long sigh of disgust as she crossed her arms and held her hands beneath her armpits. I returned her look. No words necessary.

I bent back over my task, my little plot, scrabbling at frozen earth, jabbing a dull knife with all my might into the crusty surface. It was Christmas Eve. *"Consolamini, consolamini, popule meus,"* we would sing in a few hours at Matins, Isaiah promising a redeemer. Impudent hope. . . . But still, I did love the liturgy, its empowering faith that by joining in a prayer so ancient and timeless one broke apart the bonds of time and, in some mysterious way, entered the stream of salvific history. *Consolamini.* I said the word over and over, desperate incantation against the railing of my mind. I knew all about the third degree of humility, even then. And already doubted my capacity to practise it. That day, however, in the Advent spirit, I tried. I went on digging. *Veni ad liberandum nos.*

After an hour, Sister Thomas nodded appreciatively, gestured toward her nearly full pail, gathered the knives from our raw hands, wiped the tears from her cheeks, and led us back up the front lawn — cold, tired, our cheeks like chopped meat, our hands numb and bleeding.

Merry Christmas.

That night we were put to bed early. "Put to bed" sounds odd for a group of college graduates in their early twenties. It is accurate. We were told to retire by eight thirty since we would be rising at eleven for Matins and Lauds and then midnight Mass.

I went to my cell and hung out my special Sunday postulant's veil to put on later. I prepared for bed as quietly as possible, spreading a thin white washcloth in my basin to mute the sound of the cold water I poured from my pitcher, lifting each hook of my cell curtain carefully so as not to make a zing. The dormitory was very quiet that night, each of us no doubt trying to maintain the maximum inner silence to prepare for His coming. My hands still ached from battling earth in the quest for moss. I worked at my nails, digging out dirt, but traces of it resisted. Finally I lay down on the narrow bed, turned on my side, put my hands under my pillow, and barely remembering to think of the points for my next morning's meditation, fell into a deep sleep.

Something jarred. Tearing ragged edges of sleep. Slitting dreams. Some sound. Angels? A sound unlike any I'd heard. Close by. Just outside the cell curtain. High above their blending voices rang a pure clear soprano, full and round. Sister Dolores, surely. No one else could sing like that.

"O little town of Bethlehem, how still we see thee lie / Above thy deep and dreamless streets . . . " Their voices moved away, out of the dormitory, into the hallway. Joy rang through the large silent house. I could hear them in the other dormitory, then back out in the hall, then fading down the hallway at the opposite end of the house where the two lay sisters who cooked for us slept. "Hark the Herald Angels Sing." "Angels We Have Heard on High." The very carols I'd dared on the muted organ all those weeks. Sung now legitimately. Christmas was upon us.

Sleepers wake! Other sounds began to accompany the singers — water in the pipes, slippers on hardwood floors as sisters moved out of their cells, emptied water in the sink room, donned their habits, headed out into the upstairs hallway.

Here stood Sister Thomas with the satisfied look of a mother about to watch her child open a present. (Only now does the analogy strike me.) No more moss. No more cold. She motioned us through the dark hallway to . . . the front stairs! From the day of our arrival when our novice mistress first descended them to greet our parents, it had been made clear that these were *her* stairs. No novice or postulant walked on those hallowed boards except to clean them. For two months, in fact, that had been my charge. In the early days of my postulancy, morning after morning I'd knelt on each step, carefully wiping away invisible dust, hating every minute of it.

And now we were motioned toward them, to descend.

The bannister had been wound about with shining tinsel. Through the window at the top of the stairs (I stopped to look out, it was Christmas Eve) I saw snow falling heavily. And at the bottom — there, surrounded by singing novices watching us, smiling, a Christmas tree! A huge tree, floor to ceiling, bedecked with garlands and lights and balls and small figures (not only liturgical symbols, either) and tinsel icicles. Red and green and yellow lights winking in the darkness, their dance reflected in the patio doors at the far side of the room whose panes we'd polished that very week. Small bright lights, colorful static against the snow-falling dark.

The novices were singing. Mother Theodore stood there with them, gesturing us five to join in. Her ageless face — was she fifty, sixty? — usually stern though not unkind, looked relaxed now, softened by the Christmas lights shining on her. She watched us as if to say, "See? Christmas isn't so bad here. It's special." Even before this we had noted in her hints of humanity. She was what we called in those days a woman of prayer.

After a few moments, she gestured us to silence, indicating that we should follow into chapel.

The sanctuary glowed, bathed in light. Red poinsettias

everywhere — on the steps leading to the altar, beneath the side altars, and gold vases holding other red flowers on the altar itself. What were they? Gold and red everywhere. Tall golden candlesticks. The only other lights in chapel came from two tall tapers standing beside the gold lectern in the middle of the nave. From here, choristers would intone the invitatory.

I took my place, opened my liber, waited. Chapel was still chilly but it would warm up. My stomach was on edge. Getting up for midnight vigil always brought on nausea. Sister Dolores and Sister Thomas walked to the center of the nave, bowed, faced the altar.

Never had I heard anything like it! Not even on the cold darkening afternoons when their voices cut the blue light of a December sky. Shadowy chapel, brilliant sanctuary, nuns in their white veils standing in choir on either side of the nave, two choristers in the center by the lighted tapers — calling into the dark, toward the lighted sanctuary, those same divisions of history I'd heard before.

I watched them. I wasn't to watch them, but I did. I couldn't see their faces, just the black habits, the long soft white novice veils. I closed my eyes to listen to words I'd practically memorized in the weeks before and could now easily translate. I followed as they counted from Adam, from the flood, from Noah, from Abraham, from David — from all the points in Time Before that marked the inevitability of His coming . . . until that great beginning moment, the moment of new time, which, as they chanted, we knelt to acknowledge.

" . . . in the sixth age of the world, Jesus Christ, eternal God, and son of the eternal Father, desirous to sanctify the world by His most merciful coming, having been conceived of the Holy Ghost, and nine months having elapsed since His conception, is born in Bethlehem of Judea, having become Man of the Virgin Mary."

Their voices dropped. They bowed, turned, walked back to their places in choir. Who cared if their arrangement of history was a fiction (what arrangement isn't?), an ingenious device to help memory. We knew about literary forms, multiple authorship, synoptic boondoggles, the perils of translation. We knew things could be only *so* literal. Still . . . the beauty, the urgency of it.

Our own voices followed — less dramatic, a sustained singing of the Hours that told us Christmas was almost there. "Take comfort, my people, says your God. Speak tenderly to Jerusalem, and proclaim to her that her service is at an end, her guilt is expiated . . . " Now Isaiah could be believed.

The words flew by me. St. Leo telling us: "It would be unlawful to be sad today, for today is Life's birthday; the birthday of that Life which, for us mortal creatures, takes away the sting of death and brings us the bright promise of an eternal hereafter. No one is excluded from sharing in this joy . . . " Part of my mind took it all in, but underneath everything it seemed to me nothing could match that soaring invitatory, the pure high voice of longing nourished by faith, human desire singing its own fulfillment.

Near the end of Matins I must slip out of my stall and head to the organ at the back of chapel, warm it up, prepare the registration, be ready. Just before I left my place, from the corner of my eye, I saw the family who farmed for us bundle into the balcony. Five children, snow on their hats and coats, and their vigorous father who came to the back door every morning with the huge milk pails and collected the empties. Who cared for the pigs we fed once a day. Who watched the cows we did not milk. Who slaughtered the chickens yearly with our help. It comforted me, in some unfathomable way, that Mr. Riordan and his wife and girls had joined us, were part of it, waiting with us. That October he'd taken us postulants to the cornfield at the very moment when asceticism and housecleaning weighed especially heavy. The envelope of self-denial burst open as we piled into the back of his truck and headed off, singing, toward the golden ripe cornfield. Up and down the rows we moved, harvesting, our blue and white aprons hidden in the waving sea of ripeness. The hillside was bursting with life and we were part of it.

When I sat at the organ now, I felt them behind me in the small balcony. Reverend Mother was beside me in her stall. On the seat beside her lay the plaster-of-Paris baby. I saw now that she would have to put it in the crèche. That had never occurred to me. It was so concrete, so literal.

I moved softly into the carols. "Hark the Herald Angels Sing," "O Little Town of Bethlehem." I played strings, flutes, shorter pipes, one principal. We were still waiting. Finally, on the stroke of midnight, as I'd been instructed, I opened registration to a plenum and played "Silent Night." Reverend Mother rose from her place, took the battered looking babe, carried it down the center of the nave to the crèche. I couldn't watch, though I'd already caught sight of one thing when the lights went up on the side altars. Moss. There it was, lining the crèche. Our scraping and scrabbling had found moss on which to rest the baby. I noted this almost casually, busy as I was finding the right keys. Already that afternoon excursion and my contest with resistant earth seemed as remote as the world I'd left six months before. A remnant of dirt remained beneath my nails, but my fingers were busy making music. The sisters sang quietly, three full verses. Reverend Mother returned, eyes down, to her place.

Into the sanctuary padded the small Capuchin who served us. Tonight he wouldn't need the basin of steaming water Mother Theodore usually prepared for his bare feet. He wore heavy white socks inside his sandals.

"*Dixit Dominus ad me . . .* "

Mass began, the organ quietly underlining voices that rose now to heights and depths not heard in the stuffy library on Advent afternoons. I could forget the literalness of the plaster baby. It seemed so pitiful in the midst of this sacrament of history we were creating, enacting, so pitiful to carry a plaster baby to the crib and put it before kneeling Mary and Joseph. But what would I have had? An empty crèche? The child mysteriously appearing there when no one was around to see where it came from? Perhaps.

Mass proceeded. The *Gloria* shone, bells and voices shimmering praise. The sisters had never sounded better. I felt my power. My feet moved as I wanted them to, found the right pedals, my wrists did not tighten, the organ merged with their voices in a satisfying Christmas harmony. Incense. Bells. No sermon. Our Capuchin spoke little English. Communion. Palestrina.

Then, quickly it seemed, it was over. The lights in chapel were dimmed as the sisters knelt to make their thanksgiving. Sister Henry moved about the sanctuary, dousing candles, fixing the altar. I stayed at the organ, waiting. After a few moments, Reverend Mother rang the bell she kept on her stall, a small silver dome like the nuns in elementary school had on their desks.

Eyes down, hands in their full sleeves, the sisters left their stalls, met by the lectern, bowed to the altar, and proceeded out, two by two, past the organ. I was into "Jesu, Joy of Man's Desiring," playing carefully, hoping I'd get through it. Reverend Mother left last. No one else in chapel except Sister Henry out in the sacristy. I'd keep playing to the very end, let the sounds fill the chapel. I opened the swell box. Behind me the Riordans were still sitting in their pew. I played for them. If I delayed now, I'd get to bed ten minutes later than the others.

The sink room would be empty. I could go through my ablutions undisturbed.

The end. At last. I closed the organ, clicked off the switch, slid from the bench.

I went through the library, in darkness now, oak chairs in their perfect rows, piano keyboard covered. Through the foyer — usually dark, lighted now by the winking Christmas tree. I headed past the stairs, her stairs, still festooned with tinsel. And into — the refectory. *Lighted! Full of novices and postulants!* Candles on tables, a beautiful full wreath suspended on the wall behind Mother Theodore's table where usually the white alabaster crucifix of the suffering Christ gleamed. Food. I took my place.

"*Benedicamus Domino,*" said Our Mother quietly. "Merry Christmas."

Never had anything like this occurred. Talking — at midnight in the refectory, a place of great silence. And presents on the table! In front of my place were two small packages carefully wrapped. And candles, lighted, spaced along the table. Perfect miniature chocolate logs, candles in them, decorated with holly and red berries. By each place a whole unwrapped candy bar.

Such were the gifts: a toothbrush, a box of notepaper. A candy bar. And the greatest gift of all — joy where I'd expected none. Human warmth I recognized, partly of the old kind, partly new. Novices and postulants, weary from weeks of prayer and preparation, celebrating together.

Tomorrow would come intrusion, the other world, parents arriving with their gifts, their anxious concern. But for this moment, for just this one hour, the wholeness felt different.

SPEAKING BODIES
A Trinity of Dancers

Summer, 1955. DANCE AS MEMORY

Compose a world.

Not this one in which you gobble Raisin Bran, fill the gas tank and roar out to purposefulness. Not this one in which you cherish your partner, humor your children, worry about meeting bills. Or don't. Another world entirely.

Where partners are not the issue, nor children, nor even meeting bills. Where only one thing matters.

Where heat is not only felt but visible, a shimmering scarf blanketing fields of vegetables and corn, burning backs of cattle and bulls, weaving gauze about the outermost limbs of appletrees bent now to late summer ripeness. Somehow, heat is important for this picture of a farm hidden away in Vermont.

The key word is "hidden." We are not usually privy to this world. In fact, it's no longer there.

The figures in our imagined world are twenty novices and postulants in a religious order. They seek God. Their quest may seem dated, their motives unfathomable, their piety tedious, but grant them in your sympathetic composing intelligence, bodies, feelings and will. They've been here only eight weeks, having left far behind them that other world of cars and noise, flesh throb and heartache, interest payments and debt. The fleshpots of Egypt. They knew it well and rejected it.

Sometimes, though, on these sizzling afternoons, they're tempted, like Ruth, to weep amid the alien corn. Nonetheless, they strive to control their emotions, pray daily for perseverance. They hadn't expected to spend long afternoons weeding, bent silently over rows choked with carrots, beneath the burning sun. It's a medieval scene: long skirted peasant women tending the fields as they wait for the Angelus. But these, after all, are college graduates.

So our diligent neophytes bend in obedience beneath the sun, thinning carrots and beets, picking beans, trying to rid their minds of distraction. This is God's work. That's all that matters.

The body cries out against such labor. Muscles knot and complain after hours of kneeling upright in chapel, or crawling about to wax already gleaming floors, or bending over zinc boards to starch linens against disintegration in the heat.

Seeking holiness can only confuse.

And exhaust.

Their knees grow callused, their muscles harden.

Their minds empty.

They have been called together this particular August evening for a special occasion.

An important visitor has come from Rome, from the Generalate, a representative of Mother General herself. Reverend Mother Augustine will survey the beaming healthy faces of these young postulants and novices, then return across the sea reassured that there are still young women in this world willing to forsake all for Christ.

But wait: tonight they will have a treat.

They sit in a double circle of straight chairs in the novitiate library, a room whose books they are as yet permitted only to dust. It is safe to assume they are tired after a long day in the fields. Usually this evening recreation period, the one time of day when they are permitted to talk, is a time for general conversation and mending. Tonight, though, no one has brought mending. They will keep their black laps empty, attend to the Visitor.

"We have a surprise tonight, Sisters," says Mother Theodore. She glances about the circle at eager young nuns, hers to form for God.

"Sister Albert, you may go out now and prepare," she says quietly.

Sister Albert, a roly-poly sister with high color and large pale blue eyes behind hornrimmed glasses, rises immediately, bows to her superiors, and leaves the room. Sister Albert has been here eighteen months. She graduated from college *magna cum laude*.

The library opens into a large central hallway where a wrinkled gnome named Sister Hélène has been hovering. Ancient and French, she is a lay sister. She speaks little English and takes heartfelt delight in fattening the bodies of the young sisters she feeds. She has been here thirty years.

"All right, Sister Hélène," says Mother Theodore toward the doorway. "You can bring them in now."

In shuffles Sister Hélène carrying two brooms. Her cracked shoes are unlaced. Arthritis slows her. With some difficulty she bends over and sets the brooms on the floor in the midst of the circle of black skirts. They form an X.

"Now, Sister Patricia, do you need to get ready?"

A slim, pale, nondescript-looking sister nods to her superior and leaves the room. Sister Patricia came in July. This is her eighth week. She is hiding profound homesickness.

Re-enter Sister Albert — *carrying an accordion!*

A murmur of surprised pleasure runs through the room. Reverend Mother Augustine smiles, large white teeth cracking a granite jaw. Her hands lie loosely clasped in her wide black lap.

Sister Albert was famous at college for her accordion

playing. She and Sister Patricia both hail from the same section in the Bronx, the old Irish section, where yearly minstrels and weekly dancing lessons kept alive in the body what Masses and novenas and rosaries were meant to keep alive in the soul.

Sister Albert beams at them all, her round face flushed, her eyes bright. She has taken off her guimpe, the semi-circular celluloid piece that usually covers her breasts. Without it, she looks strangely incomplete. She holds the accordion — all buttons and knobs and glittering ivories — against her black pleated chest. With a gentle heave, she expands the bellows.

Now Sister Patricia hurries in, her veil pinned back, away from her face, and her skirts pinned up behind her, exposing a long shiny black petticoat. She looks at no one.

She steps into one V formed by the broom handles and stands there facing her superiors, eyes fastened on some distant spot behind their heads. She places her hands on her hips. For a long moment she simply stands there, eyes remote, as if awaiting a secret signal. She might be a statue. Then, with a swift subtle movement, she goes up on her toes.

Sister Albert begins to play. The bellows breathe, her fingers race across the keys, her left hand pushing all those silver buttons. The strains of a lively jig resound through the library.

The black shoes come alive!

Above them, Sister Patricia's body seems barely to move, her hands clasped now behind her back, her long black skirt hiding the folding knees. All that shows are the nimble feet in their shiny black Oxfords, falling and rising, as she dances above, across, into the V's formed by the broom. Faster and faster the music races. Sister Albert's fingers fly. Sister Patricia's usually pale face grows slowly pink, then rosy. Small beads of perspiration glisten on her forehead. On and on she goes — up, down, in, out, faster, faster. She closes her eyes.

Will that dancing body never stop? Moment by moment, it

gathers to itself all the other bodies in the library until they become as one — one set of eyes, one set of bending knees, one organism of breathing — rising falling, rising falling — caught up in the weaving magic of the dance. Ancient Sister Hélène, sitting near the doorway, usually too shy to appear for any recreation, looks happy in her wizened way, her wrinkled face turned toward Sister Patricia's rising, falling, rising feet.

In and out the bellows fold. Sister Albert's fingers race. Over and over, into the V's, the feet dance, never touching the broom handles. She seems weightless. Bodiless. The sisters begin to clap. The two superiors are smiling. Mother Theodore is nodding her usually sedate head in time with the music. Mother Augustine rubs one finger up and down the back of her other hand. Small beads of perspiration glisten above Sister Patricia's parted lips.

On and on she dances, higher and higher, all effortless grace. She is breathing hard. Her mouth is opening further. Her feet seem barely to touch the floor, grazing that polished surface for a fleeting instant before they rise again to midair. Her eyes stay fixed on the spot behind the visiting superior. As if she's remembering, hearing from some other world. As if an invisible force lifts her, carries her, holds that black body aloft, suspended, gravity-defiant.

The music stops.

Sister Patricia drops her eyes.

She is coming to. Returning.

She looks about the circle, at her superiors.

Then she bows, dropping suddenly into the chair she'd vacated. "More. More!" the novices clap.

"I can't" she gasps. "I can't." Her clear face shines. Small red patches appear high on her cheekbones. She accepts a large white handkerchief someone offers her and wipes her face. "No more breath!"

This was harder work, more taxing than weeding carrots, than meditating.

It took almost all her breath.

She sits there heaving, gasping.

Sister Albert beams.

What voice called forth from oxford-shod feet patterns of movement that young sister had striven to forget?

Obedience. "You will dance for us, Sister."

Obedience to what?

Her superior.

Don't you believe it. She danced, yes. But not because she'd been told, although that had something to do with it.

Obedience to another power. The power of memory itself. As if muscles and tendons could remember, as if her flesh, tamed as it was, willed to hold intact rhythms from a former time, that other world so recently left . . . rhythms ready at a moment's notice to break out through instep, arch, and ankle . . . turn silence into speaking flesh.

On that hot August evening, in that hidden valley, in that vanished time and world, Sister Patricia's dance was pure gift. For a brief period, something split open in that room, cracked apart by remembering hands, remembering feet, remembering body. Fresh bracing air whooshed through cloistered rooms, soothing cloistered bodies. David danced before the Ark. His dance was integral, beauty in flesh, a service of spirit. Her nimble black feet and that oh so still young nun's body spoke of memory, of power.

The flesh does not forget.

Winter, 1972. DANCE AS TEMPTATION.

Compose a second world.

No convent now. No idealism. No setting of earnest piety, focussed dedication. No anxiety about the hereafter. This time we are plunked squarely in the moment. In time itself.

The scene is more familiar: a busy hotel in a large Canadian city. Time: nearing midnight. The bar in this hotel features evening entertainment. And a small dance floor.

You are sitting at a round table next to the dance floor, close enough to see perspiration form on foreheads nearby trying to remember the cha-cha, close enough to observe muscles rippling as hips shift in the effort to look oh so authentically Latin.

A few feet away, behind a silver microphone she grasps as she sings, a tall curvaceous blonde in a spangled white sheath belts it out. The V of her dress plunges deep, spangles shimmer and ripple across her full breasts as she sways. Her voice, throaty and sexy, assaults, coaxes, teases. There is no way to tune her out. You either leave the room or submit to this beat, this voice, this music. Behind her the drummer, the acoustic keyboard and bass players watch the sheathed body, decoding cues. Now and then they eye each other. The drummer looks bored. He may be stoned.

Two couples move about the tiny dance floor. The couple next to your table fascinate you.

How could eyes look so hungry?

If the music stopped, you might hear him panting. He wears a dark suit of fine cloth, his black shoes shine, his white collar gleams, and a subdued silk tie announces him as prosperous. Or wishing to appear so. His white hair, thick and wavy, reaches just to his collar. He wears rimless glasses that cannot obscure the hunger behind them. He is tall, his legs long in their subtle pinstripes, his arms also long. He is a mimic. A puppet.

How can a man look so hungry?

His partner — can we call her that? — has eyes both distant and intimate. Cool. Insinuating. Her eyes seem never to leave his, as though some invisible wire bound him to her. Not gold to airy thinness beat. No, more like an electric current, connected when they move in sync. She moves, he moves. Always, she moves first by a fraction of a second.

Her face is rather long, her eyes dark and almond shaped, her full lips a brilliant red. Except for the magnetic eyes, you wouldn't notice her in a crowded room. Here, on this tiny dance floor, she displays her singular gift: a speaking body. To his stiffness, she is supple, to his groping, speech. Her bones and muscles seem capable of melting; she is all insinuating curves. *Come . . . dare . . . let's . . . let's not . . . can you hold me . . . just try. . . .*

We'll call her Susannah.

For all the articulateness of her body, there's a certain carelessness about Susannah's grace.

The silky blue of her dress seems glued to her slender body.

He, on the other hand, is awkward, trying too hard, his earnestness embarrassing beside her cool. He struggles to answer her steps, her gestures, bends stiffly toward her gyrating hips, her thrusting breasts, her slim legs scissoring, bending, retreating, advancing.

Her hazel eyes are cold. Between her slightly parted scarlet lips the pink tip of her tongue shows. Long, ringed fingers wave scarlet nails close to his mouth. Silver-braceleted wrists weave signals in midair, slender and graceful. Eyes, lips, fingers, wrists, breasts, hips, ankles: everything teases, undulating before him, inviting, rejecting. Liquid courses through her. She is hot. She is cold.

We'll call him Guy.

He came alone tonight. Home is far away, a small town in the prairies. He lives in a new split level which, at his wife's request, is painted powder blue. His wife loves flowers and keeps them in the window boxes. Red geraniums. She insisted on white shutters and even now, at forty-three, still enjoys her nest. A woman easily satisfied.

He has acquired the habit of loving his wife.

He flew here yesterday to complete a business deal. He buys and sells condos. The deal fell through. Beneath fluorescent lights, in a room deadened by plastic plants and calculating eyes, he lost his bid for property. The exchange was marked by courteous expressions of regret, vague wishes for better luck next time, firm handshakes. He hasn't yet called home about this. A three-hour time difference separates him from those window boxes. He has time to kill. . . . A worm of despair gnaws at his heart.

He wears his fine cloth. He feels well-dressed, if disconsolate.

At the bar, sipping his Johnny Walker, he saw her come in: a single thirtyish woman in a fur jacket. Spike heels. Black hair to her shoulders. She stood in the doorway a moment looking over the room as if she knew its every cranny. She turned toward the bar.

The tall glass grew wet and cold in his manicured forty-five-year-old hand. Before she came in, he'd been observing its veins.

She sat rather daintily at the far end of the bar. He couldn't see her legs. The Scotch burned his throat. In the mirror behind the bar, he studied the graceful curve of her arm. Her breasts, high and pointed, pressed against the polished dark wood of the counter. He undressed her. Slim waist. Small pointed breasts that didn't droop. Dark nipples. Skin like velvet with a salty taste. Small, firm curves of the buttocks. Watching her, he felt a throb, a pulse. He grew hard. Desire coated his throat, his mind, invaded his nerves.

Evidently, she knew the bartender — a heavy man with two chins and grey bushy eyebrows that met above his small nose. They exchanged a few quiet words. She made him laugh. She didn't share the laugh as he passed her a transparent liquid in a tall glass.

Guy's wife loves to please. She has recently begun going to evening classes in creative writing. "For fun," she says. The instructor, a bearded guru with an earring and boundless enthusiasm, encourages her. "I think I'll write a book," she said last week after class. She has a hundred cookbooks, spends hours flipping through recipes. She sits up evenings in her housecoat sipping Weight Watchers hot chocolate as she watches the late news. He's tried, fruitlessly, to interest her in a cruise. She cannot dance, would miss her flowers. Besides, she's going to write a book.

Why not tonight? he thought. He'd done it before. Nothing major. He moved down the length of the bar and took the empty stool beside her. He bought her a drink.

Asked her to dance.

Susannah saw how hungry he was. She's used to reading the eyes of thwarted males.

He's no Herod. He doesn't want a head. Just a body.

On the dance floor, she thrusts her hips forward. *"Let me touch you,"* belts out the singer.

He moves in. Leans over, as if to lick her breasts. The sharp electric blue of her dress outlines perfect breasts. He can taste the round firm nipples. She retreats. Retreat is too strong a word. She is suddenly not there — dextrously. Frustratingly.

"Tell me what your body says, your body says . . . "

The chase. He moves again, mimicking her steps clumsily. His shoes are size twelve. She's behind him now. He imagines her arms reaching around him . . . But she never touches him. "*Show me what your body does.*" She throws back her head, black hair grazing her shoulders. He turns quickly. He throws back his head. She makes a small circle around him, tantalizing. Her arms ripple, her elbows melt.

"*Whisper now your body's words . . .*"

He turns to follow her. His arms reach out from his sides awkwardly.

"*Whisper now your body's touch . . .*"

The white spangled sheath weaves and bends with the microphone. The strobe light whirls. The drummer looks stoned. He stifles a yawn.

"*Show me what your body does . . . says . . . does . . .*"

This is a choose your ending story. Does the ending really matter? For example:

1) Several hours later:

A sliver of weak light penetrates thick motel room drapes, crosses the rumpled bed, touches a streak of red in the conservative tie thrown across a table, shines on a pool of black silk underwear heaped on the floor by the bed. Two forms sleep, breathing heavily. Susannah feels the tender dawnlight, hears a sound somewhere (was it her dream?), wakens suddenly. She looks at the naked lump beside her. He is snoring lightly. She sees a small red spot on the side of his nose. Her mouth feels stuffed with cotton batting. Carefully, she eases from the bed . . . tiptoes across the room.

She rummages through his heaped-up trousers for the wallet. He stirs but does not waken as, a few minutes later, the door clicks shut behind her.

2) Half an hour later, at a table above the dance floor:

Susannah dawdles over her drink. She is thinking, weighing. It doesn't require much wit to read his eyes. Is he safe? What's in it for her? She's had her fun. Her feet are killing her.

She gathers her purse, feels the small hard outline of the revolver inside. He follows her to the door of the bar. She pauses there, looks at Guy, sees again the raging hunger. A thrill flashes through her, the sharp deep pleasurable stab of power.

"Sorry," she lies. "It was nice to meet you, Guy. Thanks for the drink. And — I enjoyed the dance." Her cool eyes defy hunger.

She murmurs one last remark he barely catches. Then she turns and clicks quickly away through the doorway, down the carpeted hallway, out into the night.

He watches the fur jacket, the tight electric blue behind as it turns a corner, disappears. Damned good legs.

What had she murmured?

"The dance was it, Guy. That's it for tonight."

He returns to the bar.

That's that.

She's gone. Susannah's gone.

She is not. He doesn't know this yet.

He will discover it as he reinvents her: evenings, yawning by the TV; mornings, munching cold cereal; noonhours, suppressing self-doubt. Driving through a featureless snowed-in world, he will recreate her electric blue, taste her salty flesh, watch her teasing tongue, suffer anew the cold dare of her distant, measuring eyes. Lying on the unforgiving sand of a Pacific beach, he will plumb again the ambiguity of her flesh.

Just so will he discover, again and again, the memory of flesh, his own flesh, holding within himself his Susannah of the dance more securely, more intimately than if he'd taken her to bed, where there was no way he could ever hold her, ever know her.

She will never and always be his.

It's written in his aging bones, his fragile nerves, inscribed in the tension of his ligaments, the reach of his dreams.

Susannah's dance. Her speaking body.

Summer, 1982. DANCE AS ART

Compose a third world.

This time you are visiting an obscure French-Canadian village on the Bay of Fundy in Nova Scotia. It's called Pointe d'Église.

It is late August. Early in the morning, mist and fog shroud this spectacular coast. By midday fog has lifted to reveal an expanse of deep blue water, a sky brilliant and clear. Tides climb an extraordinary fifty feet to pound against ancient rocks, or recede to uncover beaches pebbled with pink and purple stones, mounds of driftwood. Often at night the fog settles in again, wrapping this rocky shore in an impenetrable shroud.

With or without the fog, this spot is off the beaten tourist path. You would have to search to find it.

You are one of a hundred or so amateur dancers who gather here every year for their annual camp during the third week of August. The only family dance camp of its kind in North America. It's been going on for over thirty years. Every year teachers fly in to instruct eager dancers in four kinds of social dancing — square, ballroom, folk, Scottish country. Anyone can come. The only prerequisite is an interest in learning to dance, a love of it. All kinds and levels of dancers gather here — beginners, advanced, or somewhere in between. Their ages range from two or three years old to eighty. Some come single, some come double, some bring a different partner every year.

It is Wednesday evening, nine o'clock. Fog has long since settled in over the bay.

This afternoon, after four intense days and evenings of dancing, the campers had time off. They've been busy preparing for the Ceilidh, the talent show. Every year, amazing talents emerge on this evening to surprise and delight campers. Skits. Dances. Songs. Readings. Drama. Two solid hours of entertainment.

All the campers have gathered now in the intimate college theater-in-the-round. Small children sit crosslegged in a row on the floor facing the space where the acts take place. Some are still in costume from their acts — cowboys, Indians, Acadian dancers.

Our Master of Ceremonies this year is a white haired kindhearted Nova Scotia gentleman, a dance camp regular for twenty years, an experienced English Country dancer who understands courtesy. With tact and thinly disguised anxiety, he introduces the next offering on tonight's program.

"Before our next part of the program, I would like to remind you that what you are about to see is truly an art form. One we do not often have the opportunity to see."

He looks at the row of small children sitting before him. "It is a very ancient art," he continues. He eyes their parents, grandparents. "In many countries a highly respected art."

He steps back to sit down near the spotlight he will manage.

Silence.

Eerie music floats from somewhere. What are those instruments? Flutes? Cymbals? Pipes? Snake charmers. Scheherazade. Arabian Nights. Kismet.

Quietly, from somewhere behind the audience, down the center aisle she floats, a maze of transparent scarves and bangles. Or is it one enormous scarf she wields so expertly that it seems several scarves of many colors? She floats into the center of the space reserved for her.

Can this really be the woman with one leg shorter than the other who for three days has carried a heavy, built-up shoe through intricate square dances that confuse even the nimble-footed? The woman whose lined face shows suffering, experience, no one knows what else? It's her first year here. Her skin is dark, almost swarthy. She's worn little make-up. Deep lines gouge one cheek. She's been friendly between classes but reserved, not completely into the camper style. She has talked little but shown up for every square dance class.

She is barefoot. Her legs look tanned. The toenails of her bare feet are painted iridescent purple. Gold bangles lace her bare arms.

Loose transparent gauzy purple balloon pants are gathered at her ankles by bands of gold. Another band of shining gold secures these ballooning trousers low on her hips. Above her bare midriff a small top of rose diaphanous stuff with gold trim covers her breasts, and a single wide strap goes over one shoulder.

She begins to sway to the music — subtly, quietly, almost gliding into it. Bit by bit the music grows. What are those instruments? She moves with deeper intensity. She sees no one. Her eyes look down. Sometimes they survey her own body. Lingeringly. Rings gleam on every finger. From her ears dangle gold intricacies. Her pulled-back dark hair, fastened behind with a circle of magenta and gold, hangs in a loose fall to the middle of her back.

Gyrating, undulating, moving ever so softly, ever so insistently, she bends to the music, floating her scarves — is it only one? yes, one — around her, in front of her. Her hips seem to have a life of their own. Turning. Turning. In. Out. Her legs, in their purple gauze, billow and ripple. And her feet. The ankles turn, the instep curves, even the toes seem attuned to her rhythm.

Her belly! How can hips and belly be so expressive? In, out, around, up, down she weaves . . . calling a mysterious message to the encircling campers. A message that gathers them. In thin air, it is the dance of a body perfectly controlled, perfectly fluid, as if muscle and ligament and vein and artery, as if every nerve existed to serve the lord of the dance whose inner call she hears and heeds, bodying it forth to music as eerie as the unfamiliar movement of her body.

No age here. No record of time passing.

Only naked flesh, speaking flesh, flesh that breathes and sings with rare and pure intensity of its own beauty, the beauty of all flesh. Until tonight she seemed an ordinary being. Not particularly attractive. Somewhat withdrawn. Crippled.

She never hurries. Time holds no threat. It cannot touch her. She does not fear the future nor recall the past. Her particular life is of no account. All that matters is this singing speaking body. She shows forth to us — gathered, rapt — the very life of flesh, of body, moving to its own song — expressive, seductive, contained.

She is no David before the Ark, no Salome before Herod. No saint. No seducer. No head will come in on a tray except our own. These she holds, the heads of all of us, every viewer — grandparents, parents, children, adolescents: caught and held.

Moving hips tell all. And shining scarves. And limbs that breathe.

She speaks to us through curves and spirals and sweeping lines her hips describe in air that seems itself transformed by movement.

She needs no partner.

We are her partners.

In the discovery of what body can do — alive, disciplined, sensuous, speaking, calling, flesh to flesh. She shows us now, in this golden moving moment, bodied forth and floating before our bewitched eyes, the enchantment of a body speaking.

The music stops.

She stays a moment, suspended.

Scarves gently fall.

Time returns.

No one claps.

She sees no one.

She turns away.

Floats out.

And then the clapping starts.

INHERITING

My oldest son is fourteen, about to make his confirmation. I've thought lately about the meaning of this word *confirm*. I know it means to make strong or make certain. I do not know what this means in the world of 1984 — post-Holocaust, pre-Apocalypse, the world of Michael Jackson, Woody Allen, a movie-star president, a jet-set pope, Boy George, COUNT DOWN, break dancing, sperm banks, AIDS. Tomorrow night the bishop will strike my son gently on the cheek and pray that he be filled with the Holy Spirit, a worthy prayer. I'm certain, however, that getting a set of army fatigues is at this moment more important to Peter than being anointed by the bishop and declared a soldier of Christ.

When he was born, we named him for his Great-Uncle Peter. Around the age of four or five, he began to realize he had this very old great-uncle, a bachelor, who showed up at holiday gatherings with camera, new bow tie, and clear if unspoken designs on the family. Not that a four- year-old knew what those designs were, but he responded to them instinctively, playing up to the needs of his silent uncle in the way a canny child can.

This is a story about inheriting.

I'd been told by that uncle that one day little Pete would be taken care of, that I needn't worry myself about his education. This, in days when worry about higher education was as remote as Mount McKinley. When you're immersed in managing the successive challenges of diapers, Fisher Price dump trucks, training wheels, Big Bird, Miss Piggy, and Legos that seem of their own volition to climb into your son's bed or roll down the toilet, the dilemma of financing higher education is hardly compelling. So for some years that promise of Uncle Pete's was more a matter of occasional curiosity than anything else. The will of a shrewd bachelor uncle pushing ninety is bound to tease anyone's imagination.

Uncle Pete died when little Pete was ten. I'd never imagined just what it would feel like to inherit. Then suddenly, on a Friday like any other, there it was sitting in the mailbox along with the catalogue from Harry and Davids, a bill from the telephone company, a letter from mother and a flyer from Sears: *Last Will and Testament of Peter C. Delaney.*

I took it to my room to read in peace. Little Pete was out with his dad, and Anna was playing with cars and trucks in the back yard. With luck, I'd have an hour to myself.

I was unprepared for the surge of emotion that swept me as I read its opening words: *I, Peter C. Delaney, residing at 1432 Linden Lane, in the City and County of Rochester and State of New York . . .*

A voice from the dead, from one who sat silently through years of family gatherings sending the felt message: fuss over me.

Being of sound mind: no doubt of that.

"Sharp as a tack, still," pronounced my mother, a mere eighty herself, returning from a visit to Uncle Pete's nursing home the year before he died. "Even at ninety-three, Claire. He hates being there, of course. But he quoted the Dow Jones Index for yesterday. I hope I'm that way when I go."

Hope takes the oddest shapes.

. . . and memory: did he do anything else all day, near the end, but remember? Sitting by the barred window, excruciatingly thin, always put together — the string tie, the bushy moustache, the faded blue eyes. His skin grew transparent; the

veins in his long thin hands turned the color of dry ice. He was the venerable family archivist — a role hard to sustain in a family too separated now, too busy living to notice.

A year and a half before the end I did the right thing — took the two oldest children to see their Great-Uncle Pete, who was, the doctor again thought, dying. We happened to be spending six weeks in the East that summer, southern Vermont, close enough to make the trip both ways in one day. Extracting them from the town pool, I bribed them into clean clothes and drove through shimmering July heat for three hours to the handsome brick building on King's Way. *The King's Arms* it was called, an embrace he despised to the end. Past the front desk ("Mr Delaney? Room 10, right through those doors."), past the Visitors' Register, past the blaring TV room and down the long air-conditioned corridor I hustled them. On one wall a sign: *Today is Thursday.*

The door pushed open noiselessly.

Was the long, thin figure lying on the bed in his maroon silk bathrobe and unpolished shoes asleep or just resting? I'd never before seen him rumpled. Tacked to the light green wall above the bed a handwritten sign said: *Hard of hearing. Please speak up.*

His sister, sitting in the corner, tiptoed over and touched him on the shoulder. "Pete. Pete. Wake up. Claire's come to see you. She's brought the children."

"Uh. Uh." He blinked, startled, and stared at the three of us. "Oh. Claire. So you came."

Gradually we helped him up (bones bones bones, where had the flesh gone?) and draped him in the wheelchair. Aunt Jo put in his hearing aid.

"Turn it up, Pete. *Up.*"

The scene could could officially begin.

"Little Pete's into soccer," I yelled, trying not to disturb his roommate, whose radio was spouting static. "And we're riding horseback together. Anna's about to get her beginner's badge in swimming."

Not a flicker of interest. Anna, with a five-year-old's genius for getting attention, planted herself by the wheelchair arm and demanded a response. She winked, first one eye, then the other. I went on shouting inanities about the summer while Aunt Jo refilled the water glass and fluffed the pillows, pursuing her lifelong vocation of seeing to his comfort. Anna winked. Uncle Pete winked back. It was the triumph of the visit.

Little Pete, uneasy, just stared. "Why do they have bars on the windows?" he finally asked.

"Eh?" Uncle Pete turned up his hearing aid, between winks.

"Why do they have bars on the windows?"

"So I can't get out." Uncle Pete tuned out again and went on winking.

Now Anna discovered the brakes. She pushed Uncle Pete back and forth a few inches, but the black shoes interfered. She squatted down close, studied the footrests, then pushed them into place. "You put your feet here," she bossed. Uncle Pete winked, and obeyed.

Little Pete, meanwhile, picked up a framed certificate from the bedside table. He held it out before his great-Uncle's eyes. *Faithful Navigator,* it read, *Peter C. Delaney.*

"Member since 1912," said Uncle Pete, and turned to show Anna how to manage the brakes.

A few years before, he'd sent us a picture of Peter C. Delaney, Past Grand Knight, decked out in plumes and scarlet, preening his Knights of Columbus feathers. Now, even that vanity gland was dead. Nothing could compete with a child's wink.

When the time came, the children fought over who would wheel him to the lunch he didn't want. Little Pete won and cautiously navigated the corridor, Anna running on ahead to open doors and bow ceremoniously to every geriatric she met. "Isn't she darling?" "Come here, dear." Bobbing heads and claws. Onward they took him into the large cafeteria (nurses everywhere, cajoling, reassuring) to the assigned table, the plastic sectioned plates, the digestible food and the moment of panic: "But where's my tablemate?"

Suddenly he sobbed — a frail, petulant old man insisting we not leave.

I bequeathe . . .

I read impatiently. Of course I wanted to discover how much I'd been left. By that time we were well past diapers and I'd learned how money goes and age invades. But as the print stared up at me and I listened to this voice from the dead, I knew I wanted to discover more. What had this life, this person, really been? He'd always seemed so . . . pinched, so virginal, so locked into himself. . . . Surely this final statement would yield a clue to the secret of that life. I wanted more than money.

. . . to my beloved sister, Josephine . . .

Josephine, second youngest of seven, embraced these days by the same walls, if not the same room, where Uncle Pete spent his final years. I visited her once this year. She's grateful to be so well cared for, as she puts it, and spends most of her days in the past. "Last twig left on the tree," she says of herself. After Uncle Pete died she lost her desire to get out of bed in the morning.

It was a tall, many-branched tree, the Delaney clan, of which I barely know the trunk and a branch or two. I'm made aware of my ignorance when little Pete and Anna come home from school with the annual *Write Your Family Tree* assignment.

Occasionally I'd press Uncle Pete to tell me about the family. Once we had an hour together on the couch at the old homestead in Rochester, his pale fingers turning the dark pages of a photo album. Bearded men in high starched collars and solemn-eyed girls in long frilly dresses looked out at us. I was already forty. That would have made him eighty-six. It all sounded so ordinary, so unglamorous. Perhaps that's why I forgot details even as he said them. Grandfather Delaney over from Limerick. Potato famine. Farmer. Married on this side. Nellie — who? They raised seven to adulthood. Grandfather taught in a one-room schoolhouse in upstate New York. Oldest boy, Peter, born 1887. Helped father and mother with chores on the farm, taught in the schoolhouse when old enough. The three youngest brothers went to the war in 1918 and came home safe. Not one murder or suicide in that family. No drunks, no divorces. Can it be true? Adultery didn't exist. Premature death, yes. The youngest sister, Emily, died in childbirth. The brother after Uncle Pete, my father, died before he knew he had grandchildren. Uncle Pete outlived all his brothers.

The uncles told some tall tales, but not enough to create a real myth of the Old Days for us children. There were stories of five brothers digging through twenty-foot snowdrifts to reach the barn and lurid descriptions of slaughtering hogs — told for the benefit of us city-bred children, my brother and me, eating dinner from a linen tablecloth in our large airy New England dining room forty years later.

But none of this holds for me the living resonance of one small story.

"Will you ever forget the Christmas morning John ate the peanut?"

That was how Aunt Jo began the story the only time I heard it told — seriously, you understand. The snowdrifts reached to the top of the barns. The buggy was hitched, the children scrubbed. They lined up. Their mother checked behind their ears. Mass first, presents later. This was in days when fasting from midnight was required for all communicants. Uncle John, the third boy down, confessed he had eaten a peanut that morning. Where had he found a peanut? It spoiled their day. There were only eight at the altar rail that Christmas, not the whole Delaney family. Their mother wasn't angry, just disappointed.

It rings with a truth I recognize: a felt incompleteness in the family Christmas, the perfect circle of shared faith broken. Later stories echo it. How Uncle Pete — in his thirties, forties, fifties, when he and Aunt Jo still had a housekeeper — would hang a sign on the refrigerator on Thursday nights. *Friday: no bacon*. How next morning Edna, their Protestant housekeeper, would open the fridge out of habit and fry bacon anyway. "She means well," they always said. "We don't know what we'd do without her." They never ate the bacon.

Or later still . . . I happened to be visiting them once on Good Friday. Uncle Pete would have been eighty-eight then. Aunt Jo was down with a touch of flu. "Would you mind driving him, Claire?" she said apologetically. "I worry so when he drives alone."

So we found our way to St. Matthew's and managed to squeeze into a pew about halfway back. Uncle Pete said his rosary, small black beads slipping through those pale fingers while the Passion was read. Then it was time for the Adoration of the Cross.

I pushed back to let others climb over us. I'd always been uncomfortable with this ritual, even as a child. Up he stood, grasped the pew in front of him, and began to work his way out into the aisle and down to the front of the church. Panicky, I followed. How would he ever make it to the altar rail in this mob, let alone kneel down, once he was there?

He never hesitated. He moved ahead with the line and I pushed in to be right behind him. At the altar rail, one by one, people knelt to kiss the crucifix the priest was holding. The person ahead of Uncle Pete got up. The priest wiped a Kleenex quickly across the corpus. Uncle Pete had already started down, wobbling. I grabbed his elbow, a sharp knot of bones, through his overcoat. Down, down, all the way down. He kissed the crucifix, then reached out to grasp my hand for help getting up. It was a slow, painful process, but there was simply no question of omitting it. My own forms of slowness and pain would have been incomprehensible to him.

When little Pete made his first holy communion seven years ago, I wondered then what it might one day come to mean, or not mean, to him. About confirmation, he seems refreshingly matter-of-fact: "Yeah, Mom. I think I'll go through with it."

I've made it clear that he has a choice. Perhaps it is a mistake to project on your children anxieties inherited from your past. On the other hand, what price do we eventually pay for overcherished certainties?

I bequeathe to my beloved sister, Josephine . . . a very large amount, enough to make her comfortable, he must have thought, for the rest of her life.

"Pete decided he could make his own breakfast," Aunt Jo told me drily about ten years ago. "So I showed him how to turn on the stove. He came down the first morning and the porridge boiled over. That was the end of that."

Too late to buy her a life. He bought her the comforts of a nursing home.

He was vain. We fed that vanity by compliments about his

clothes, his looks, his life. I asked him to give me away at my wedding, a late one at that. My father had died the year before and I'd always sensed I was a favorite with Great-Uncle Pete. He was pushing eighty at the wedding, proud and dapper. It would have been unthinkable for him to perform had there been no Mass. Even though I was marrying a non-Catholic, as they called Jim, and we had Mass out-of-doors at a secular university, Uncle Pete could still recognize the outlines of his familiar world: marriage, church, family. The bread was still consecrated (though it was a loaf, and Jewish friends shared), the wine offered. Afterward, he toasted me, reading in a clear strong voice the words he'd written out ahead of time: "To the jewel of all the jewels, my niece . . . "

When he was younger, he was good looking. I've seen the picture of the tall handsome man in his forties standing with four other men on either side of their seated father: Pete, Jim, John, Mike, and Fred, all in dark suits, white shirts and dark ties, dark shoes. Only one figure breaks the staid symmetry — Uncle Mike, sticking one hand in his trouser pocket, exposes a gold watch chain on the vest beneath. Uncle Mike was the liveliest of the bunch. The paternal figure is handsome in age, with thick white hair and white moustache. To me he was only a picture, but the uncles I knew, all of them. I have sat many a long hour in the room where they posed; I know the pattern on the wallpaper, the cracks in the molding. My children have crawled through styrofoam blizzards on that floor.

The brothers looked like businessmen, not farmers. They'd moved into town from the farm years before. Uncle Pete went first to stay with the priests and did odd jobs for them, getting through high school. Later he went to business college. "Thought of being a teacher," he told me once when I was still teaching. "Went into the business world instead." "Thought of being a priest," he told me another time when I was still a nun.

Did he ever go into any other world instead?

They had been poor.

Uncle Pete's dresser drawers, when I knew him, were crammed with shirts, ties filled his closet and were draped over the lamps in his room.

"You've never known want," my mother explained to me. "Uncle Pete probably never had more than one good shirt as a child. When he could, he filled his drawers with shirts and his closet with suits."

Only later, in his seventies, did he loosen up and begin to wear plaid flannel shirts. After eighty he dared the bolo tie and moustache.

On holidays he'd hold us captive in his living room after dinner. The grownups would fortify themselves with a "bracer," as Aunt Jo called it. Good Scotch. Or sometimes cheap Scotch poured into expensive bottles. It depended on Uncle Pete's mood. Then he'd haul out the slide projector. There we'd sit — nieces, nephews, in-laws — subjected to hours of his life: "John Casey, the one on the far right, he used to work with me, met him over in Syracuse in '41"; "Harold Simes, the one with the dog there, had a good time at his place on Boon Lake"; "Last K of C banquet when they honored me . . . "

One after another they appeared, blurred Kodak faces certifying the existence of a world in which he was important.

We sipped and watched, bored stiff.

Did he want anything except attention? Yet how could one offer simple attention to an uncle who sat mute through holiday gatherings and with a flourish offered your husband ties twenty years out of style, the original gift ticket still inside the freshly wrapped box: *For Pete, Merry Christmas, 1950, from John Casey.* Or calendars preserved until date and day would again match and this happened to be your lucky year.

For fifty years at least the despairing question went round before Christmas: "What can we get Uncle Pete?"

That day, when he opened the inevitable socks and ties, he'd mumble: "For me? You shouldn't have gone to the expense. I don't need anything."

It went with the not-wanting-to-be-any-trouble formula. "Don't go to any trouble," he'd say, thinking he meant it.

At eighty, he drove from Rochester to Auburn, New York, to visit another niece "Don't go to any trouble," he said. "We'll eat lunch out. Something light."

She took him at his word.

They went to a place that served fancy sandwiches. Later, she discovered he never ate sandwiches. For fifteen years Aunt Jo had been making him three hot meals a day. "Ever since the housekeeper left. Pity we couldn't keep her, but she was getting on in years, poor soul, and needed to be taken care of herself. So now it's all up to me. Pete tries to help out, you know, but . . . "

A year later he visited the same niece again.

"Don't go to any trouble," he said.

This time she decided on Howard Johnsons: bland and safe.

"I hope everything was okay, Uncle Pete," she said, as they left the restaurant.

"Fine. Fine." He hemmed and hawed as he fiddled with car keys. "Though I found the Jello a bit tough."

"My niece, Claire, my nephew John, my niece Caroline, and my nephew Henry . . . "

He worked to remember us all, combining family and memory.

It was his hobby. Each year we'd go through the ritual: "Just line up now. Where's Claire? Squeeze in there, little Pete."

He'd stand too far away and tip the camera, then rock back on his heels. This was his moment. "That's good. Hold it now. Don't anybody move."

Click.

A month later he'd send everyone a copy — the Delaney clan out of focus, standing on a slant. In light blue ink he'd write time and place on the back: Rochester, 1952; Boston, 1960; Windsor, 1965. He was intensely conscious of dates.

He wanted to see something growing.

Money grows. He invested. In the years of the string tie and moustache he'd prowl around the front hall in the late afternoon waiting for the thud of the evening paper on the front porch. Then he'd settle into his chair and study every last dot of the stock market before he tuned in to *The Price is Right*.

"Over the years we bought quite a bit of property," he once told me, "the brothers went in together." I must have been twelve or so, and we were walking the three blocks from the family home to the nearest store. He pointed out a corner lot with a four storey commercial building on it. "See that? I'd always thought I'd build there. We boys bought that lot years ago. Your father was only eleven when we came in from the farm. He was about eighteen when we moved to where we are now."

Where we are now . . .

It stands empty these days, prey to vandals, the square three-storey house on a quiet street, with a broad front porch, and a swinging hammock I covet. Aunt Jo refuses to sell, in case she ever returns home from The King's Arms. One corner of the dining room holds the daybed where I'd fall asleep as a child while aunts and uncles played penny ante Red Dog. Against the opposite wall stands the Philco, topped by a lace doilie and African violets. Pius XII sends a Holy Year Blessing down his long thin nose toward the violets.

Number of the house: debatable. "They rezoned in 1940," Uncle Pete explained. "Our number is really 1432. I had everything changed. But Josephine kept the old number, five."

Perhaps it was important to her to feel she lived at a different address. His checks read 1432 Linden Lane (Old Number Five).

Numbers tell part of the story: the house, the property, the care to think it all out, divide fairly. What's fair? What have I done to earn remembrance, anyway? Sat year after year at holiday meals teasing him about his love for mashed potatoes? Named my oldest son for him, aware that Uncle Pete grieved the dying out of the family name? This was the best I could do.

I sat there and read the news that I was an heiress.

After everything else was seen to — funeral, debts, taxes, Josephine, Masses and enrollments, I would receive ten thousand dollars. The numbers on the page, $10,000.00, were as real as vapor. I was grateful. But there was no living person to receive my gratitude. Only a *memory*, an unsatisfying one at that. *I wanted more than the voice from the page, a voice reduced to prose so reasoned that nothing could be revealed.*

He committed himself to the final embrace of the church, faithful mother. One thousand dollars was set aside for Masses for himself and members of his family. I tried to imagine his state of mind as he wrote that: anxious? afraid? believing?

He was proud of the niece who chose religion. "Talented and beautiful," he once wrote of me in a short family history he put together. "She is now a member of a religious order." He came to visit me more than once, at Christmas. He sat silent there, too, in the convent parlor. No grand-nephew played about his feet, nor did any of us suspect there would ever be one.

Uncle Peter understood virginity.

It's strange to think of a man that way. He was shy. You couldn't imagine him howling at an off-color joke. Perhaps I misjudge. Perhaps in those knotty pine cabins up at Boon Lake a glass was tipped, a joke passed. It defies imagining.

As I sat on the bed that summer afternoon I could hear Anna downstairs. The car had pulled into the drive. Little Pete and his dad were back.

I still wasn't satisfied. I wanted more.

I wondered if the emaciated figure who in the last five years of his life took pills to help his appetite but divided the dose in half to reduce the cost, if this remnant of a man had once known passion. Love. Anger. Rage. Gnawing frustration.

There was an incident. I'd all but forgotten it until I sat holding the legal document in my hands, wanting more than print could offer me.

We were visiting Rochester. Little Pete was seven. He suffered the living room relatives with their bracers and talk as long as he could. Finally, he pulled me aside. "Can I go to the attic, please, Mom?" He'd heard tales of the crammed attic and was in his treasure-hunt phase.

"Ask Uncle Pete or Aunt Jo."

Uncle Pete needed no coaxing. He lifted himself out of his chair and left his highball behind. He would host us — little Pete, my husband, who'd never seen the attic, and me — in our ascent to he past.

They'd been cleaning out the attic since 1960. The moment we reached the top I saw the change. The unicycle was gone.

And the feather beds. The parlor organ was gone. Most of the remaining stuff had been stacked or boxed. I sensed little Pete's disappointment. He'd expected the musty chaos that had fascinated my brother and me when, forty years before, we'd gone up there for relief from grown-ups and prowled through dust and junk, fascinated.

Uncle Pete seemed unaware of us. He moved slowly through the dust toward a stack of cartons. Little Pete went off to explore under the rafters. Uncle Pete worked at the yellow string around the top carton. He seemed intent. Folding back the cardboard cover, he reached inside and lifted out a newspaper.

"Where's little Pete?" he asked, looking around.

"Pete," I hissed, "get over here!"

The child hurried over and squeezed in beside his uncle.

"Do you know what this was?" asked Uncle Pete, waving a yellowing newspaper before his grand-nephew's eyes.

Pete looked to us for help.

"Pearl Harbor Day," said Uncle Pete smugly. "Collector's item." He refolded it and returned it to the box.

In a flash little Pete was gone.

Now Uncle Pete was moving toward a clothes press. He paused, looked at us in some odd way and, as if satisfied, went on. He pulled at the door of the press. Stuck. He yanked hard. It gave. His head and shoulders disappeared inside. We waited.

He re-emerged, holding a small oval framed picture. Ignoring me, he addressed my husband, holding the picture out toward him.

"Florence Brady," he said.

I couldn't make out the features: hair, two eyes, a nose and a mouth. Female.

"Met her in '45 down in Syracuse . . . fine women." He took the picture from Jim and turned back toward the press. "We corresponded a bit . . . " This was barely audible as he set the picture inside and slammed the door. Again he turned to Jim. "Last wrote to her in '53," he said. "Never heard back."

Taking Jim by the arm, he began to move away. I was just behind them. He stopped suddenly and turned to look Jim straight in the eye, man to man. "Might have been Claire's aunt," he said, "if she'd played her cards right."

Oh Florence, you missed your chance. He left you behind in the press for moth to corrupt what he never had. You might have been the beloved wife. He might have fathered seven as his father had before him.

How odd that this attic encounter with Uncle Pete comes back to me now, on the eve of little Pete's confirmation. What connects the seemingly immaculate past of a rich bachelor uncle with his namesake's entrance into spiritual adulthood? That's how the religion books would describe this sacrament: the serious commitment of oneself to a way, a life. Confirmation.

Surely most parents long to leave something lasting to their children. In our case, it won't be money. It's hard to imagine little Pete as a man sitting on the side of his bed reading my bequest to him of ten thousand dollars.

But there are other things to hope for, deeper inheritances, a way of seeing, ways of seeing, that life's experience will not entirely invalidate.

Is it too much to hope for that?

Uncle Pete made a final bequest, one that affected me as I read the words.

After all the above is taken care of, it is my wish that a chapel be built and designated so as to honor my parents, Mr. and Mrs. Peter D. Delaney, formerly of Rochester, New York.

This was the distinctive clause in the will, the one nobody could have predicted. Having insured that he himself would be remembered, in Masses and money, he reached back to re-

member his parents, that proud-looking man with his handle-
bar moustache, that shadow of a woman about whom I know
nothing. He would perpetuate them in the most lasting way he
could imagine: a chapel.

It was a way, no denying that. Holy Mother Church: eternal midwife. Inflation might negate it, as it has, reducing
edifice to memorial plaque, but sound mind couldn't think of
everything. The impulse was honorable, to remember his parents.

Still, as I read them that afternoon, his words made me feel
heavy. It was as if all the carefully reasoned prose, the measuring and dividing to honor every family claim, were all qualified
or undercut by a desire so passionate it could only fail. It was as
if he sensed that leaving money to an heir might be a gesture
too easily forgot, especially when it came from an uncle who
had given so little of himself for ninety-four years. He had
spent over three quarters of a century acquiring money. He
could give that. But how could he who had spoken so little
vanquish the final silence and guarantee a place against oblivion?

He must have puzzled over that one long and hard, worrying about it as he checked nightly stock market reports or
stared at passing seasons through the barred windows of the
King's Arms.

Finally he summoned those resources he knew and trusted
most: type, seal, secretary, mortar, stone. He would order
space enclosed, made sacred, and named for his parents — remembering himself also in the gesture, for he bore his father's
name.

Even as I think of it today, that final gesture carries with it a
sadness.

I see Uncle Pete with his full white moustache, his string tie
and flannel shirt, bending toward me over his Scotch to assure

me I'd never have to worry about his namesake's higher education.

I finger the white shirt little Pete will wear tomorrow. I must fish through his crammed drawers for a tie. This will be a dress occasion.

I do these things — find the tie, check the trousers for spots, resolve to make him shine his good shoes — automatically, with the expertise 14 years of motherhood confers. After a while you develop an inbuilt checklist for all occasions.

He will be freshly scrubbed and dressed up. He will move down the aisle with others in his confirmation class. The bishop will strike him gently on the cheek and anoint him with the oil of salvation. Little Pete will once again renounce Satan. And all his pomps.

And all the while, as I kneel in my pew and feel the inevitable pride, I will know in my heart that inheritance cannot be predicted, measured, divided. He will be what he will be.

However that may turn out, I fortify myself with the thought that a good dose of the Holy Spirit can only help.

SCORING

"Weren't there snakes in the shower?" asks Peter. "That's what you told me the last time."

He eyes me. Tell it, Mom. Tell it now. Here in the dining room of the Sheraton in Ithaca, New York, surrounded by potted palms, earnest young waiters in their black and white. I want Karen to hear it.

"Yes, snakes. There were snakes. I don't know how many."

I see them. Feel them. Narrow and tough, they wriggle beneath my toes, beneath the thin soles of my black slippers. I stand firm above them on a small square of wallpaper. Tension tightens my back. Am I strong enough to do the job? I press with all my weight, bracing both bare arms against the metal sides of the shower for balance. I swing the heels of my slippers back and forth as if maneuvering on a skate board, grinding them. Only I am not in the world of skateboards. I am in a dark damp cellar. I am alone, in a shower stall, with snakes. When I lift the wallpaper, will they be mashed? Or will one raise its ugly little black head and hiss?

I want to believe I killed them all. He thinks I did.

"Garden snakes, right? No killers."

"Probably not. They were pretty small."

"In your *shower?*" asks Karen. Setting down her fork, she eyes me with sudden interest. Her eyes are blue, like water at the shallow end of a lake, and opaque. This latest girlfriend of Peter's is not easy to read.

"You had to be there," I murmur.

Conversation stopper.

Evidently they want distraction, relief — these seventeen-year-olds on their college tour, minds stuffed with SAT and Achievement scores, campus layouts, admissions requirements, core curricula and the pressing question, *Will I get in?* It's late August, almost Labor Day.

Peter has had it with information sessions deftly engineered by smooth admissions officers, anxious parents in dresses and sports jackets herding their ragged offspring around on the campus tour, posing the crucial questions: "Are the dormitories co-ed?" "Are the scholarships need-blind?" "What is the security on campus?" "What are your counselling services?" "What are your basic requirements for a B.A.?" We've watched kids eyeing each other, covertly measuring themselves, second-guessing interviews. It's a giant lottery, this college admissions business. As we've moved from campus to campus — we drew the line at five — I've watched his self-confidence plummet. Unless you're a genius or a drone, and maybe even then, this process doesn't build up the ego. Now we're at the end of it. Finally. Cornell. Where, if he knew the questions to ask, he might uncover a secret or two.

But he's asking the questions he does know. "Weren't there snakes in the showers?" Entertain us. Get our minds off this admissions hassle. Tell us about YOUR world, back then. Something *different*.

Wouldn't he be surprised.

"Yes," I say, nibbling the last bit of an overdone roll as our student waiter eyes us from behind a potted palm. "There were snakes in the shower. But you've got to understand, it was better to have showers at last, snakes and all, than none."

"You mean they didn't let you have showers?" Karen grows wide-eyed. She wipes her small pretty mouth with the white cloth napkin and sets it back on her lap. Even in ragbag jeans and a rumpled Ecuadorean shirt, she has a dainty manner. Beside her, I feel like a moose.

"When I first entered the convent we had no showers," I say. I'm already beginning to bore myself. It's a B-movie rerun, *Mrs. Minniver*, Jennifer Jones in *The Song of Bernadette*. "Our novitiate was in a rambling old country house. The water pressure there was poor. Besides, in those days we had a notion of penance — "

Her eyes are blank.

Our waiter circles the table discreetly, eyeing our almost empty plates.

"You should hear about Camp Leafytrees," she says, suddenly confiding, leaning forward on slim tanned arms. A cluster of narrow silver bands circles her wrist. From one ear dangles a spear of silver. "I told Peter about it. My parents sent me there when I was twelve. It was in the Adirondacks. You had to kill an animal while you were there. Our year, it was chickens. I hated it. I ran away. Overnight. I stayed out in the woods. The whole camp was in an uproar. They called my parents. Went searching for me with flashlights and dogs. When they found me they sent me home. I wasn't ready for it, they said."

The waiter retreats.

"*Ready* for it," mutters Peter. "Tell her about your chickens, Mom."

He has his cues down pat.

"I had to kill an animal, too," I oblige. He's tired. They've forgotten about the snakes. "We ate chicken a lot in the novitiate."

Her pale eyes grow puzzled.

I spot our waiter two tables away, conferring with another waiter. They are hotel school students. We are the last ones in the dining room.

"A novitiate's sort of like boot camp," I explain. "Mine lasted two and a half years."

"I know about boot camp. My dad was in Korea."

"Anyhow, at the novitiate we had a farmer who raised and milked our cows, planted the corn field that we harvested, took care of the pigs. Once a year we novices were invited to help him slaughter chickens. I'd been there a year then."

"More water, Madam?"

I nod. The rush of clear water, clinking ice, reassures. Some things are forever. Elemental.

"So we put on our aprons and boots and went up the hill to the chicken farm. It was very hot. I can't remember many cool days from my two summers there. My overwhelming impression when I think of it now is of sweat running down my face and my body. We wore heavy black wool." Pre-polyester: ancient history. Twenty-five years later, they've reverted. She and Peter gather wrinkles, subsidize Banana Republic.

"Did you have any *choice*?" asks Peter.

"About what?"

"About going to slaughter chickens."

Their generation is hooked on choice. *Requirements* is the dirty word. Admissions officers eyeball anxious parents and talk about maturity, options.

"We practised obedience, remember?"

"Awesome," says Karen. "They could make you do anything?"

"Within reason."

"What you thought was reason."

Peter can be arch.

"You'd be a disaster there, Peter." Karen offers him a smirk.

"Would any of you care for dessert?" Our waiter, his Adam's apple working, waves his small pad above our heads.

"Cherry cheesecake, with whipped cream, please." Peter actually licks his lips.

Karen studies the menu. "Well . . . "

Can this child possibly worry about her weight? She can't be more than a hundred pounds, wet.

"Do you have any sherbet?"

"Orange and lime."

"Lime, please."

The waiter inclines his head toward the elder. "And you, Madam?"

"Just coffee, thanks."

He vanishes through the swinging door to the kitchen, though not without one quick glance at Karen. Summer on the Delaware beaches has left her golden.

"So you went to kill the chickens . . . " she urges.

"There were probably fifteen of us, all told, decked out in our habits, heavy boots, blue and white checked aprons to our ankles. Something out of a Bergman movie." That may give her a picture. She's never heard of Jennifer Jones. Details don't really matter. What I remember is the feeling. The zest of climbing the hill toward a challenge. Fresh breeze rippling my veil. Relief at being out of doors. A sense of freedom. A chance to prove my mettle, up my eternal score. "Mr. Riordan, our farmer, opened the gate to his chicken yard and brought us all into the chickenhouse. It stank. Can't remember too much except for the smell and the squawking chickens running around. Anyhow, he gave me a long piece of wire with one end bent around to make a kind of hook."

"Why you?"

"I suppose I volunteered. Sister Claire always was a Goody-Two-Shoes."

I *know* I did. Eager beaver for spiritual advancement. Who

was I to decide a chickenyard no arena for the practise of virtue? Charles de Foucald went into the desert. Simeon Stylites climbed a pole.

"Anyhow, Mr. Riordan told me to catch a chicken."

"How?" This from Karen.

"He must have seen my great eye-hand coordination."

"Hah," snorts Peter. "You can barely chew gum and walk at the same time."

"I had to snap this long wire toward some unsuspecting cornered chicken and hook onto one of its legs. Then pull it toward me, quick. As soon as I could, I had to grab the two legs in one hand, then carry it outside, squawking and flapping."

"But didn't you have to kill them, Mom?"

"Yes. I'd bring the poor chicken out into the yard. I remember there was a high chainlink fence all around. Mr. Riordan's children — he had five — stood behind it watching us. We didn't have any contact with those kids all year, of course. We were cloistered. But there they stood that blistering hot day, noses pressed against the links, watching. In the middle of the yard stood one bloodied tree stump. Headless chickens were running around. Mr. Riordan wanted someone to wield the axe. I volunteered."

"What was *he* doing?" Peter wants every detail.

"Your sherbet, Miss."

A perfect mound of light green is set before her.

Peter eyes his cheesecake. Digs in.

"Directing this show, I guess. I don't remember some things. I only remember myself on this stage. I know someone held down the chicken on the stump. My aim wasn't all that great, either. Anyhow, I smashed down the axe on the chicken and chopped off its head."

"Didn't it make you sick?" Karen spoons her sherbet daintily.

"Your coffee, Madam."

"Not really. But after that I couldn't face chicken for several months. The fact is, Karen, you can nerve yourself up for anything if you try. I was motivated. I wanted to excel."

"Yeah. I know all about motivation." She gives a short grim laugh as she brushes back a strand of fine sun-bleached hair from her forehead. "My mother thinks I was motivated to put Cornell on my list just so I could have a rendezvous with Peter at the end of summer."

"Well?" He eyes her.

She rolls her baby blues.

Suddenly I'm tired of it all. What has it to do with them? Why has he put me up to this?

They're in their bubble. There come these instants when you actually think you've penetrated it.

"We're going swimming after, Mom. You coming?"

He scrapes the last bit of graham crust from his plate, pressing the tines of the fork against the china.

Why didn't his mother teach him manners? This young man is not dainty. He's not even couth. What does she see in him?

"Don't think so. I'll stay here and nurse my coffee."

"Come on, Karen. Pool's only open till eleven."

❧

"Sisters, I am having four showers installed in the cellar," the new novice mistress, Mother Patrick, announced that September day. "We are living, after all, in the twentieth century."

A new sense of historical awareness, this. The novices and postulants had been steaming through the twentieth century for some months, oblivious to the Cold War. Absorbed in their own war, they fought daily to transform their battleground, through prayer and grace, into a garden of heavenly fruitfulness.

Mother Patrick, rumored to be more forward-looking than her predecessor Mother Theodore, seemed determined to bring her new charges into what she considered the twentieth century.

So she had four showers installed in the cellar. Showers every night. It felt almost decadent.

Sister Claire liked being first. She was born to excel. Her scale of measurement, though, was gradually changing. Achievement no longer meant making the dean's list or getting honors. Nothing that simple. This school of the spirit in which she'd so recently matriculated had its own methods of measuring advancement in virtue.

And so, after night prayer, she would hurry out of chapel, walk quickly through the silent dark novitiate building, climb the winding back stairs to her dormitory, close her cell curtains and change from her habit into her nightgown, bathrobe, slippers and nightveil. She'd take a bar of soap from her washbasin, a washcloth and towel, and close her cell curtains behind her. She wanted to be the first one down the two flights of back stairs to the new showers in the cellar.

Why?

Because, as she learned that first night, the cellar showers offered an opportunity for spiritual advancement.

Cellar means cellar here. Not subterranean rec room. No television, no pool table, no cosy Franklin stove, no built-in bar. Ancient stone walls, packed earthen floor, shadowy darkness, a few dim light bulbs here and there, cartons stacked neatly in corners, shelves of preserves and root vegetables, bits of old unused furniture.

An enormous coal furnace dominated the cellar. Throughout the winter the novices took turns shovelling coal into its maw from mounds beside it. Around the edges of the cellar, against damp spidery walls, stood saw horses and zinc boards for rainy-day starching. Nearby, the newspapers which only the novice mistress read were tied and stacked, their yellowing edges carefully evened out. A novice might raid that pile for only one purpose — to extract a few sheets for covering freshly washed floors.

Posture improvement took place in the cellar.

Brides of Christ should walk erect. For five minutes a day each sister was to balance a sizeable library book on her head and walk about carefully, maintaining silence, modesty of the eyes, and perfect balance.

To this cellar Sister Claire hurried that late September night.

At the foot of the stairs she pulled the string of one dim lightbulb. Shadows sprang forth and wavering fingers of light stroked the stone walls. She hurried past the furnace to the far corner where books of wallpaper samples were stacked. They had been instructed. To avoid standing with wet feet on cold concrete, the novices were to take one sheet, the *top* sheet, out of the wallpaper book, bring it to the shower stall and place it on the floor of the outer stall where they'd stand to dry off.

She pulled the string on the twenty-watt bulb hanging above the wallpaper pile. From the top sample book she tore out a sheet of pale green and white lilies against a beige background and carried it to the first shower stall. She pulled back the shower curtain.

She stifled the urge to cry out.

Snakes!

Three or four of them, small and dark, lay curled around the drain of the shower.

She was not a country girl. Were they harmless? They were repulsive.

Quickly she pulled the curtain shut. She listened. No one

else down here. The others would be changing, upstairs. Were there snakes in every stall?

She walked to the second stall, gingerly inched the curtain back. One dark snake lay stretched out in a straight line beside the drain. Did it twitch?

She pulled the curtain shut. Her heart pounded. Along the back of her neck she felt something like prickles. She might vomit. Where should she do it? Down the drain?

The third stall.

A few inches from the drain, two lazy green reptiles curled into an almost perfect number eight. Their symmetry mesmerized her for an instant. They looked dead.

Now the last.

She thought she wouldn't throw up after all. The tingle on the back of her neck was subsiding. She knew she wouldn't faint.

Ease back the curtain . . .

Nothing.

She stood a moment holding the edge of the gray cloth shower curtain, looking at the new shower stall with its shiny gray metal sides. She closed the shower curtain carefully.

She must decide.

Who would know?

Only God.

What would he know?

That she'd missed an opportunity.

For what?

To conquer herself. To do an act of charity for her sisters. A hidden act. Because if she did it quickly enough, they might never know how heroic she'd been. That was the best kind of virtuous act.

Sister Claire moved quickly.

She returned to the first stall. She slammed an inner clamp on her feelings. This was becoming habitual. *She knew what she was doing.* She clung to that now. This was *commitment.* Even if it came down to killing snakes in a shower.

Though killing a garter snake by hand, or foot, in a shower on a hot summer evening in an old house in Vermont didn't feel much like leaving off the Old Man and putting on the New.

Nonetheless, she set about doing it.

This was obedience of judgment.

So she stood in the first stall, praying all the while as she pressed down hard, balancing carefully, bracing herself with extended arms, willing the damned critters instantly, thoroughly dead.

It took a little work.

Years later, nursing her coffee in a distant motel, watching her lanky son and his dainty girlfriend depart for the pool, she thinks: *Who forced Sister Claire? What is freedom? Have our children been freed of that question or do they simply recast it? Does anyone ever really know what they're doing?*

Sister Claire was quick and efficient that night. She moved from stall to stall. She took two fresh wallpaper squares — poppies on the diagonal, a pattern of flying geese, and stamped on those squares, grinding down the snakes. Later, she'd notice how the statues of Mary showed her foot on the neck of a snake. It didn't make her feel any closer to Mary.

She wanted to get it all over with before anyone came downstairs.

So she did. And carried each limp dead victim in its wallpaper coffin to the large trash bin near the furnace.

When she heard someone coming downstairs, she was already at the third stall, grinding.

Since the sisters were in the Great Silence from after night prayer until the next morning after Mass, even if she met someone, no words would be spoken. She ground her final snake, carried him (she thought of it as a him) to the trash bin, and returned to take a shower, passing only one figure in a black bathrobe, Sister Augustine, who kept her eyes down and hurried past her into the next shower stall.

Did it happen several times or only that once? She's never been sure. Memory of those days carries odd lapses.

Nothing was ever said about it. In fact she didn't, as far as she can recall, ever talk to anyone about it until twenty years later, meeting a friend who'd shared those strange weeks, years, with her.

"Do you remember the snakes in the shower?" she'd asked her friend Genevieve as they downed Manhattans and grew boisterous in their hilarity one memorable winter evening not so long ago. Indulgent, amused husbands, comfortably outside that circle of shared experience, watched the spectacle of two educated, middle-aged women laughing until their sides hurt as they called up story after story of earnest misguided piety. Stories that seemed to erupt from places deeply hidden, forgotten even, until some spark struck them forth from oblivion.

To her question about the showers, though, Genevieve replied, "What snakes?"

That was the puzzle. She could still see them snoozing lazily near the drain, still feel them beneath her heel. She could still call up the sense of anxiety and revulsion that had gripped her that first night.

Perhaps no one else encountered those snakes.

As a story, the snakes have served her well, rescuing occasional family dinners from the banality of turnip and onion, the sadness of lumps in gravy. Even salvaging one disastrous party.

They have won the attention of a teenage son.

What is their power? For him? For her?

"Camp Leafytrees," says Mr. Klenman over pancakes next morning, "was a camp children hated and parents loved."

They'd met briefly the night before when he and Karen arrived exhausted after their six-hour drive from Pennsylvania. Peter had hovered by the front door of the motel, peering out through torrential sheets of rain. When he saw the Buick drive up, he'd rung her from the front desk to come out and meet Mr. Klenman and Karen. Dutifully she'd slid into her shoes and hurried out. Karen and Peter had been phoning each other for weeks, comparing notes on parental obtuseness and planning this final meeting before they both returned to their boarding school in Connecticut after Labor Day.

He had seemed a shy man. Not someone you'd notice in a crowd. Medium height, mild-mannered, alert eyes, and a hesitant smile that could open up his entire face unexpectedly. A warm and seemingly gentle man. A high-powered chemist of some sort, he went about the world testing the quality of water. She already knew that from Peter. He had a dominating wife. She knew that also. Meeting this kindly gentleman in the lobby of the Sheraton, she'd been struck by the strength of his handshake and the mildness of his manner.

He had disappeared to his room quickly and left Karen and Peter to her.

This morning they had decided to eat breakfast on campus in the Willard Straight. Cornell's food was famous.

"At the last college we visited, the campus guide told us if we wanted good food not to go there but to come here," smiles Mr. Klenman, mopping up maple syrup with an edge of pancake.

"Brown's campus tour was cool," says Karen. "Can it ever kill a place if you get a lousy guide."

"Tell me about it," says Peter. "Did you get the guy at Amherst who kept pointing out the thirty tennis courts?"

This is an in-joke. He hates tennis.

"I didn't go there."

"Karen wants theater," says Mr. Klenman, as if his daughter weren't beside him. He speaks with resignation, a seasoned actor on the stage of life. I feel the edges of his imagination curling protectively about her naive ambition.

"Yes," I say, "she's told me."

Karen glances up quickly. Will I betray her confidences of last spring? She'd come home with Peter over March break — anxious, he said, for relief from her own mother. We sat a long time at the kitchen table, she nibbling rice cakes while I guzzled coffee, and she told me how much she wanted to be on stage. How her parents were convinced she'd waste her life in Starlet Purgatory, never make it onto the Real Stage.

"You got an interview here?" asks Peter.

"No. I called too late to get one. You?"

"Right after lunch."

After breakfast we make our way slowly past the bookstore, Olin Library, across the Arts Quad littered with students soaking up the last rays of summer. Cool in my sundress and sandals, I wish Mr. Klenman would take off his sports jacket. It's just past nine o'clock and beads of sweat already line his forehead. The humidity is killing. But he is born and bred New England — a man of settled proprieties and not without charm. Now that I've learned to look at men, I see I could like him a lot. Could I run away with him?

This is a test question I've devised. It loosens up an imagination bound overtightly for many years.

Peter and Karen walk ahead.

"Gorgeous campus," says Mr. Klenman. "I'd never been
here before. Peter says you went here."

"I did my Ph.D. here."

We pause by the huge statue of the Founder surveying the
Quad.

"*Ciao*," says Peter to Karen and her dad. "See you at the
tour." Karen sends him a thumbs-up and we leave, heading for
the humanities building. They head across campus toward the
new theater arts center.

We begin to climb the steps.

Ghosts ambush me. From the left. The right. I wasn't prepared for this. I try to live in the present. *Concentrate on Peter.
This is all new for him. It's his trip. Mothers clutter things up. Slay
the demons.*

But I know the very grooves of these hollowed stone steps.

How scared Sister Claire was the first time she climbed
them, her black skirt swinging against her ankles as she para-
chuted into the world of Vietnam protests, civil rights marches,
voter registration, agitation for peace. She felt so conspicuous,
so . . . out of it. She was.

We enter the building, turn left past crowds of students
finding their way, checking schedules, shoving, pushing. They
eye door numbers, names. We pass a small auditorium where,
during one long semester, Sister Claire tried to master the in-
trigues and disguises of Restoration Drama as she grew daily
more uncomfortable with her own.

Near the end of the hall I stop, check the name on the door,
knock.

"What're you doing?" whispers Peter.

He's in no mood for surprises. Karen's grade point average is higher than his. She wants to come here, too. The campus tour is in half an hour.

"Shh — "

Inside, we hear someone getting up, moving, approaching the door.

It opens slowly. A whiff of tobacco envelops us. I see the familiar eyes, nose, mouth. The pipe.

Screw up your courage, Sister.

"Professor Dodd?" The small eyes blink as the head nods. "I'm sorry to disturb you. I don't know if you'll remember me. Claire Delaney. I was a graduate student here about twenty years ago. I happen to be on campus with my son, Peter, who's doing the college tour, and I hoped we might just say hello and have him meet you."

Breathless. Schoolgirlitis.

I'd forgotten this heavy anxiety at disturbing a Famous Scholar. It came every time you knocked at his door.

"Of course. Of course." The door opens wide. He seems to recognize me. "Of course I remember. Come in. I'm delighted to see you again."

With a nod, a firm handshake, he brings us both inside.

I have measured out my life in chocolate chips. Seasons of mothering have transformed me. I'm back in the world where brain is power. I see Peter eye the bookshelves, the signs of mental industry. Where are the dreams, the ambitions of yester year? I'm being seduced again — by the pipe smell, the books, the atmosphere . . . of seriousness, of weighty unhurried reflection, of time to study a text, plumb its meaning, take part in the great push toward truth. All this simply from entering his office. I always was a pushover. We have interrupted his work. *What have I to show?* It's standing there, with holes in its jeans.

Professor Dodd moves quickly to clear places for Peter and me, removing books from two chairs, placing them somewhere. We stand for a moment, then position ourselves as indicated. He settles at his desk, leans back in the chair, tamps his pipe in the ashtray. Behind him a high window, open at the bottom, shows waving green and, beyond that, cars moving along a road.

"Well now . . . how have you been, Claire? Let's see, you were in the class of . . . "

I can relax, sort of. He'll take charge. Same deliberate manner, kind, courtly, a gentleman. Impossible to imagine him dishing out stew, scrambling after Legos, whipping up Kraft Dinner. This is a setting for serious pursuits. He will direct us, initiate topics, bring us quickly up to date on his beloved university, his home of — would it be forty years? At least. He looks exactly the same. Same brown hair carefully parted in the middle. Same lines about the eyes that deepen when he smiles. Same craggy forehead, almost too high for the rest of his face. Same large ears with lobes that seem overlarge, somehow. Same deft, competent manner.

"That was Al Gaffney's class, was it?"

I shake my head. Peter is studying a Blake print on the wall above the desk.

"Oh, earlier then?"

"We finished in 1968," I tell him. "I was in your Medieval Studies seminar."

"Yes. Of course. I remember. Carole Longley was in that class. Did her dissertation on Yeats. It's been published. A good book. She stopped by just about five years ago. She got a position at — was it Tufts?"

You create your place.

You stake it out.

If you're lucky, it's one you can name. You claim it. *Yours.*

This is a good and satisfying place, here in this booklined cocoon. Professor Dodd leans back in his chair, puffs on his pipe, surveys us. From every shelf and corner they also survey us: Chaucer, Pope, Coleridge, Shakespeare, Dante, Cervantes, Eliot, Austen . . . Dodd himself. His books are arranged by size.

He of the legendary memory enjoys remembering. He entertains us, his voice taking on that gently hypnotic quality that was death on a long hot afternoon.

I could entertain him.

"Professor Dodd," I could say, "I discovered lust in your seminar. I knew all about the seven deadly sins. I could have written a learned paper on them. But this time I was in the grip of one. Beneath my black I hid a churning heart. Did you know, as you expounded on 'The Pardoner's Tale'? At times you seemed to enjoy having a medieval remnant in your Chaucer seminar. We made little jokes about *Amor Vincit Omnia*. Little did you know. I was undone by the power of swaggering maleness imperfectly concealed in ragged jeans. We were seven or eight gathered about that glass-topped seminar table. He sat directly across from me. I felt challenged. Scared. The throb of an awakened body so easily defeats an awakened mind. Sometimes in the evening he and I would go for walks. He confided his troubles to my chaste ear. A habit hides much. . . . "

If you could listen and if I wanted to, I could amplify your stock of jokes and anecdotes, that drawer of your filing-cabinet mind you'd pull out now and then to enliven your class. I could tell you now that those weekly arid afternoon seminars were redeemed for me not by your wit and learning but by the presence of a graduate student on the other side of the table who fascinated me. The invitation issuing from him — from the muscles bulging beneath his T shirt sleeves, from the shrewd glance of his wise green eyes, from a chest that looked strong and hard, from a square jaw that often showed a dark stubble, from long fingered hands that gestured with elegant grace — that invitation dug far beneath my earnest efforts to pronounce Middle English correctly, reached into my heart and soul. . . .

The young nun kept her eyes demurely on her book while the room spun with her desire. Her bones began to melt. At times, she wondered if she could stand up at the end of the two hour class. . . .

Peter is eyeing me.

"We really must go," I say quickly. Apologetically. "We have to find our way to the next campus tour."

"Well, Claire, you'll see a lot of new buildings, some of them grotesque." He's not stirring. I remember that now. He sets the pace. "You may have noticed. If cranes and tractors are a sign of progress, Cornell's in the vanguard."

Drawing deep in the eternal pipe, he turns now to Peter, addresses him for the first time.

"You know, Peter, I have a great story about your mother. I don't know if she's told it to you."

"She's told me quite a few."

I have entered his mental files. What drawer am I in?

"When she first came to campus as a graduate student she lived, as you know, in Sage Hall, the dormitory for graduate students."

Peter nods. He had his eyeballs directed that way earlier. "That's where I met dad, Peter."

"One day, after she'd been here just a little while, I met her in the hall. 'Well, Sister Claire,' I said, 'How are you getting along?'"

He would have asked her. He would have been courtly, charming. She would have been self-conscious but reasonably frank. He would have encouraged her. She would already have been worried about failing. The community was counting on her to excel.

"'Pretty good,' she said."

Peter remains opaque.

"'But to tell you the truth, I do have one problem. It's very noisy in Sage. I find it hard to study there at night, especially on weekends. There are a lot of beer parties downstairs in the lounge.'"

"'Well,' I said to her, 'yes. I'm sure that's hard for you, Sister. But just keep going. Keep trying. I'm sure everything will work out for you eventually.'"

He knocks his pipe against the already full ashtray at the edge of his desk. He sets one polished loafer with its shiny penny on the floor beside the other solidly grounded foot as if he's about to get up. Somewhere outside a steady grinding sound has begun, as though they're excavating another hole for a new building.

"Then, one day a few months later," he continues, smiling broadly now at Peter, "I happened to meet her again. 'Well, now,' I said to her. 'How are you getting along these days, Sister Claire? Are you still troubled by all that noise or are things going better for you?' She looked at me with a smile. 'I thought about what you said,' she replied, 'that day I complained about the noise. I finally decided there was only one thing to do: if you can't win against 'em, join 'em.'"

Pipe in one hand, the other palm resting on his knee, he leans forward toward Peter, his eyes bright.

Peter offers a weak smile.

Professor Dodd stands. He escorts us to the door.

Once there, he pauses. Peter and I step outside, into the hallway.

He eyes Peter. "So you're interested in coming here, Peter?"

"Yes."

"How were your scores?"

Wary, Peter shrugs. "So-so. 1395."

"Hmmm. Not bad." The small wise eyes study my son.

What do they see? The silver bat dangling from one ear? The dyed hair? The intelligent eyes? The feigned indifference? The son of a nun?

"Of course you can easily bring that up, raise it a good forty points next time you take the SATs."

Standing there in the doorway, Professor Dodd grows more serious, focussing on this imagined challenge as if it were a bibliographical conundrum. "Lots of kids waste time, get stuck the first time through the SATs." He opens his left hand and holds it palm up as if a pad of paper rested on it. He forms the other hand into position as if holding a pencil. Then he bends over the nonexistent paper, marking with the nonexistent pencil the nonexistent test. "Just be sure to keep going once you've started, Peter. That's the trick. Don't waste time. Tick off the answers you know." He ticks them off against the imaginary page. "Then, when you've finished, go back to the ones you didn't know. So many kids get stuck." He pauses, looks at Peter thoughtfully. "Yes, you can easily raise your scores."

Peter looks embarrassed.

Then — a cordial handshake between men, a wishing of luck, a hug for the lady.

Out again into the now burning sunshine, the brilliant day. The radiant blue sky harbors not one cloud. A fat pigeon squats on the shoulder of the Founder. Two dogs frolic at the far end of the Arts Quad.

We descend the hollowed steps, pass students bent over

books and newspapers or lounging on the lawn. One fellow in cut-offs plays a strange instrument as he sits crosslegged at the bottom of the steps.

"Balalaika," says Peter as we pass. "I've never seen one with four strings."

I consult our map. Campus has changed. We point ourselves in the right direction.

He is quiet as we walk, morning sun hot on our heads. I'm grateful again for uncovered shoulders. Skin bare to the sun is something I do not take for granted, even now. Or soft breezes against my hair. The roots of his are growing dark again.

He speaks quietly, firmly, as we walk. "You might as well know that I'm *not* retaking the SATs, Mom. That's one form of pain I'd prefer not to go through again."

I'm silent. I hear the challenge. I'm not up for it. I'm too busy coping with a different urgency, the push from somewhere deep within to make things somehow more right, truer, more accurate. The human mind craves clarity, understanding. The very air of a morning like this begets such desire, feeds it. Is there no way, then, to put together murdered snakes and the longing for God, no way to combine motherhood and wisdom, no certain route to the Ur-text of memory, no definitive edition of THIS IS HOW IT WAS?

Is there no window into the soul?

"And I hope *you* realize," I say, stepping briskly onward, "that the whole story he told you was made up. It never happened. Not a bit of it."

Surely if it had I would remember.

Peter glances at me, irritated.

"What do you take me for, Mother? Of course I realize it." He looks away, toward Karen and her dad standing up ahead at the edge of the gathering tour. Mr. Klenman has removed his jacket. "The question is . . . *did he?*"

SEDUCING PIETY

I haven't much time. In a few moments we leave for the party. Now, in the cold of an overlong Canadian winter, we're to go dressed for heat. The host and hostess promise to turn up the thermostat in their house and make as if we're in Algeria. I still have to fix my veil. We're to go dressed for a kasbah and bring our own liquor. My daughter is downstairs attaching silver sequins to the transparent veil that will cover the lower part of my face.

Before I go down and complete my disguise, I must tell you. The need to do this catches me by surprise. The event itself was quiet, no bitterness. Just a kind of distanced curiosity as I watched myself read your words. Whether you'll ever see my words I don't know. But I must say them.

I'd decided years ago not to focus on you. I'd watched too many women pine for mirages from the past, then swallow hard to suppress rage when the past turned up with pot belly and bad breath. Our illusions, found out, shame us.

For me the process of disengagement had been simple. I would have preferred complications. But you went away. Two years later I too went away. To a new life.

A long time afterward, unknown to you, I saw you once.

Chance had brought me to a university library. My oldest boy was checking out colleges. We'd driven hundreds of miles in the Northeast and were both exhausted. I'd ducked the campus tour this once so I could prowl around by myself for a while, smell library stacks again, browse through the campus store, observe the blend of brashness and avidity that marks an

American college campus. Many years had passed since I did my time in such a setting.

Suddenly, there you were, leaning against the card catalogue, talking absorbedly to a young woman with long blonde hair and a green backpack. I stood at a distance, by the Z drawers. It *had* to be you — still slim, balding now with graying hair — same expressive gestures, same way of standing with your long legs crossed, your head bent forward as if hearing her words, responding, was the most important thing in the world at that moment. I'd seen that pose before, felt its power, watched freshman girls sit at your feet in your apartment listening to you teach an extra section of English 101 before vacation started. A charmed circle. You in the center, as convinced as they that before long you'd enter the stream of poets fattening their Norton anthologies.

Observing you in the library that day, I felt nothing. That pleased me. No desire to announce myself, invade the stage of your life. It seemed to say that I'd grown up. However late. In such matters, what is late?

Hadn't I moved a whole country away, not to say several lives?

Then today, without my seeking, there you were again. That you found me through a poem is appropriate. You wrote swathes of poetry in those days, long metaphysical meanderings that set my mind confused and even bored. Nonetheless, I was flattered that you'd show them to me. And I read them gratefully. In the privacy of my dormitory room, removing my veil and headdress, I'd bend over them to baffle my way through overwrought syntax on women and sex and despair about impermanence. What was so devastating about impermanence? From childhood I'd been trained to acknowledge and accept it. *All things are passing; God alone suffices.* The great St. Teresa. *All flesh is grass . . . the grass withereth, the flower fadeth* . . . I'd had years of access to poetry greater than yours.

So I struggled to decode the late adolescent ramblings of the secular male mind. I'd already had quite enough experience with the maturer ramblings of older, "religious" male minds. As I read your poems, it seemed to me you lived in an enviable spot that could never be mine, a no man's land between adolescence and maturity. By any conventional figuring I was already a woman. Too late to seek the female equivalent of your youthful flaunted freedom. Did it exist? (I didn't know then that you'd grow bald early, that you'd still, twenty years later, be hurling your attention toward undergraduates, seducing them with warm understanding eyes into, at the very least, a kind of hero worship.)

In any case, today I found your poem.

It was long and unrhymed. In an obscure Canadian magazine from B.C. I saw the name, Hardwick Gunning. It can't be, I thought. But who else would have a name like that? So I sat right down in the periodical room, parka unzipped, boots dripping, and abandoned myself to the pleasure of the middle years — looking both ways.

Time was short. I still had to get home, cook supper, devise a costume, prepare myself for tonight's foolishness.

So I had to skim. But I caught the essence of the story. It went on for some ten or twelve pages. I doubt it was poetry. Perhaps now I'd say this to your face. As I skimmed, I felt this piece should have been a story, not a poem.

Your hero was an artist. A painter. He had a studio somewhere, a loft or a barn, something remote and private. Inaccessible.

Like you in those days. You lived in a world I had yet to inhabit, explore: *the world,* as we called it. You were good-looking in a professionally poor way. These were the sixties. It wouldn't do to appear rich. Your jeans were appropriately ragged. You zoomed around campus on your motorcycle. Not tall, you had a walk, half swagger, recognizable a block away.

After I arrived mornings at the library, locked myself into my booklined carrel and resolved to bore through fifty more pages of Shakespeare's shenanigans or Wordworth's musings before coffee break, I'd watch out the window for your arrival. The professors obviously considered you intelligent. You wrote good seminar papers. Your students idolized you, innocent freshmen who'd lucked out with this stimulating and sexy grad student for their English prof instead of some stodgy, learned and famous professor. You wowed them with trenchant remarks about Yeats and Auden, offhand observations about life. You took yourself (and they took you) so seriously.

I don't know what I felt in those days.

It puzzled me even then.

The shining glass-topped mahogany table separated us.

"Today we shall discuss the medieval notion of love," said our learned and famous professor.

I watched him pull out the file drawer in his mind labelled *LOVE: MEDIEVAL.* He leaned back in his chair, placed his leather elbow patches on the arm rests, drew on his pipe, his small quick eyes studying us. "What can you tell me about it? Did they have a notion of the sublime?"

Someone had prepared a paper.

The liquid fire in my knees, my stomach — could it be my heart? — had about it nothing sublime. My bowels loosened, my palms grew damp. That night we would again walk about the deserted football field and you'd tell me about your latest conquest, spelling out for me the moral perplexities that dogged you as you threaded the maze of relationships with (ah, let it now be said) consummate pleasure. Oh, the impermanence of it all. But then, you wanted nothing to last.

Your hands were strong-looking and well-maintained. You

wore T-shirts that revealed rugby-trained muscles. The long taut lines of your throat, your mouth. . . . It was the mouth that drew me, the fuller bottom lip, the generous curve of it, the —

I'm too old to be going through this, I thought, gripping the seminar table to keep hold of myself, maintain the even untroubled mien of a disciplined sister, the well-adjusted committed life plopped there in the midst of Vanity Fair. I held my black knees together, stared at the page. I wanted to do well. Get an A from the learned man. Justify my presence in the academy.

But yearning knew no controls and at moments the seminar room tipped — as later, I discovered, it also might from too much wine.

Well, then . . .

Your overlong poem, today's surprise, centered about this artist and his hidden retreat. The secret place where he did his painting. Somehow (the pages I skipped set up this situation) he met a girl. A girl much unlike him, a waif-type he said he'd take in overnight. Motivation wasn't clear. Some kind of half-baked compassion. She seemed to be one of those wandering about the face of the earth with knapsack and running shoes. They met, I think, at a party. He was older, successful. Glamorous, perhaps.

After the party or whatever it was, he took her with him. A long quiet drive through the night. She didn't talk much. When she did her speech was awkward, tactless, lacking in charm. He took that in. I remember that in the poem, specifically. *"Whatever else he might say about her afterward, it wouldn't be that she had charm."*

I've come to suspect charm. I've been told I have it. The

term puzzles me. Does it mean I lie well? What are its uses? Those short on charm lead lives less encumbered.

Tonight I'll try to be charming. My skirt hangs long and gauzy and the veil is seductive, so my fifteen-year-old daughter tells me. We are to stand among academic artsy types and look interested. Since I've lost my belief in charm, such functions have become a problem. My husband, the mayor, must attend, for this is a small town and absences are noticed. He's a funny man, Hardwick. It would be difficult to find someone more thoroughly your opposite. He loves public functions, wears exquisitely tailored suits. Since you've never met, it's pointless to go into that except to satisfy your curiosity . . . which probably, these twenty years later, is non-existent.

I climbed into your bed. I no longer feel mortified at my aggressiveness. I see it now as normal, given the circumstances. I'd never been in bed with a man. All year I'd suffered from longing for you. Our late night walks might have shocked some, the sight of a longskirted nun walking the football field in moonlight with a young man in jeans and windbreaker. I doubt anyone knew. What the secular mind might have concluded was quite true: the campus Romeo was telling me his troubles. We'd cross the swinging bridge high above the gorge, and those hurtling roaring waterfalls below had nothing on the colossal swings and surges hidden beneath my black. What privilege, what intimacy: out beneath the stars with an appealing younger man sharing an insight into his sex life. What absurdity: longing for touch, committed to distance. He was safe.

I loved being with you. I hated being your confessor. Once in a while, over a stone wall, down a pebbly path, you took my hand. I wanted more.

So I climbed into your bed. Having at last shed my black and white a few weeks before, I'd returned to campus in technicolor. Mistress of my own life.

I went to your apartment — driven, it seems to me now, by an inner fire I could not control. Your roommate was in the front part of the house. I doubt he heard me come in the al-ways-open back door and head through the kitchen for your bedroom. I knew my way around from having been the invited guest at several of your extra classes. You had the upper bunk in the small back room.

The story in your poem went like this: at the end of the party, as I said, she goes home with the artist. And as he drives through woods and over hills and past deserted landscapes of nothing much, he realizes that he's taking her to his secret hideaway and he regrets it. She's smoking, saying nothing, looking out the window opposite him, all curled up in herself in a way that defies breaking through. Not that he really wants to. But he can't turn her out here, in the middle of nowhere.

So they go on.

And finally come to the isolated spot, a small cabin in a clearing, not of clay and wattles made, the secret space that is his own. Where no one else ever comes. Where day after day he paints desires and dreams and regrets on canvas and some-times, later, sells them. They go in, he turns up the few lights, she looks around. He arranges a couch for her, makes it up in a fashion and heads for his room.

He lies on the thin mattress and stares up at the low ceiling. He is thinking of the painting he's in the midst of. He's seeing the eyelids, half-closed, over wine-purple eyes. He's imagining the curve of the eyelashes. He has already forgotten the girl. She'll leave in the morning. He'll see to that.

In the middle of the night, unbidden, she comes to him. She glides naked and light through the cool dark, pulls back his sheets and slips in beside him. He doesn't say no. He isn't even excited at first. But he takes what is offered and that, eventually, with pleasure.

The next morning she makes him coffee. He shows her all around his workshop, even to the cast-off canvases in the back room behind the bedroom. She doesn't say much. She smokes and looks at his canvases coolly, then turns back to the sink to do their breakfast dishes. She will not be easy to dislodge, he senses. He starts to paint.

It goes on like that for several days.

I climbed up, I remember, in my slip. I was just getting used to a slip, to the pressure of straps on my shoulders, lace against my breasts. We are not, after all, constantly aware of our bodies. Certain lives train us to forget them.

I kissed you full on the mouth, that wonderful mouth, and waited . . . I hardly knew for what. I was neither cynical nor overly hopeful. My imagination was remarkably uncluttered; I hadn't seen a movie, read a magazine, in eleven years. I was simply following the longing of my heart. I sensed danger, what I'd once called the occasion of sin, but I didn't care.

You held me a moment, your lips soft against mine.

Then you told me to go away.

I had my pride. I wasn't immune to shame.

I struggled down awkwardly from the upper bunk, pulled on my sweater and skirt, left the dark room without a comment. Burning.

An instinct I would still affirm told me that my chastity spooked you. Perhaps you wanted me still pure and untouchable, even outside the cloth. You wanted your confessor. Something permanent. I could be wrong.

In the poem it is different.

She stayed several days. They ate together. During the daytime he painted and she walked about outside, seemingly content. She watched birds, sucked the sweet ends of tall grasses, and breathed quietly. She had a way of being indolent, of lying around watching him, of not caring to do anything herself. She made him nervous.

So, after days of work on the half-closed lids, he decided to send her away. One morning he said, "Pack your things, I'll drive you to the highway."

"You won't," she said, and stood there breathing.

He watched her small pointed breasts lifting her pink paint-spattered T-shirt, and round her he seemed to see an aura, an effulgence that defied analysis. Nonetheless, he held firm. He wanted to paint. He could not do it with a woman around. He would get rid of her.

He helped her into the car. It seemed unnecessary. She was perfectly capable of helping herself. Not once in her four or five days there had she asked him for help. That was the odd thing. Several times he'd been tempted to ask her to help him move a canvas, to tell him what she thought of a color or a line. Some secret caution held him back.

They drove on down the road past thickening fields of corn, past waving ochre grain and a deep blue lake. He knew she'd be all right. Fortunately, it was late summer. She could go anywhere.

He'd asked if she needed money and she said no.

Near the main intersection with Route 191 he dropped her.

"Thanks," she said, and never looked back.

He did, through the rearview mirror and then, when the road curved, through the side mirror. He saw her standing there as if she had all the time in the world, no place to get to. She looked lost.

Back home, he tried to work.

I felt that in this part you were stretching things to make a poem. Nevertheless, I went on reading.

I don't know what I did that very night. Memory sorts out moments to keep alight and darkens others. Probably I roamed about campus, aware of soft evening spring air against my bare legs, relishing wind in my hair. I doubt I prayed.

Everyone knew you were involved with at least one undergraduate, as well as heaven only knew how many other women in places remote and exotic. You'd perfected the look and manner that say *experienced*. My oldest son is presently working toward it.

There come times when impermanence makes itself deeply felt. This was such a time for me. I'd left one life, begun another. Shed one skin, revealed another.

And you were leaving at the end of the year. I had at least two more years to go.

The campus itself was held for those weeks in a numb state of shock. In an odd way, that bore on my situation.

After Easter I had returned early from my convent to campus to face my major decision. I needed solitude. A friend who'd gone home for the spring break lent me her apartment at the edge of campus. This was part of a special building complex Cornell had built for five-year Ph.D. students, the best and brightest from around the country. My friend was a don there.

For two days I walked those deserted fields trying to sort

out my life, my mind. I took off my veil, let air circle my head. I spoke to no one. I don't think anyone knew I was in the building. It was almost empty. Most had gone home for the break.

On the third day I returned to my own graduate dormitory. Everyone would now be returning. Classes would resume the next day. I had made up my mind to leave the Order at the end of the term.

As I lay sound asleep in my own bed that night, I heard footsteps pounding outside my room. Voices. I slipped on my black bathrobe and nightveil and opened the door.

"Sister Claire, there's a huge fire," said Bonnie, the girl in the room next door. "Terrible."

"Where?"

"The FUD building."

That's what they were called, those bright students. FUDS. I shut the door.

The building was levelled.

It was said that later that outlines of the victims' bodies were visible on the ash coated rugs of the burned-out dorm.

I could have been there.

It could have been my body.

The old cliché took on sudden urgent meaning. *I had one life*.

Three days later I left campus to negotiate my own trans-formation.

After that night I felt embarrassed with you. We'd talk, of course. Our paths crossed every day in the library where, along with dozens of other grad students, we were cramming toward the ultimate certification of brains and endurance. We'd leave our cages at every excuse, head toward the student union, kibbitz over coffee, always in a group. No longer confessor, I longed to be lover. Now, apparently, I could be neither. Still, I rejoiced to be part of the world of color.

And carried deep within the sense of having been miraculously spared. For what? The consequences of that tragic fire were, for me, anything but tragic.

I had a new life.

Well, in your poem the painter goes back to his cabin and starts to paint. Although he works harder than ever, he can't seem to do it. The quality of the air, the very ends of his fingers, seem altered. Everything is strange. What had been his alone is marred, somehow, because another has walked through it, seen his half-finished pieces, commented or just stared.

At the end of a frustrating day he decides to pack it in and take a break. He can't clear out the air in the cabin, but maybe he can clear out his own head.

Two days later he returns. From where, I haven't the faintest idea. I guess I skipped that. The essential is that he went away and came back, expecting to reclaim his own place.

The minute he pulls up outside the cabin he senses something different. Then he goes inside . . . and sees. Every canvas has been slashed. On the unfinished canvas, the head with the half-closed eyes, green paint has been dribbled down the front. He goes into the back room hoping she may have left something, some shred of the past. Nothing. Wherever she could find his dream or desire or half-articulated thought, she slashed it.

He stands in the room and looks about. A lifetime down the drain.

As he stands there, you say, he realizes something: that he

has violated her also, perhaps more than she could ever violate him.

I don't get the ending.

I want to argue with you about it. I want to accuse you of tacking it on just so something neat can click and the reader can set down the journal and walk away with that everything-has-come-together feeling.

I want to argue with you on several counts. Things don't come together like that, neatly balanced: you did this to me, I did that to you, now we're even. That's the world of children's marbles.

I'm glad you sent me away. It was a good thing. I didn't know it then, and I'm sure some would say to me now, "You're just saying that. It's never that simple."

It wasn't that simple.

The complication I yearned for would have been simpler than the one you handed me.

Who was there to tell? And who now? These children who in a moment will adjust my veil and say, "Okay, Mom, you'll pass," or "Wait a minute, I'll fix it" — eager to make my disguise complete?

That's why I think of sending this to you — a voice discovered today, twenty years later, on a library shelf in a foreign country. Your words read by friendly eyes, knowing eyes. Read quickly. You'd be insulted at that, but then I doubt you've children waiting for you somewhere saying, "What's for supper?" You never wanted that complication.

Life is full of them, complications.

I put down the pen, know you still live, know you still write, know that somewhere in the thicket of Manhattan a man the curve of whose jaw I've traced and the hollow of whose cheek I've caressed, that man writes now of an artist in the woods who is destroyed by the woman who invades his privacy. And then disappears.

I don't think I'll send this. I'll let it sit. I'll come back to it tomorrow, and maybe the next day, and stare. I don't want to impose a false ending. The ending had come. I felt that. Then today — a new ending. Like Haydn when he really got going . . . finding one resolution after another. Fooling the listener, and maybe even himself.

So I'll let it sit on my desk. Perhaps in a few days or weeks you'll get a letter that tells you, years later, how a picture can be repainted and new words found, how nothing is undone forever.

LIFELINE

It's the trembling head, the abstracted look of the near deaf. You can't tell when she hears you. You can't count on her not to hear.

It's the feel of sharp fragile bones through the thin nightgown you've helped her into, trying all the while to numb your awareness of the ninety-pound once-beautiful body which fifty-seven years ago thrashed in passion (you hope) and suffered extremes of pleasure and pain in getting and having you. Difficult birth. High forceps. You've heard it all many times.

She sat gingerly on the bedroom chair, one leg out straight, while you knelt to ease off her underpants, knee stockings. Ah, those legs. Shapely. Trim ankles, even yet. What unkind blip in the genetic process left yours so thick?

You lift her bad leg into bed as she maneuvers the rest of her surely aching body and soul. You smooth the sheet back down over the top edge of the electric blanket, pull both up snug beneath her freshly dewhiskered chin. ("Could you find the tweezers in my top drawer and pull the big ones? My hand shakes so, and I can't see them.") It's July in southern New England. Ninety-five degrees Fahrenheit. "We'll leave the electric blanket on the bed," she said. "It's none too warm." You wonder: does the body prepare itself for the ultimate chill?

"Leave the door open and the nightlight on. Put the walker there in the corner where I can reach it. Where will you be? Are you going to bed soon?"

"Soon. I got The New York Times. I'll read in the living room for a while." As if murders on the West Bank, corruption in high places, wars and rumors of wars, one more air disaster, could mute this whispering death.

"What time is that lady coming in the morning?"

"Nine-thirty."

"Don't stay up too late. And be sure to check the locks."

As you leave the room she's lying all tucked in, eyes wide open, staring at the ceiling. In half an hour, if the buffered aspirin work, she'll be snoring like a bull moose.

Your son, here for two days, one night, has tried to jolly her.

"Here comes Steel Foot," he said at the sound of her walker rattling and clonking through the kitchen. "I hear you coming, Grandma!"

She smiled uncertainly. "What did he say?" Wanting to be sure to laugh at her grandson's joke. If it was a joke.

Supper over, he has closeted himself in the back bedroom to read *The Crack in the Cosmic Egg*.

This leaves you to sleep tonight on the twin bed next to the cosmic snore.

Lifeline Day.

It has taken months, years of persuasion and cajoling to bring her to this day. It has taken the agony of lying broken and afraid, alone in the locked house, despairing of rescue. It has taken the misery of the convalescent home, of brusque therapists, impatient aides, of querulous voices calling in the night for help, for release from their private hells.

"You stay near Grandma in case she gets confused," you tell him, wishing he'd shaved in honor of the Lifeline Lady. In honor of Grandma. In honor of you? At least he got out of bed.

She is deft, this lady come to hook Mother up to the hospital. Tactful, reassuring, Betty Sullivan, who arrived at nine-thirty on the dot, wears a matching skirt and sweater of dusty rose, small round pearls about her short neck, and plain low-heeled navy blue shoes. We are in the sun room, Mother's favorite spot, Betty on the straight chair opposite Mother's cushioned chair. She speaks clearly, in an even tone, as Peter and I hover nearby.

"Now first, Mrs. Delaney, we'll give you the Lifeline medallion," she says, unwrapping the apparatus from its packing. She sets a small plastic box on her lap and leans forward toward Mother, holding out a square piece of plastic suspended on a light chain.

"Now, you feel it, hold it. See? It's not very heavy. This is what you'll wear around your neck."

Trembling veined hands accept the unwelcome plastic intruder, test its weight on the palm.

"You're right," Mother concedes. "It's not too heavy. I thought it would be heavier than this. Mabel Doran had one. She was my friend who broke her hip, she's gone now, Mabel had one and it was much heavier."

"They've improved them in the past year. Now we'll just slip it over your head — like this."

Betty stands up to slide it easily over thick white hair which needs, as Mother tells me hourly, a cut and a perm. Eight weeks in a convalescent home would leave anyone a wreck and besides the girl there who did it — well, she was nice enough but didn't know how to do it right. The old way, brushed out. Nobody brushes your hair out all the way now. They just leave the waves in place and spray it to hold.

Over the hair it goes, past thick glasses obscuring clouded eyes — oh rare and beautiful pale blue eyes due for the second cataract surgery as soon as she can summon courage. At last the plastic medallion comes to rest on the shrunken chest.

There it nestles, Lifeline medallion, a gentle dent in the pink and blue Talbot's blouse donned just for this occasion. Beneath it, inside the blouse, hides another medallion, a gold miraculous medal. In case the official Lifeline fails.

"Once we have this all hooked up, Mrs. Delaney, you just press that little section in the center, the smaller square that pushes in." As Betty leans her round unwrinkled face forward and quietly explains, Mother takes in every word and presses the indicated spot. "That's right. Now a buzz will sound in the hospital and a light will go on to indicate you're at this address. The hospital will call in turn each of the three people you've designated to be on the Lifeline until it makes contact with one of them. You've notified three?"

"Yes, yes. I've asked three."

"And then, if there's no answer at any of those places — this doesn't often happen, Mrs. Delaney — the police come."

"They break in?"

"Well, of course they'd try the doors first. But they have to get in somehow. Don't worry about damage. They're very skilled at this. They usually do it through one window."

Mother looks about the room, imagining doilies out of place, statues chipped, the Sacred Heart of Jesus askew.

"Now, then, Mrs. Delaney — "

"Please call me Vivien," she says. "I'd like you to call me Vivien." Gracious. With a social sense, even now. Creator of the perfect bridge party, the elegant dinner, the comfortably furnished home. At our wedding reception, in the garden of a country inn, she asked my newly minted spouse: "Where are the napkins? Perfection *is* perfection."

"Don't get too friendly," she mouthed at me from her hospital bed as I chatted with the lady in the other bed suffering from her own fractured bone and destined, it turned out, to heal more quickly.

"Don't get too friendly," she admonished as I jollied up the nurses, the therapist, the head admissions person in the nursing home, hoping thereby to insure some decent steady attention when I left eight weeks ago to face my own domestic duties a thousand miles from here.

"Do you need a modular phone outlet?" cuts in the grandson. Technological whiz. Bearer of Electronic Age savvy. Unshaven Einstein. Granny looks at him — puzzled, proud, half-hearing. "He mutters so," she often complains. "If you need a modular outlet," he says to Betty, "There's one here and one in the bedroom."

"Good." She leans toward Mother. "Do you think it would be best if I make the hook-up right here, Vivien?"

"What should I look up, Betty?"

"The hook-up, Vivien. Would it be best in this room, do you think?"

"I think so, yes. I spend most of the day in here." On the small table beside her chair lie her Rosary Novena booklet, her beads, her magnifying glass. The TV stands a few feet away.

Betty fiddles with the outlet near the desk.

Once a place of pleasure, the desk with its stuffed cubbyholes has become a nightmare warren of bills: ambulance, doctors, X-rays, medication, Medicare will and won'ts, Blue Cross/Blue Shield, drawers of old bank statements, IRS forms, the unbalanced checkbook, the CD that matured. And then, in the bottom drawer, the will, to be changed tomorrow. After the grandson goes back to his summer job, earning moola to support his needs. Another year of higher learning. Dollars to send him once again to the Grateful Dead while Grandma squeezes out her monthly check to Covenant House.

"I hope he always stays the way he is," she says periodically.

I see a paunchy balding man zooming around the U.S.A. unshaven, cigarette dangling, racing from one concert to another, one ashram to another, seeking the guru who'll lead him, once and for all, to the ultimate laid-back lifestyle.

"Now we have just one thing left to do before I call the hospital. We have to install this box somewhere in this room," says Betty. "Shall we set it flat on a table — near where you'll be sitting, Vivien?" Betty surveys the corner of the room near Mother's chair: a desk, a bookrack, a dresser holding dozens of family photos and unused tablecloths, dead letters, life litter. "Do you usually sit in this chair?"

Mother eyes the square white plastic box with its three buttons on one side: red, yellow, green. Innocuous looking.

"Yes," she murmurs. "I love this chair. I say my rosary here first thing every morning."

Betty moves aside some photos and sets the box on top of the black dresser, an arm's reach from Mother's chair.

"There. You push this green button every morning at the same time, Vivien. That's important. Choose whatever time you want for the first morning. After that it will be the same time every day. You make it part of your morning routine, like brushing your teeth. It tells them at the hospital that you're okay."

"What if I forget? I'll never remember, Betty. I'm getting awful. I forget everything."

"Don't worry, Grandma. You only have to remember one thing. Push the button at nine-thirty, or whatever time you decide. If you forget it, no big deal. If they don't get your call, *they* call you five minutes later. That's all you have to do."

A male voice. Reassuring. She listens to him. He sounds so knowing. She sits back, relieved.

"He's right," says Betty, shooting Peter a grateful look.

Later that day we'll shop for the alarm clock to put near the breakfast table set for nine twenty-five to remind her to push the Lifeline button on the box. At the clock counter in K Mart, she'll reject a louder wind-up alarm because she would forget to wind it. Insisting on an electric alarm, she'll discover after we bring it home that it's useless. She cannot hear it.

"Now, Vivien, with Peter's help we're going to try this buzzer all over the house to be absolutely sure it works."

Betty hands the small square medallion to Einstein Junior and he is off, in his T-shirt and Bermudas, his huge bare feet and hairy legs propelling him from room to room.

We stand near Mother, waiting. She has closed her eyes and her head drops slightly forward. What is she thinking? Is she falling asleep?

We hear the back door open, then slam shut.

Suddenly a loud buzzer sounds. Her head snaps back, her eyes flutter open. The red light on the box flashes.

"What's that?" Her eyes grow confused.

"The warning from outside," says Betty. She sets a reassuring hand on Mother's shoulder. "Everything's fine."

Moments later Peter lopes back in, exuberant. "I went out in back as far as the trash cans before I pressed it. Did it work?"

"It worked fine," says Betty.

"Awesome."

Betty is about to leave. She has set the Lifeline instructions next to the rosary beads on the table by Mother's chair. "Later, when you have time, you can go over all this, Vivien. If you have any questions, just call me."

Before she leaves, she tells us, she'll make a test try to the hospital. They are expecting it. Following Betty's instructions,

Mother presses the square center of her new medallion. The yellow light goes on. After a few seconds, the phone rings. Betty picks it up.

"Teresa? Good. All's well. Thanks." As she sets down the receiver she nods with a smile toward Mother.

"Now, Vivien, it's all set."

Mother seems not to hear her. During the test call she's been eyeing the exact position of the square box on the dresser top.

"Before you go, Betty, do you think we could change the location of the box?" she asks. "It's off-center there."

"Of course. As long as it stays here where you can get to it easily first thing in the morning. I'd be afraid you might trip on the cord if we put it on the desk. You just tell me and I'll move the pictures around it wherever you want."

Delicate business, this. Rearrangements of a life. Pictures, pictures: the babyhood of this galoomph near her wiggling his toes. No recent shots. She's waiting for him to cut his hair. See him in the long baptismal dress, hers, in his mother's arms, my arms. I feel that small warm body, see his proud grandmother beside us. Do we really look that much alike?

Evenings, when she was in the hospital, I sat in her chair, the one she now occupies, with its rose flowered slipcover. I wore her pink velour bathrobe, having travelled light, a hasty journey, drank her Scotch, fingered mementos extracted from nearby drawers, scanned *Modern Maturity* and the large print *Reader's Digest*, fiddled with the remote control, tried to suppress the sense that I was turning into her. The insanity of the evening news brought me mindless balm: riots, rapes, betrayals, murders — stupefying elixir of mortality summoned to stave off murmurings of soul less violent, more penetrating, impossible to deny. *Must daughters eventually turn into their mothers?*

"Try spacing them evenly," she says now, pointing, as Betty moves framed family snapshots, setting them first on a diagonal, then a straight line, then in a semi-circle, all the while holding in one hand the carved madonna around which they'd been clustered, as if by some magic that heavenly lady could zap a remnant of faith into this faltering faithless clan.

When I was fifteen, President of the Children of Mary, I crowned the statue of the Virgin in May, Mary's month. I wore a long white dress and my court, all Children of Mary, wore pastels. The church was packed. Afterward, on the outside steps of the church, someone took our picture beside Father Hanrahan, the pastor, with his long narrow jaw and close set eyes, his nervous half-smile. Awash in a sea of nubile virginity, he looked like a drowning man. Surely that picture is here still, buried in one of those stuffed drawers.

Betty has finished rearranging.

"Now, Betty, that's better. Why don't you try putting Our Blessed Mother right on top of the box?"

Betty obliges.

"What do you think?" Mother eyes us all.

"Fine, Mom."

Peter's pale blue eyes, her eyes, hold a look I've seen many times. *Who needs this?* One more hour to go. He must pack, leave before noon.

"Now remember, Vivien," says Betty, waving Mother back down as she reaches for the walker to escort her visitor to the door, a matter of training. "If you have any questions after you've read all the material I brought you, just call me. I'm sure you'll find this a big relief. And I know your daughter will."

"She'll have to take me out to get an alarm clock," says Mother, leaning hard on the walker. "I'll need to be reminded to push the button. What time was it?"

"Nine-thirty, Grandma," says Peter.

"I know I'll forget."

She's right.

The notes are everywhere. "Take pill at 9:00." "Doxidan before bed." "Get paper towel." "Call Stella." "Hair." "Weekly envelope." "Rent."

You'll make a new one, attach it to the bathroom mirror. **Remember: 9:30 — push button on Lifeline box.**

Assuming she gets up in the morning.

Later, in the car she is secretly wondering if she will ever drive again, we set out to purchase the unusable alarm clock.

Which loss to accept? Which to fight?

"Would you consider a hearing aid?" I asked her again recently, pained anew at the confused withdrawal in those faded blue eyes when two or three people were gathered in a room, talking.

"Absolutely not. I spent five hundred dollars for one eight years ago and it was no good. Didn't help me one bit. Elizabeth Molloy had the same experience."

"It might make you more comfortable, Mom."

"I can hear all right. The answer is NO."

Sometimes Fortune smiles, sometimes she leers.

My trip here to spring a healing mother from eight weeks' incarceration in the convalescent home coincided with my college reunion. Two hours away. Why not take in a small dose of it before beginning this troubling ordeal? Just enough to satisfy the curiosity, all these years later, of an aging GCG (as we called ourselves, Good Catholic Girls), uneasy hostess now to a thousand viruses of scepticism and doubt. I deliberately skipped the keynote address by a famous Catholic sociologist: "The Sandwich Generation."

"My mother is ninety; my husband's mother is a hundred and one," a chic silvery-blonde ex-classmate told me. "We still have kids at home. I'm going to visit my mother after the re-union. She's still in her big house, alone, moving toward a decision. We're going to have to do something. She won't give up driving and refuses a hearing aid."

Two nights later as we three sat in the sunroom facing the boob tube and eating dinner from plastic TV trays, I tried to drown out an inane commercial with a bit of humor.

"You know what the sociologists call my generation, Mom?" I shouted to her, careful to smile. "The Sandwich Generation."

Peter eyed me.

"Don't EVER give me one!" she shouted back. She set down her fork with a sharp clink against her plate. "I hate them. I've always hated them. They gave me enough sand-wiches in Forest Villa to last me the rest of my life. Your father never liked sandwiches either. You know I always saw that he had a hot meal in the middle of the day."

Some losses can be held at bay, minimized. You can dare them to get you.

Memory, for example, can be helped. You learn little tricks. Always put things back in the same place. Establish a routine, keep to it. Write yourself notes. Reminders.

Then comes the Ultimate Note, the one in the bottom desk drawer. Compose it with exquisite care. Scrutinize your conscience, worry your tremulous way through every detail, every implication. Brood over it, night after night, alone, watching *Jeopardy*, sipping sherry with the ten o'clock news and weather, applying your one good eye through a thick magnifying glass to the big print *Reader's Digest*, deciding finally it's time to take your bowel-softener.

How you long to be remembered! Some evenings, as you sit alone, desire spears you like pain, passes right through you, fighting that other sharp sense you strive to hold down. You will not let it get you, you will not. *I am alone here.* After that comes the ache, the longing to be thought of, *remembered,* in the secret corners of other minds, to float forever in the roto-gravure of their memory, an image distinct and cherished. But not just in any old memory. Oh no. To float forever in the holding hearts of those you call blood kin. Those are the memories that count, finally. It becomes a desire so strong you can taste it: metallic, lingering, obsessive.

So you've decided to change your will. You've told your faithful daughter. "You write it down," you told her. "You deal with the lawyer tomorrow. You can express it better than I can."

Your daughter will never forget you. Your grandchildren might.

Now, after a night of terror, the hour has come. . . .

This is no slick, pinstriped, hotshot lawyer come to redo the will. No. This is a nephew of Mother's friend, the one who never got her Easter water. Michael Dunovan. We went to school together, could swap anecdotes about Sister Gabrielita, whom we christened Gabriel Heater and who favored whack-ing a yardstick on the backs of recalcitrant eighth grade fingers. Michael's Aunt Lou, a daily communicant, was hard of hearing and rattled her beads against the front pew at Mass. A visibly tired man now, bald and beginning to fold in on himself, Michael shows his years of contending with widows and probate, large schemes and fine print. I remember him as an eight-year-old with a shock of red hair in his eyes, socks that sank into the heels of his shoes, and a sweet voice that set old ladies aquiver when he sang "Mother Dear, Oh Pray for Me."

He sits patiently with us at the dining room table this morning as I spell out the changes she wants, article by article, and see the grandchildren grow fat and prosperous.

"I would never tell him how much I have," she declared five years ago, in the midst of yet another discussion about the will.

"But Mother, he's your own lawyer. You chose him. And you need advice."

"Yes, but still . . . I wouldn't want him to know."

"Is it because you have too little, too much, or you don't trust him?"

"No. I trust him."

"Well?"

"Well . . . It's just that people are always curious about what other people have."

"True enough. But if you feel that way, why not get a new lawyer? Someone you don't know. A perfect stranger. Better yet, get a crackerjack accountant, or a financial adviser. You need some advice on protecting your money."

"It's not that I don't trust him. I know he's honest. And he's smart. It's just — "

It's just that you wanted your privacy. Intact.

Now even that is gone.

I wash the body you would never expose to me.

I pay your bills, arrange your care. I measure out your pills, confer with your physician, violate your cubbyholes.

I spread out before your lawyer your assets. You are past the time for secrets.

Exhausted after the night, you sit at one end of the dining room table watching us, straining to hear, trusting me to tell him exactly what you want.

Out of such scenes great novels grow.

This one lacks the essential conflict.

I tell him what you want.

"Be sure on her Money Markets you have Rights of Survivorship," he says quietly.

"You're afraid I've let *what* slip?" she asks quickly, leaning forward. Her blue eyes grow milky, bewildered.

"No, no, Vivien — " Michael eyes her soberly over his half glasses, his veined and spotted hand surrounded by sheets of paper covered with notes. He's brought the last will she made, and the one before that.

"He's just cautioning me to make sure both our names are on you Money Markets," I say, "so I can get at them if I need to."

"With *or*, not *and*," he says.

She shifts on her chair, adjusts the disposition of weight on her extended leg, which rests on a footstool beneath the table. Then she sits back suddenly, lets her hands fall to her lap.

Is she in pain?

They picked her up from the marble floor of the church sanctuary after she fell. They sent for an ambulance, got her to the hospital. I was called. Surgery on the knee. *Come*. Her pulse is low. There is no one else.

A cruel joke which almost severed the family line for good. After Mass, she wanted to fill with Easter water a small vial she'd carried to church in her purse. She planned to bring it to Lou Dunovan, languishing now in a convalescent home. The holy water, freshly blessed at Easter, was kept in a container in the sanctuary. The priest had left the altar before she moved out of her pew, went forward, and climbed the three low steps into the sanctuary slowly, mindful of her recently healed hip. She bent and filled her vial, screwed the top back on.

Then, as she turned to leave the sanctuary, she met the pastor, Father Sullivan, coming back to the altar unexpectedly. With the reflex of a lifetime, she paused to greet him. Her foot missed a step. She fell, smashed the bottle and her knee. The two or three parishioners still in church ran forward to help. Until the ambulance arrived, Mother lay nearly unconscious. At least not alone this time as once before, with the hip.

She and Michael's aunt both loved to sprinkle holy water about the rooms of their homes at night. Even now, in pain, she grasps her walker and clonks through the house just before retiring, sprinkling a few drops in each room. Bless this room. Keep us safe.

A green scapular is draped over her bedstead near her pillow. When she goes to bed these nights, she hangs the Lifeline medallion over it.

On her bedroom dresser, the small silver Infant of Prague stands watching, between the perfume and her earrings.

A rosary dangles from fingers gripping her walker, beads to tell hour by hour the mysteries that color her imagination — joyful, sorrowful, glorious — beads to number hopes and desires thrumming through her aching body, her anxious soul.

Above the bed hangs a hollow, cross-shaped box with a pale plastic Corpus attached to its top. As children this fascinated us, for it hid a secret. If you held onto the Corpus and pulled gently, the top part of the box slid off to reveal inside two candles and a linen cloth, items the priest would need when he came to anoint a dying body.

Viaticum we called it. A comforting notion.

Yet when the pounding started at three o'clock this morning, neither Mother nor I turned to holy water, rosary, scapular, or priest. We never thought of the Lifeline. We turned to the cops.

Two squad cars came.

No cop cruises alone at night in this city. As children, we played unafraid in this residential neighborhood, even after dark. We'd take flashlights, prowl around outside the windows, find an unshaded one where we could look in on adults gathered for drinks, socializing, cards. No TV in those days. We'd knock on the window and hold the flashlight beneath our chins, shining it upwards as we distorted our features into grotesque masks, pulling down our lower eyelids to show the pink undersides, stretching our mouths into leers. We wanted to spook the grownups, ghostify their windows of light. The dark was ours to invade, dominate, play with. Sometimes we frightened ourselves.

Then we had only to run inside.

Last year an eighty-year-old lady was attached at dusk on the next block.

This very apartment where Mother insists on remaining has twice been broken into in broad daylight, oriental throw rugs and silver tea service carted away in green garbage bags by two men in ties and sports jackets as neighbors watched with casual interest, supposing them legitimate. Both times she was out. She returned to jimmied locks, dumped out drawers, a sense of violation. She had her triumph, though. They never found her silver hidden under the dresser in the sunroom where the Lifeline now sits. Both times she insisted on sleeping here that night. "I'll have to get used to it sooner or later."

Last night was different. No lock was jimmied, no door broken through. No one appeared. Nothing was taken.

Still, I called the police.

The pink walls of her immaculate kitchen felt like cardboard. The house itself felt like cardboard. After we stumbled from bed at the sound, we went into the kitchen, turned on the light and sat there trembling. Fists pounded on the front door. The bell rang repeatedly — *bong bong bong*. A voice shouted, then muttered, then shouted again: "Let me in! Let me in!" *Bong bong bong*.

My fingers, dialing the police, shook. When they finally answered, I could barely speak. "Please, someone is trying to get into this house," I whispered into the mouthpiece, its plastic smooth and warm against my dry lips. Could he hear me? *Bong bong bong*. The pounding continued. "Please! Come immediately!"

"Let me in! Let me in!" cried the voice on the other side of the door.

The cardboard box shook.

It seemed forever before the squad cars arrived. Mother and I didn't speak. She sat by the kitchen table, her hands clasped in her lap, her cheeks sunken. She'd left her teeth in the glass by the bed. I stood near her feeling I should offer some strength, some words of reassurance. I had none. This was not the way I'd planned to die.

"Let me in! Let me in!"

The muttering was worse than the shouting. Though he was three rooms away, we could hear the outside front door rattle as he pounded.

Finally, a knock came at the back door. That doorbell didn't work.

I forced my cold feet across the floor, dared my eyes to look out the high window.

Into the soft brown eyes of our savior in navy blue.

I let him in.

"I'm all alone, Officer," whimpered the little old lady on the kitchen chair in her pink velour bathrobe, head trembling. "What would I have done if my daughter wasn't here?"

Panic laced her pale eyes.

"Must've been some drunk at the wrong house, Ma'am," he said. "We looked everywhere." He was burly, important, olive-skinned. MANCINI said the metal nameplate above his pocket. "Couldn't find anyone." He planted black shiny boots on the linoleum beside the kitchen table. "Found a few items on the front porch: a pair of men's trousers, a pair of sneakers, a piece of birthday cake."

His voice was like music. It didn't go with the heavy black boots.

"You placed the call?" he asked, directing soft brown eyes upon me.

"Yes." I wanted him to hold me. A gun rested on his hip. He wore fingerless gloves.

"Name?"

I gave it.

He produced a small pad, held it in his left hand, pulled out a pen, and began to write with his half-gloved hand. I watched his slim fingers reduce our terror to a police report. I wanted his fingers to touch me.

"You never saw anyone?"

"No. Whoever it was just banged on the door, over and over, and kept shouting 'Let me in.'"

"When did it start?"

"He woke us up over half an hour ago."

"Did he say anything else?"

"He muttered something we couldn't hear."

Mancini finished writing, slipped the pad into his pocket.

"We'll look around some more outside," he said. "But I don't think anyone is around now. He must've seen us coming."

Together we crossed the acre of kitchen floor toward the back door.

"It's her nightmare," I said (as if it weren't mine), pattering down the outside steps with him. He was a big man, well over six feet, solid. Cold damp concrete shocked my bare feet.

He nodded. "It's everyone's these days, Ma'am."

His buddy was coming around the corner of the house, flashing light into the leafy dark, illuminating bushes, litter.

"Nothing," he said.

Cold sucked at me deep within, spreading through my bones. If I stayed there a moment longer I might suddenly disintegrate, melt down, turn into a puddle of liquifying jelly, dribble away into the cracks of the sidewalk, vanish . . .

I left them, went back inside while they walked around to the front strafing bushes, leaves, dead hydrangeas with their beams. I turned the latch on the kitchen door, hurried past mother still cowering on the kitchen chair, went through the dark dining room past the table where we'd meet the lawyer and rewrite the will, past the sunroom with its Lifeline box, through the carpeted living room now in total darkness, opened the inside door, then the outside, and stood in the doorway watching them cross the lawn, go down the steps, cross the sidewalk, open the car doors, and slide inside.

"We'll cruise around here for a while," Mancini called back to me through his open window on the driver's side.

Mothers eat their daughters.

Not in one gulp, bit by bit.

It takes effort not be swallowed whole.

No one tells you this.

The first time, with the broken hip, she lay on the floor in the back bedroom, far from telephone, window. Three hours it took her to drag herself, inch by inch, to the window a room away where she could pound and bang with failing strength and heart, hoping at last to be heard over the lawnmower just outside.

This was before the Lifeline.

"When I was a young girl," she said once, "I'd walk down the streets by big comfortable homes in the rich section of town and dream. What would it be like to live inside such a house? Sometimes, in summer, the windows would be open, the curtains fluttering, and I'd see inside — linen tablecloths, china teacups. Lovely pitchers holding milk. I dreamed of being inside those houses, pouring milk from such a pitcher. My mother was a wonderful woman. I'm sorry you never knew her. She worked hard. She was a lady at heart, but she had no family on this side to support her. Always the outsider. Lonely, away from her own. I hope you never have to know what that is. She didn't have money but she worked hard to make us a good home."

Some stories have endings. Neat tidying up. A sense of closure.

Some characters remain stable, intact in their pronouns.

This is not such a story.

The *you*, the *she*, the *I*. As I tried to tell it, tried to keep them separate and distinct, I felt them sliding. They wouldn't stay put, resisted the necessity of remaining only themselves. Grew mushy, slippery, wanting somehow to merge. "Person" turned out to be an elusive grammatical concept.

Why must any grid of characters remain forever separate and distinct?

Let's give Betty her due: a kind efficient minister of hope and reassurance in her dusty rose skirt and sweater, with her pleasant even voice.

Let's leave mother and daughter pushing against the odds as they emerge, while grandson moves on to discover the crack in his own cosmic egg.

What then of the lawyer? A man with his own lifeline to sustain — wife, children, who knows what? For our purposes merely the lawyer, a formidable figure with certain powers. We'll leave him poring over the rewritten will, translating into legalese the Final Notes of a dying woman transcribed by her daughter. Leave him scratching his pink head and crushing one more cigarette into the already full ashtray as his secretary longs for a smokefree environment.

Don't forget the burly cop with a musical voice. Mancini. His walk-on part carried peculiar weight. Badge, muscle, voice, gun. Laconic efficiency, terse reassurance. He's still cruising around out there in the dark, hooked up to the main desk downtown, listening for calls, training his beams on suspicious dark blobs in the night. He waits for something to move in the shadows. His hands grow sweaty on the wheel of the squad car, inside his fingerless gloves. The gun prods his hip as he and his buddy cruise, on the lookout for trouble.

Which brings us to the intruder, the one we never saw. Who tried to break in, whose loud voice, whose brutal knock vanquished dreams and woke us to nightmare. We felt him more powerfully than any of the others. He struck mortal terror into our hearts. Next to him, the lawyer becomes a wimp; the grandson a pewling adolescent. The sunroom, the kitchen, the bedroom, the very walls themselves shook at his knock, that powerful knock yanking exhausted sleepers from the depths at three in the morning. That pounding on the front door, that muttering and shouting. "Let me in!" "Let me in!"

The front door held.

The cops came.

Wrote it all down.

The intruder disappeared into the night.

No more voice, no more knock.

He left remains.

We never touched them.

Mancini carried them off.

As I leaned out the front door to watch the officers depart, squad car headlights shone against empty pantlegs, dangling. For just an instant I saw them swinging there in the light, limp, bodiless, mere cloth, a vestige. . . .

I never saw the abandoned sneakers.

I never saw the piece of cake.

How did Mancini know it was a birthday cake? Did it have a flower of pink frosting? Was there part of a message?

Someone had a party.

That's all I know.

Going home, he found the wrong house, knocked on the wrong door.

That's all we know.

Despite our terror, the lifeline held.

THE MAGIC MONASTERY

Its doors were immense and golden. The polished wood catching the light of early morning almost reflected the face of the child knocking. She made a fist and knocked harder. The doorknob was above her reach, a square metal knob with intricate designs on all sides. She pushed her whole small weight against the golden flatness but nothing gave. Somewhere far off birds had begun to sing. Soon the sun would be fully up. No sound came from within.

Until she heard a step — light, faint. And then — just beyond her reach, for she had stretched to test — just above the light soft curls she had pressed against the door, she heard, then saw, the knob begin to turn. It made one complete revolution, like some alien metallic planet, and the door began to open, inward.

"Yes?"

A soft voice, almost a whisper.

"Please may I come in?"

"You wish to come in here?"

"Yes, please. Or at least to see."

So far the child could see nothing. Something held her back from pushing her way in. She wasn't that kind of child anyhow. She had been trained to manners.

"What was it you thought you'd see, child?"

"I — I don't know. But the house is so huge, so fine, and all the windows . . . " — here the child sounded breathless, as if stretching to discover words with which to answer this voice — "so brilliant. . . . I was coming up over the hill back there and your windows on the top, they gleamed like emeralds, and on the other floor — all red, ruby windows. . . . I came because I'd never seen light like that. And I thought it must be very beautiful inside."

"Indeed."

The door opened a little wider. The child stepped forward, one step, and found her head at the waist of a tall figure in a long black robe. A face looked down at her, not unkindly.

"We do not usually have visitors," said the figure.

"Never?" The child had her persistence up now. She had got the door opened. "Never at all?"

"Seldom." The face looked down at her gravely, a fine face — nose straight and chiselled, lips parted now in a half smile, eyes dark and welcoming. Her head was covered. "But we love to see children."

"Then can I come in?"

When the child bent her head back to look up and plead her case a small crick started in her neck. So tired from all that walking . . . would they be looking for her yet?

"Come in."

What a warm voice, promising nothing. But welcoming.

She entered.

❧

The large square hall in which she stood dazzled her when she looked down. Little bits of gleaming stone made intricate patterns all over . . . rivers of shininess here, glistening stars, sapphire mountains, topaz animals crouching, or running, or leaping — like those wonderful lines her eyes would trace on the page as her mother read to her at night, a wilderness of line and color. If you listened hard and looked closely you could find the shapes. Her favorite was *Where the Wild Things Are.* She would bend her head down close to the page and nestle against her mother's warm body before darkness came and she was left listening to voices of grownups floating up from downstairs. She knew something about lines like these.

Only these seemed to hold no threat. Forgetting for a moment her welcomer, she moved across the brilliant floor studying it. An animal here. A lamb? Knees bent. Huge round golden circle. She traced it with her feet in her new Mary Janes her mother had bought her for the party. One toe touched blue, a glorious deep blue, truer than the sky of yesterday. Today's sky had not yet grown blue. When she'd left the world it was still grey, a pink mist rising above distant trees, gathering to disappear. Soon the sun would be up.

Tap. Tap. Tap. She traced the figures on the floor with her shiny patent leather.

"Do you like that?"

The voice imposed no response. It waited.

"Is there more?"

Her mother had often accused her of asking for too much. "Take what you are offered, Claire. Do not always ask for more."

She remembered that now with a stab of guilt, but she felt disinclined to settle for a front hall. Surely there was an upstairs, a downstairs, a milady's chamber. Where were the ladies? Who were the ladies? Now and then her father, a tall serious man with ideas, had said, "That place has nothing to do with you, with us." And they'd passed on by. But when she'd twisted around in the back seat and peered through the exhaust puffing up behind their car, the tall spired building with its brilliant windows and high walls had looked . . . well . . . interesting. Only this morning she had felt it to be compelling. That was more than interesting.

The figure came forward. "Yes, there's more. Would you like to see?"

The child took her hand. "Yes, please." She took care to remember the please. One felt this to be a place of politeness.

They started out.

The corridor leading back from the brilliant front hall was dark and narrow. Claire was disappointed but didn't let on. The ceilings felt too low, the walls too close. She held the warm dry hand tight. They were walking straight ahead. Somewhere far behind her she still felt the huge front door. . . . Would they be looking for her yet?

Her arm scratched against the wall. Stone pulled at the sleeve of her voile blouse, the new one Mother had said yes, she could wear just today. Did it make a hole, she wondered, but dared not ask to stop and look. The hand holding hers was firm and propelling. They were going somewhere . . .

They came to another door at the end of the corridor, directly opposite the front door. Her guide put her hand on the silver knob and turned it.

Inside — a vast chamber with a black and white floor. Lines of black, perfectly symmetrical, parallel to the doorway. Claire stared.

"Look up," said her guide.

Ah! How brilliant, how crystalline . . . as if someone had taken iridescent markers and traced with the most exacting care all over the ceiling a sky more brilliant than real, galaxies deeper than space, purple and green and gold and magic silver stars shooting an arc through time and space. Her heart leapt.

"But why?" she asked, looking again at the dreary floor. "Why only the ceiling — "

And then her heart gave a sudden spasm. Could it be? Near her, one of the black lines squiggled. Then another. And another. Until it seemed the whole floor was alive with black worms which turned and turned until she saw . . . they were figures. Human. Like her guide.

Horrified, she looked up.

"What *are* they?"

"They are learning."

"But what *are* they?"

"Learning to be humble."

She could think of no response. It wasn't a familiar word. She'd heard it once or twice. Was it Hansel and Gretel? It certainly wasn't Babar. *Humble.* . . . Giapetto, maybe, for didn't he struggle to make a shirt for Pinocchio? But what had Pinnochio to do with these black forms lying there pointing their noses at the white floor? At the very least couldn't they turn over and stare at a ceiling so brilliant it must dazzle, perhaps blind them?

"Do they ever get up?"

"For a while. When they're ready. But their struggle is to learn to be humble."

"Have *you* been there?"

Looking at the grave knowing face above her, Claire felt impertinent. Like the time she asked Mother if *she'd* ever got Messy Work written on a paper. Miss Sticks was always after Claire to stop peeling her crayons and get to work. What was the point? More interesting to feel the thin paper give way, touch the smooth colored wax beneath, then look for the crayon sharpener and grind that smooth color way down to a soft point leaving little piles of colored shavings behind. Blue. Green. Red. She like primary colors. That's what they were called, she remembered now. Primary. And here was a whole primary ceiling overhead and they didn't, or couldn't, look. But why wouldn't they look at *her*?

She longed to ask these questions. Something made her not. She'd had that feeling before, of course. Lots of times she wanted to say things out loud at school, or home. Like what was so bad about boring a hole through the soap when you sat in your tub surrounded by bubbles? It was fun. You held the smooth slippery soap and rubbed it lathery, then took the nail-file from the closet and pushed it in, turning, digging, until right through the middle of the soap was a hole you could put your finger in. But Mother didn't see it that way. "This is *not* what you do with soap," she said. But it was. And what was wrong, too, with opening the big bag of white stuff in the garage and pouring it out in designs all over the floor? Of course, that was long ago. Ages. Beautiful hills of soft white sand, enough to create a whole world. But Father snarled and made you help him sweep it up. "This isn't what it's *for*, Claire." He tried not to sound mad but he was, his face red and knotted like it sometimes got. "I need this for the lawn."

So there were lots of questions she never asked.

She took the hand that was leading her out of that room. Quick! One last glance at the ceiling, its searing blue seeming to open on a vast beyond, the swooping stars. Hadn't Mary Poppins come down from just such a sky?

They were moving now through a small hallway, this one narrow and dark, too. A few pictures hung here and there, too high for her to make out.

She smelled something yummy. Was it chocolate? Rich and thick and sweet, like the cocoa they sometimes had in winter, marshmallows melting into a gooey sticky mouthful on top. Surely it was chocolate.

Just before they opened this door, her guide squeezed her hand.

"You must touch nothing in here," she said.

Claire's heart contracted. She had thought this would be different. *Don't touch.* Like when they went to the dime store and she wanted to handle a few toys. *Don't touch.* Some things

were all right to touch, though. At school the teacher sometimes said, "Feel this." She could tell the difference between
velvet and silk and wool. At home, when she got a chance to
touch in the kitchen, how she loved to stroke the smooth shiny
surface of an eggplant. . . .

Once, she'd broken a dish. She remembered it well. They
were visiting — special friends, her mother said. In a dull room
with no toys. There was one interesting dish on a table near the
couch where the two ladies were sitting. A china rooster, white
with red wattles. He opened at the middle. "Go ahead," said
her mother's friend, a big smiley lady with a musical laugh.
"It's all right, Claire. That's what it's there for." So even
though she felt her mother watching, she did. Inside — dark
brown chocolates, each set in crinkly paper cups, and one in
gold. She held the rooster top by his cold wattles with one
hand and reached inside for a chocolate with swirls on top. She
pushed against its bottom. Soft. Ugh. Quickly she set it back in
the dish and took a long thin candy with edges of nut showing
through. Her mouth had already begun to water. She could
taste the sticky sweet hardening on her teeth. Then — clunk!
Down it went! Three pieces of white china on the floor. . . .
Afterward, she couldn't answer when her mother kept saying
Why? Why? Finally, she stamped her foot and ran out of the
room. That had been the worst. She flushed the chocolate down
the toilet, then worried it might stop up the works. It didn't.

And now the door was opening.

Another large room — white, with smells. Along the sides
of the room were tables heaped with food, every kind, fresh
and warm. On the table nearest her she saw platters of fresh
steaming bread, mellow golden loaves, some shaped into rolls
and crullers. She looked on down the table but nothing
reached her stomach like the smell of bread. She was hungry.
She'd walked a long way from home. What had awakened her

this morning, anyhow? Something about the day, a different day. Yes, Mother had said, you may walk by yourself. Yes, we'll trust you to get there. You're a big girl now. We'll pick you up after the party. You'll be tired. . . .

Tables of food. On the center table — a large golden turkey filled with stuffing, rice and sausage, maybe. A little farther down, some other stuffed animal with an apple in its mouth. A pig? She'd never seen anything like it. And on the third table, to her right, fruit — piled high: apples, oranges, grapes, pineapples, grapefruit . . .

But the strangest thing. This made a shadow cross her heart as she stood there longing for bread but afraid to ask. In front of the middle table, in the center of the room, was a small stool like a milking stool. Empty. No other chair in the room.

"Do you eat here?" she asked, suddenly wanting an answer.

"We?"

"All of you . . . whoever you are."

"Oh no, child. This is for looking."

"Why?"

"We're learning mortification."

"More — ?" Puzzled, she looked up at her guide who had begun to turn around.

"Mortification. *Mort* means death. It means we're learning how to kill certain parts of ourselves. Each of us comes here for a time every day and sits on that stool, just to look. We must sit and smell and look and never touch. After a while the appetite dies."

Crazy. As crazy as some things Father said. He was full of them. "Stand up straight now and get your body in shape." "Work first, then play." "Room inspection each morning before you leave for school, Claire. You're old enough now to make your own bed." These words had the same ring, although she didn't understand them at all. She only knew the tone of voice.

Father had tried once to explain to her about death. Out back, when Pepper died, hit by a car. But all she got was that Pepper wasn't there any longer. So she buried him. The ground was so hard she had to use mother's trowel, and later the garden fork.

As the door shut behind them, she took one last deep sniff of that wonderful bread, enough to carry her down the corridor.

The next door was round. She must lift one Mary Jane high to get over the threshold. Behind her the round door stayed open. As she went through she had the oddest sensation, as though she'd stepped through a membrane as fine as Saran Wrap. Mother kept that under the sink.

She was inside now and everything seemed fuzzy. Blurry. She rubbed her eyes and caught a sleeper in one corner. It felt sharp and hard as she took it out and stuck it in the pocket of her jumper, pressing it into the corduroy. Green corduroy. Mother said it went with beginnings. She wore it the first day of school. She loved green.

On every wall were large dizzying designs. Black lines on the nearest wall opened up spaces of different shapes and sizes, like in her Altair Design book mother gave her in honor of starting school. "Something new, Claire," she'd said. "See. You get to create your own design, within these lines. You can make lots of different pictures." The cover showed a purple, brown and red duck eating pineapple against a pink background. That was only one way to put together the lines and spaces. Immediately, she saw another.

It's harder here though, she thought.

"My eyes sting," she complained, rubbing them again.

Her guide replied, "It takes time to adjust. If you stare long enough you'll begin to focus."

On the nearest wall no one was tracing. In front of the

middle wall stood three figures holding a very long pencil. Was it seven feet? wondered Claire. One, at the far end, held the eraser. One, in the middle, supported the bulk of the pencil. One, nearest the wall, took the sharpened point and found where to trace, in color.

"But how can she see anything up that close?" asked Claire. She had a habit of leaning over too close to her desk. Miss Sticks was always after her. And mother was constantly telling her not to sit so close to the TV. "How can the one up close see anything?"

"It takes three," said her guide. "The one at the far end keeps her inside the lines, the one in the middle spots detail, the one up close couldn't do a thing without the other two."

"But what are they doing?"

"Making a wall."

"But why?"

"It's prettier with a design than blank, don't you think?"

Indeed she did. She wrote on the binding of every book. And one night when she couldn't sleep she'd taken a marker and made beautiful red designs all over her bottom sheet. That had been bad. But the worst was when she colored the bathroom wall. She had a friend whose mother kept one upstairs wall blank for children to write on. She loved to go up there and make her name in daring swirls, leave her green name huge on the wall of Emily's house while Emily and her family were asleep at night.

"Why trace?" asked Claire. "Why not just do freehand?"

"Oh, no." Her guide shifted the child so she could look at the third wall, resplendent. "No one, not even three persons, could make so beautiful and intricate a design and never make a mistake. You have to learn first just how to see relationships. We practice and practice. The walls are erasable. These three are just beginning. They'll stay in here three months — "

"Three months! Do they eat or sleep?"

"Oh, yes. Now and then."

"And at the end?"

"An inestimably beautiful wall. If we didn't do this, how could we make windows like you saw from the outside? For we have made our own windows, too, out of fine bits of glass hitched together with lead, and heated. Stained glass it's called."

"Oh."

Claire could say nothing more. Never had she seen anything so strange. But her head was beginning to ache and she wanted to get to the second floor, at least.

"Is there an elevator?" she asked.

"Are you tired?

"Yes. I've come a long way, you see, and my shoes are new." She looked down at the pretty T-straps and shoved out a foot for her guide to notice.

"There's no elevator, but there's an escalator, just for children."

As if from nowhere it appeared, a long moving staircase with a golden rail, and instead of those metal grooves she was always scared of getting caught in when they collapsed at the top, this had alternating gold and silver steps, smooth and shiny.

There was room for only one person on each step. She stood behind her guide and held the rail.

Suddenly they were at the top. They stepped off and into a warm windowless inside room which seemed made of echoes. Objects crowded the room, musical instruments of all kinds, large and small, familiar and strange. All looked new — several trumpets, a curly French horn, an oboe, clarinet, tuba, and more. Claire could recognize many but not all. Some instruments were being played.

She watched the fiddler, a tall black figure whose dark draped arms sawed back and forth rhythmically. The arm stopped. The music went on.

"How come the music doesn't stop?" Claire asked.

Though no one was playing the piano, the ivory keys went up and down.

"The music never stops," replied her guide. "It's a question of learning to hear it. We prepare to hear it by learning how to make it."

Three sides of the room were lined with silver pipes — long, short, thin, fat — all polished to a dull gleam. Sitting before the pipes at a large console in the middle of the room was a black figure, her back to the two of them. Beneath the bench her feet went back and forth on something that looked like a huge wooden keyboard. Beside her, seated on a low stool and bending over an elegant golden instrument, sat another black figure, her face invisible. She plucked strings. From them came a haunting sound. Claire knew that sound. Her father had once taken her to a Marx Brothers movie. How she loved Harpo! He made music seem fun.

Even the fiddle was golden. She had thought of playing fiddle.

Some children in her school did, Suzuki method. Only all they ever played was "Twinkle, Twinkle, Little Star" and she thought it stupid. Besides, their mothers — or worse, their fathers — had to go with them to every lesson. She didn't want *that*. If she made music she'd do it on her own. Later, maybe.

Suddenly the sounds bored her.

"What else is there on this floor?" she asked. How long had she been there? Would anyone be looking for her? They were expecting her early at the party, for it was an all-day outing. Surely there was more to see. . . .

"Most of the rooms on this floor are music rooms," said her guide. "We all learn how to make, then hear music. But perhaps you are too young. . . . Shall we go then to the observatory?"

Ah, an *observatory*. She knew what they did there. Father insisted she know something about space. Not the *Star Wars* sort of thing, real space stuff. He'd gotten them a telescope. She was the only one in her class with a telescope. On cold nights he took her up to a flat spot on the roof to look through it. One night last year when she'd been only five he'd wakened her.

"Come on, Claire. You may not see anything like this for years."

She slept deep but he kept pulling at her and afterward she was glad. Her mother was already up there, and some of the neighbors. It was this giant display in the sky, colors of all kinds, lots of green, and even reds and blues. Primary. Aurora something, he called it. She stood there until her neck ached, staring up at changing shapes and playing lights. It made her feel small and happy and excited, there between them, looking up, not knowing how long it would last. They put her to bed before it was over.

"I know what an observatory is," she said brightly as they stood outside the music room. "But I really have time for only one more room. I've got to go."

"Fine. Did someone bring you?"

They were climbing a winding staircase now. It must be the tower she'd spotted first, just as she climbed over the hill from home.

"No. I came all by myself."

"A little girl like you?"

"I'm not so little. I can walk to school all alone. I've got my own two-wheeler. I'm off training wheels."

The stairs grew narrower and narrower. The figure ahead of her pulled in her skirts around her black ankles for the last few steps.

"I wish you had a balloon I could jump out the window with," said the child as she puffed up over the final step and stood inside a small room with eight sides.

"Perhaps we do."

The room had windows on all sides, in fact every side *was* a window. At each window, on graduated stools, sat four silent black figures looking out. Each peered into a long black telescope. How strange it must look from the outside, thought Claire. She hadn't been able to see the black cylinders from the ground. Some telescopes pointed upward toward the sky now red with morning. Some pointed straight out over the rolling green hills she herself had climbed. Where was the valley that held her house? Pushing over between two figures who never stirred, she peered out. How high they were! Had she really been down there just — how long before? Where was the door at which she had knocked? They were too high for her to see it, or perhaps they were on a different side of the house. She had lost her sense of direction. It didn't matter, she'd find her way home. But first she had to get on to the party.

"What time is it?" she turned from the window to ask her guide. She didn't have a watch. She couldn't tell time yet. It confused her, though they were constantly drawing her little clocks on paper plates and saying "Sixty minutes in an hour. Twenty-four hours in a day." She knew that much. But what *was* a minute? She could never tell. When she came home late from school and Mother opened the door to glower at her, "You're late, I was worried," she felt guilty for a second but didn't know what to say, for she didn't *feel* late.

What difference did it make? It would make a difference now. They would be looking for her. Maybe Mother and

Father had started out already. Maybe they'd heard she hadn't arrived at the party. Maybe the Robinsons had called. Maybe the police were out.

Sudden panic nibbled at the bottom of her stomach, the way it did when the fat black man who stood at the corner after school said to her, "Hello, little girl." Hadn't she been told not to talk to strangers?

She looked around the room at the black forms. They were strangers. All strangers. Even this tall lady with the warm hand who had answered the door and taken her around. How had she gotten into this?

"Please," she asked. "How do I get out? Do you really have a balloon?"

She hadn't even felt it. With no warning, her guide had puffed them up behind her — large pink wings, like a great angel.

"Ohhh," she said, feeling like Superman. "You put them on me?"

The two figures nearest her suddenly drew away from their window. Her guide unhooked the latch and pushed the window outward.

"Here," she said. "Just jump. You'll be all right."

"Really?"

She wanted help. She wanted at least a hand, someone else there. Like when Mother took her to swimming lessons on Tuesdays and Thursdays, and then she got so she could swim at the deep end of the pool, and then they said the children had to go up on the high dive. She'd walk out on it all brave and look down, then over toward the bleachers where the mothers sat, and she'd say to herself *It won't hurt* and look down again at the water trying to feel how it would feel . . . and then she'd stand and stand, and the swimming instructor would grow impatient, for children were lined up behind her all the way down the ladder, but he'd promised not to force them, so for two bad weeks she'd had to walk back in from the high dive because she couldn't, she just couldn't let go. Then, just last week something happened inside and almost without thinking she'd gone out to the end of the board and jumped and that was it. When she landed, she touched the bottom and still had lots of breath left to get back to the surface and swim to the side.

So she jumped.

And felt around her the soft morning air and felt the wings holding her up. They made her go slowly. It was much better than the high dive and besides she was doing it all alone, and she couldn't even look back because she was too busy floating, seeing out there all the golden maples of fall and the gorgeous dark trees she'd come through earlier — when was it? — and feeling the soft air smooth against her legs above her high socks, and seeing her skirt billow out just like an upsidedown tulip, and wondering how long this could last, this long soft float, but then, as she came nearer earth, she saw she was going to land standing upright, and that it wouldn't be in a treetop or a dump or a flowerbed but that everything was going to turn out fine.

And when she stood there and wondered how she would shed her wings, she turned around to see.

But they were gone.

RUPTURE

He smells of hair tonic or shaving cream, something faintly sweet and sickening. She looks out the window, trying to see down, but today there's cloud cover and nothing to be seen.

"Going far?"

He's determined to be friendly.

"Toronto."

"You're from the Maritimes?"

"I'm from the other world," she murmurs and, squeezing her elbow close to her side, tries to cut into the hunk of mystery meat Air Canada has served up for this flight.

He begins also to chew.

Claire Richardson is on her way to a TV show.

She is fifty-eight years old, in good health, reasonably good-natured, a bit flabby, going gray. She's decided not to touch up her hair. She has a husband, Jim, fifty-five, three children: Peter, twenty, away at university; Anna, sixteen, aggressively adolescent and recently tattooed; and Jerry, about to turn fifteen, a budding couch potato with a quirky imagination. She is resolved to accept wrinkles. She has been looking forward to this trip, a break from home routine where she teaches high school French and does occasional freelance editing.

She has left behind an angry daughter. It tugs at her now, Anna's anger, as she, escaping mother, sits high in the clouds, heading toward a guest appearance on Laura LeMonde's talk show. She thinks she's nuts to have said yes. Especially, given the topic.

The call from Toronto came several weeks ago, injecting excitement (fake, she thinks now) into a particularly gray November afternoon. She'd just come in from a brisk walk and was in the kitchen, near the phone, watching the vegetables and warming up the leftover stew for supper.

"Mrs. Richardson?" said the voice.

"Yes."

"We're putting together a program. Perhaps you've heard of the *Laura LeMonde Show*?"

"To tell the truth, no. I haven't."

Proof again of how thoroughly out of it she is. Anna was right. But she has better things to do with her time.

Like read her daughter's mail, she thinks now, staring out at cloudy heavens. It gnaws at her, this violation. She's particularly sensitive to the intimacy of letters, having resented for years the fact that hers were routinely read by censoring eyes. *Why* did she have to give in to that momentary impulse? She rarely invaded Anna's room. Privacy matters. How well she knew! We all need to feel some things are our own. Letters, certainly. But that day she needed the hairdryer. It wasn't in the bathroom. It could be in only one other place, so with dripping hair she'd threaded her way through the labyrinth and in so doing found not only the hairdryer but the unfinished letter her daughter was writing to a friend from summer camp. Open on the unmade bed. Asking to be read.

It was the very same day the phone call came from Toronto.

"Your name has been suggested," said the high girlish voice of the assistant producer that day. "I understand you spent some time, when you were younger, in . . . religious life? The convent?"

She seemed to have difficulty wrapping her tongue around the words.

"Yes." Stretching the phone cord so she could reach the stove, Claire speared a carrot and eyed a crumbling potato. "But that was ages ago."

"You've written some articles on that experience?"

"Well, yes. But again . . . that was a couple of years ago. Largely an editing job of other people's views."

She tried to gather her wits. The carrots were still hard.

"We're putting together a show on women who have been in the convent and have left," said the voice. "The statistics are interesting and we thought it might fascinate our viewers."

Our viewers.

"Why do you want to do this?" she asked. Through the kitchen window she could see Hal Jones, their next door neighbor, pulling into his drive. Jim would be home soon. Jerry had basketball after supper.

Late afternoon was always the worst time. Leaden. "I'm not interested in participating if this is simply church-bashing," she said, surprising herself. She harbored major gripes about the church. "If you intend to treat the subject seriously, I think you should have a theologian on the panel, and someone who's chosen to remain in religious life."

"What a good idea."

The response sounded genuine.

"I could give you some suggestions for names," she said. "Not people I know personally but whose articles I've read. Articulate women do exist."

Snide. She'd have to watch it. It was too easy for her to slip over into gratuitous irony. Already she was seeing herself on TV. What would she wear? What was she letting herself in for? TV was a medium for selling, as she was forever telling the children. Period. Boob Tube.

"We'll get back to you, Mrs. Richardson. Thank you for your suggestions. Before the show airs, we'll have a substantial telephone conversation with you to fill in background."

What, Claire wondered, stirring the stew, did they consider "substantial."

The people at Laura LeMonde took her suggestions, contacted the women whose names she offered, then phoned her back a few days later with a panel of four all arranged.

"We're calling the show 'Hanging Up the Habit,'" said that voice.

O God.

"You're participating in idiocy," her husband said when she told him.

"I think it's cool," Anna said. "What are you gonna wear?"

Should I tell her about the letter now? thought Claire. *Clear the air before I leave? Would she forgive?* One never knew with Anna.

Her son, glued to *Star Trek* reruns, eyed her coolly. "Watch it, Mom. Don't get too fresh. You can come on pretty strong without meaning to."

In her heart she hoped something could be said that was serious. She didn't want the panel to be talk-show-dumb.

Now, weeks later, floating on puff, hemmed in by male smell, masticating Air Canada meat, she regrets it. Is a talk show ever serious? Shouldn't she be at home trying to deal with her daughter? Does anyone ever really hang up the habit? Misplaced moral earnestness has been known to complicate her life before. It's a dead issue. Why try to drum up interest?

Face it. They ran out of topics. Reached in the grab bag and pulled out this one. Quick fix for the three-minute attention span: today, ex-nuns; tomorrow, prostitutes; next day, lesbian marriages; next day, adoptions; next day, the new female condom. Ho hum.

What made her, or them, think religious life was such a special topic?

So here you are again, she thinks, as her ears explode and the plane hits ground, taking an absurdity seriously.

At the airport a stretch limo displaying a large LAURA LEMONDE SHOW sign in the window meets her. And to think she'd never heard of Laura!

Toronto is even grayer than the Maritimes. She rests against dark blue upholstery and lets herself be driven through this drab Vanity Fair to the Delta Chelsea Inn where, on the twelfth floor, next to a window overlooking concrete canyons crawling with fashionable ants, she discovers a china dish with four chocolate cherries and a large fresh strawberry beneath a glass dome. Beside the dish lies a note. WE HOPE YOU WILL ENJOY YOUR STAY WITH US. Signed, so to speak, by the president of the corporation.

Later that night, when she has returned from a sumptuous meal at a gay restaurant run by the brother of her good friend Millie, she will find her bed turned down and a chocolate peppermint lying on her pillow. Beneath it, a deckle-edged napkin with a message on it in gold script: *Sleep Well.*

But she cannot sleep — despite the king size bed, the satin sheets, the extravagant puff, the full liquor closet in which, a couple of hours ago, she discovered a hermetically sealed bottle of cashews and, with the glee of a ten-year-old, pried off the sealing tape, popped the lid, and pigged out as she watched the late news.

Now she cannot sleep.
One scene will not leave her.

Midsummer sun beating down on them, they stand out back of the house. This is a comfortable sprawling summer home in Delaware, on the Elk River. She is standing there, beneath the clothesline. She has just hung up her wet bathing suit. They've spent the afternoon on the beach, stripped at last of their black serge, these ten nuns on holiday at the edge of the Elk. The year is 1963. Almost thirty years ago.

She wears sneakers, protection against the tall grasses wisping her bare legs. They are on a week's vacation from the rigors of teaching, studying, praying and surviving life in community. During this week their routine is more relaxed. Once they've finished chores and prayers in the morning, except for prayer time and dinner, they are allowed to wear the students' blue gym suits. A few of the older nuns opt to stay in habits all day, but the younger ones shed cloth readily and head for the beach in mid-morning. This is living.

The scratch of grass against her calves, her knees, as she stands by the clothesline should perhaps annoy her. Instead, it holds something fresh and electric for skin too long covered.

"How come you didn't go swimming?" she asks Sister Dolores, a nun two years ahead of her in religion.

Sister Dolores is taking in some things from the line. Two white T-shirts, a long black underskirt. She is in her habit, minus veil. She has put on her nightveil. Curly blonde hair sticks out around the edges of white seersucker.

"I can't. I've got my period."

They speak quietly. Even out here by the line, there's the possibility that someone nearby may be trying to pray or doing her spiritual reading.

Sister Claire pauses. It's always risky to tamper with another's conscience, especially in a world dedicated to formation of conscience. She decides to take the risk.

"Look," she says. "That's no reason to stay out of the water. We only get here once a year and you're missing the chance to swim."

She sees the perspiration streaming down Sister Dolores's pale face — a young nun with skin the color of worn piano keys, and soft brown eyes that carry in their depths a hint of something haunted. What that is, Sister Claire does not know. She's noticed it before — as far back as the novitiate. When Claire came to the novitiate, Sister Dolores already knew the ropes. Now, nine years later, they are both back teaching at the same college they had attended years before.

They've been at the Elk for three days. Only two more days of vacation left. It's ninety-eight degrees Fahrenheit in the shade and there's no relief from heat except the luscious soothing touch of ole man river himself as they swim around in gym suits. The full split skirts swirl and cling annoyingly against their thighs, but it's better than nothing. Better that sitting on the beach lusting for immersion. That's for sure.

They are a sight on the beach and they know it. They don't care. Yesterday a motorboat with three tanned young men wielding field glasses zoomed in close to shore and ogled them. One of them called out, "Having fun, Sisters?"

The Sisters waved back, laughing.

"But I can't go down to the beach," says Sister Dolores. She drops the clothes pins into a cloth bag attached to the end of the line.

"I'd . . . well . . . it'd be messy."

"No problem. Use a tampon."

Sister Dolores looks puzzled. "What's that?"

"It's . . . " Sister Claire stops. "Look, I have my period,

too. But I was darned if I was going to miss this chance. So I went to Mother Josefa and asked her to get me some tampons."

The sisters must ask for all their supplies, which are distributed by the nun in charge from a source called Common Good.

"She didn't even know what they were, but when I explained, she said she'd send out to the store. Don't ask me how she did it."

Sister Claire feels again the embarrassed flush on her face as she dared to ask Mother Josefa, a small, kind-eyed, simple nun of about seventy who was sent to take charge of these vacationing teachers at the Elk.

"What do you do with it?" Sister Dolores wiped her streaming face with a large white handkerchief.

"I'd have to give you the instructions. I kept them from the packet I got," says Sister Claire, remembering where she put them under her T-shirts in the underwear drawer in the dormitory upstairs where five of them sleep in an orderly row. "Can you meet me in a few minutes?"

Sister Dolores agrees. They'll meet in ten minutes out behind the garage where surely no one will be trying to pray.

Now, almost thirty years later, lying alone in the extravagant suite of the Delta Chelsea, Claire thinks of that moment, feels again the heat, the prickles, the puzzle of just how to deal with a nun she'd suspected might be given to scruples.

She hasn't thought of that word in years: *scruples.*

It comes back to her in a flash, straight from *The Spiritual Exercises of St. Ignatius,* as she lies there swimming in a king-size bed, her head on a satin pillow. *Scruples* — the tendency to judge something a sin which is not a sin. She even remembers his example. How odd, when she forgets exactly how many years she's been married, or what her husband gave her last Christmas. How deeply she absorbed it all! What an apt student!

Ignatius offered the religious neophyte the example of someone who steps, by accident, on a cross formed by two straws and judges that he has sinned thereby. A trivial example, he said, but not in a class with a bona fide case of Scruples. Real, full-blown Scruples was a disease of the soul, pervasive, exhausting, perhaps even terminal. The person so afflicted lost all sense of judgment, all sense of proportion. Felt everything she was doing might be a sin. Couldn't tell the trivial from the serious.

Claire remembers, too, the old Ignatian solution, one often told them. The only solution for Scruples, he claimed, was total obedience to an enlightened superior or spiritual director. The soul must confide in someone wiser and holier, someone who would direct the soul back to the path of right thinking. It was a matter of total trust. Total surrender to someone who had that ever-to-be-desired grace called *discernment of spirits*.

Ah, there's the rub, she thinks now. Someone wiser. Someone holier. Someone capable of discerning spirits. Laura LeMonde, here I come.

As arranged, she and Sister Dolores met a few minutes later out behind the garage, the sun reflecting off the bright white rear of the building, a massive clump of tiger lilies preening beside them. She'd brought the instructions.

"Look . . ." She showed the illustration, a clinically exact drawing of the relevant parts of the anatomy, isolated from the rest of the body.

Sister Dolores took the small set of directions and studied it in silence, frowning.

"It's a little tricky the first time. You sit on the john, at least that's what I finally did, you may have to search around a bit."

Claire smiles now, her head against the soft pillow, remembering. She could have said, "We're not exactly used to searching for the right place."

These are the things you think of later, too late, when you realize you missed a chance. At that time, she could neither have thought it nor said it. Instead, she just went on explaining. "You just insert it with this," illustrating with the round cardboard tube. "You remove the tube and leave in the tampon and a string hangs down."

Sister Dolores studied the mysterious object. She held it, turning it over in her hot hand. They were both in their habits now, veils and all. The bell for supper was due to ring in about ten minutes.

"And it works?"

"It works fine. When you can, just pull on the string and it comes out. It expands inside you. It's highly absorbent."

Like Christian indoctrination, she thinks now, lying there. What a thought! This is what it is to be raised Catholic — or what it was in the old days. It's a question these days just how much of any doctrine can be absorbed. In those days, you absorbed it, it penetrated the most intimate crevices of mind, heart, soul. Yes, even body. As you grew, it expanded inside you. Not so easily removed, though. Even major surgery couldn't do that. Psychoanalysis has its limits, though she's never tried it herself. Why suppose an expensive shrink is holy or wise? Where, these days, can one hope to find a discerner of spirits?

Such thoughts were not hers that day as she stood in the hot July sun by the Elk River in Delaware.

Sister Dolores glanced behind her friend as if she saw some-one approaching. She started to say something, seemed to think better of it. Then she handed the tube and the instructions back to Sister Claire

"Thanks, but I . . . I just don't think I could do it."

"You're afraid it'll hurt?"

"Not so much that." Sister Claire didn't think it would be that. Sister Dolores was nothing if not mortified. "It's just that I'm afraid . . . " Sister Dolores blushed, bit her lip, then finally spit it out. "Well, will it break the hymen?"

GOOD GOD.

The question had never once occurred to her! This was simply a way to secure time in the water, defeat the heat, float free of routine, minimize the discomfort of menstruation. And even Mother Josefa, dear simple nun that she was, hadn't de-murred.

This was a case where the end definitely justified the means.

"Heavens, I don't know."

"Well . . . " Sister Dolores was getting ready to leave. She looked sad, almost rueful. "I just can't do it . . . I just can't."

They never spoke of it again.

For the next two days, while Claire splashed around and chased small fish, welcomed the sting of salt to her eyes and the tantalizing itch of dried salt on her flesh, she'd catch sight of Sister Dolores up on the lawn, sitting in a chair, habit on, reading or just looking out to sea.

Will it break the hymen?

Rupture. Rapture . . . So slight a change, so great a dif-ference. She sees Anna in the kitchen two nights ago, angry, stamping her foot, turning like a ten year old to leave and walk around the block. With that toss of her long snarled black hair over her insulted shoulder. "This is how you always treat me," she shouted. "Like a baby. As if I didn't have a mind of my own! As if I didn't know what I was doing."

All this outburst, this stamping, this genuine distress and tension, from a little butterfly drilled forever into pubescent flesh beneath her fragile sixteen-year-old collar bone.

She came in half an hour later, calmer.

Claire was at the dishpan, her back to the door.

"I know it's permanent," said Anna to that back as she slammed the door behind her. The deadly calm of her tone was frightening. "I *wanted* it permanent. I've always been fascinated by tattoos. Chelsea's mother has one on her thigh. A Christmas tree. With decorations! At least I didn't go that far! I *do* have some judgment, you know! Even though *you* don't seem to think so!"

Claire tries now to shut out the thought of Anna, of the kitchen that night — the lingering smell of onion, the steamed-up kitchen window over the dishpan, the soft lather of suds on her hands as her daughter threw words of challenge and hurt against her back.

Someone is running up and down the hall outside the room. A door nearby slams.

She must prepare herself for tomorrow's inane probing, the secular mind in the form of Laura LeMonde, taking on one nun and three former nuns to question them, play out their stories before an audience gathered in the studio to listen, participate and gawk. But she cannot erase the vision of Sister Dolores behind the garage that sweltering day — rueful, determined, regretfully declining. *Will it break the hymen?* The pain in her eyes as she asked the question.

Nor can she quell the sense of Anna's recent anger. Their parting had been cool. "So long, Mom. Break a leg." Then, no hug or kiss goodbye, just slamming out the door with her jacket open and her backpack slung over one still-insulted shoulder. She'd always been one to hold a grudge.

The day of the butterfly upset — was it really just two days ago? — Anna had come home after school and gone immediately to her room. Unusual. As a rule, she'd rummage for a snack, flick on the TV. Later, she sat quietly at the supper table, saying little until Jerry left for his basketball practice. Jim was still out, delayed with a client.

Suddenly, as Claire sat there nursing her coffee, Anna said, "I want to show you something." The statement held no defensiveness, she didn't seem nervous. She pulled at the loose neck of her T-shirt until it stretched toward her shoulder. The fragility of the pale, flesh-covered collarbone smote Claire's heart as she watched her daughter and waited. What was coming?

There, nestled in the soft flesh beneath the bone, in exquisite colors of green, yellow, blue and purple, sat a small butterfly tattoo.

"Why?" was all the mother could think to ask.

"I just wanted to," was all the daughter could think to say, stricken by the pain in her mother's eye. It had been a lark. A thought-out lark. Six of them had made the appointment weeks ago, gone after school, made sure it was a clean establishment. They were savvy. They knew about unclean needles.

"Was it — was it very painful?" Claire tried to keep her voice calm.

"A little. Not bad."

Anna released the neck of her shirt.

Then, Claire's control broke down. She saw her daughter on the table, someone leaning over her with a needle. Anything could have happened.

"But — but why would you want to?"

She hadn't intended to sound accusatory. She did.

"This is the way it always is!" Anna said, like a ten year old, wanting to stamp her foot but knowing better. "I just wanted to do it. That's all. So I did."

She'd looked her mother square in the eye, turned on her heel, left.

Claire found herself unable to separate her own feelings, the confusing rush of them, the sense of that flesh broken, the flesh that had once been part of her, yet she squelched that thought because she wasn't sentimental, she did love her daughter, though there was a certain distance between them she couldn't seem to penetrate. At times the air between them seemed to grow clotted with unexpressed emotion in a way it never did between Anna and her father. (Or maybe, thought Claire, I imagine this. How can I tell?) Other times, the same air stretched out thin and vaporous, acquired a strange empty-ing power, as if it could change the substance of whatever Claire wanted to say to her daughter into pointless drivel.

What she couldn't confess to Anna, or at least wouldn't, was that she'd read that letter. Had violated that trust. Now, such a confession seemed ruled out forever.

She was paying for it. The discomfort would fade. It always does. But for the moment she felt bad and unable to repair.

The lines she'd read in that letter haunted her: *I don't mind lying to my mother,* wrote Anna, *I'm just sorry I can't share. She never tells me the stories like your mom. All my friends know stories about their mother's growing up, about their sexual experi-ences . . . about, well anything.*

She'd dropped the letter, forever sorry she'd weakened, sorry she'd snooped. Her face burned. She felt caught in a lump of sadness. Nothing could really help. Nothing at all. So her trespass became her burden and that was that. No way to exorcise it.

She left the house, walked out into cleansing wind, a bitter salty wind off the bay, and walked and walked, wondering what stories she had to tell her daughter. She recognized the truth of Anna's complaint. No, she didn't tell her daughter stories. She'd never thought of it quite that way. The problem is this, she argued with Anna mentally as she fed her face to the stinging wind: what would hold resonance? No point in telling a story that holds no meaning. There has to be some way to make it connect.

She thought of her daughter's friends: Isobel with her green hair, her sad frightened dark eyes, her evasive responses, her nose ring that so perfectly matched the flesh tones of her face. Isobel always looked hungry but wouldn't touch a morsel in their house. Moody Caroline, whose parents claimed she was a genius, who had no curfew and made it tough for other parents because Caroline, already an alcoholic, had her parents fooled. Jessie, already through one abortion and now involved with another sleazebag from grade twelve. Chelsea — what kind of a name was that? — always wearing calculated tatters with designer labels, who came to the house now and then, browsed through the kitchen, draped herself over the chesterfield, picked up magazines and books lying around and made comments like, "Your parents actually read this stuff?"

What stories did she have to tell?

Plenty.

She knew another reason she couldn't seem to tell them. Because they'd sound like high comedy, and looked at from a certain angle they were just that, but she wanted them to be more than that when she told them. She wanted her daughter to hear them against an echo of recognition in her own head, her own life, that would give them meaning. And that seemed strangely absent in the 1990s.

So she never found words to tell the stories she might have. Weren't they better simply forgotten, anyway? She'd thought so.

Though one couldn't really forget.

And now Anna's words: *I don't mind lying to my mother. I mind that I can't share. She never tells me stories . . .*

Anna was right. The loneliness of her comment reached deep inside Claire, touched a nerve she couldn't name.

She returned from that brisk, sad walk at five o'clock, chilled to the bone, ready to prepare a supper of leftover stew.

Laura LeMonde is tiny — five feet, perhaps. This morning she wears a black leather mini skirt, black heels and stockings (over excellent legs), a blazing green sweater, black beads. She has large dark eyes, short curly red hair, and wears shining red lipstick. Energetic, focussed, she is all business with her four guests in the ten minutes they have together before the show starts. She has rushed in to meet them after taping another show. She holds a sheaf of papers in one hand, notes on her guests furnished by her assistant producer, and sips coffee from a YOU'RE THE GREATEST mug as she talks to them in a firm business-like voice.

"In segment one," she says, "we'll talk about why you left the convent. What made you reach that decision — after so many years."

They are crowded into a small space outside the make-up room next to the studio. The four guests have just had their faces improved for the camera. Their hostess's make-up is already perfect.

"You" — Laura eyes a small slim woman in a flowered split skirt sitting to her left — "it is Rachel Beaubassin, isn't it? Am I right? You were in the convent how many years?"

"Thirty-five," says Rachel quietly "I just left last year."

"My. What an adjustment," breathes Laura. She shifts forward to the edge of her chair, crosses her legs, and swings one black leg as she talks.

"And you?" to Claire.

"Thirteen."

"And of course I know about *you*," she says with a wicked grin to the younger woman on Claire's right. "But tell me again, Judith."

Judith Frank, a slim well-tailored woman of about forty, carries herself with composed confidence. Obviously she knows how to dress for TV. Cool colors. A specialist in child management, she has visited the LeMonde show several times, offering seasoned advice on how to manage difficult children. "I was in only three years," says Judith, in a husky voice. "I went in at sixteen."

Doesn't qualify, thinks Claire. *Too young to know what she was doing. Adolescent.* She remembers well her own adolescent yearnings. The crushes on nuns.

"They took you at sixteen?"

"I had to fight for it," says Judith. She holds her coffee mug with both hands as if to heat them, though this windowless room is very close. "I had an aunt who was a nun in the same community. That helped."

"Ah, fascinating. You can tell us all later." Laura eyes each guest in turn. "Now then, I have all your names straight, I think: Rachel, Claire, Judith . . . "

She turns to the fourth woman, a nun wearing a brilliant blue suit. She is attractive, fortyish, with a gentle voice, a radiant smile.

"And your name is — Sister Clothilde deAngelis? Right? I'll have to practise that. *Clothilde deAngelis? WOW!*" Laura says it with italics, then swallows and laughs lightly. "Right?"

She eyes Sister Clothilde, who nods. "Okay. After we've dealt with that question, how and why and when, there will be a commercial break."

The audience is already waiting in the small studio next door.

"Then, in the next segment of the show, I'll ask you *why* you entered? What made you make that decision."

"I — " starts Sister Clothilde.

"Four minutes, Laura," says a voice from the doorway. The assistant producer.

"Okay. Okay, thanks. We'll make it."

"I — " starts Sister Clothilde again.

"Sorry, Sister. You'll have to hold it for the show. Now then, for the third segment I'll get into what everyone wonders, of course. Why is this life a life of celibacy? Why does the church require . . . I mean, it's not natural, is it? This is everyone's question. How do you live without sex?"

Claire imagines her with a different lover every night. The assistant producer has told Claire Laura has an eighteen-year-old son. She too has a hidden life. It's hard to believe.

"I mean the church is really down on women, isn't it? Can you talk about that? You can't be priests, can you?" She laughs. "Not, of course, that any of you might want to. But just the same. . . . And I understand that there are many . . . aberrations in religious life," Laura sets down her emptied mug on the small black table beside her, "and I'm sure it would interest our audience to hear something about that. Wasn't there was a book a few years ago about lesbianism in the convent?" She addresses her question to Claire.

Ah, on to something juicy.

"I never experienced it," Claire comments. "Though yes, there was a book on it. And no doubt it existed. But I don't think that's the real issue here — "

"Now just relax," says Laura. "Everyone is eager to hear what you all have to say. It's going to be an exciting show. I can feel it. And then, for the final fifteen minutes, the audience can question you about anything they want to." She stands, shakes her small red curls a bit, and pulls down her green sweater. "All clear? Any questions?"

The assembled guests eye one another.

What are we doing here?

The nun by the clothesline was named Dolores. It fit. She would have her share of dolor. But oddly enough the memory Claire has of her from the novitiate is of a relentlessly smiling face. That was encouraged in those days: compulsory joy. The children of God should be joyous. What does it mean if one who lives a life of faith is dour?

Sister Dolores as a postulant and novice, in the days when they were all learning how to be religious, set the example of joy. Upbeat. Bright, no doubt about that. She had memorable brown eyes, a round face, a wide generous mouth, a complexion of peaches and cream, and gorgeous blonde curly hair. That of course was covered now. She spoke in a slightly breathless voice and sang like an angel. The sound of that sweet pure soprano singing "Hark, the Herald Angels Sing" to awaken the postulants for their first Christmas was etched forever in Claire's memory. When Sister Dolores was assigned to teach the novices Latin, she greeted them daily with a Latin motto for them to translate. *Amor vincit omnia. Per aspera ad astra. Ad maiorem gloriam dei. Miserere mei Deus. Nisi Dominus aedivicavit domum.* Offering her Latin thought for the day, her eyes lighted up as if she were offering them a bonbon from heaven.

Sister Claire found it off-putting. Yet fascinating. She saw the tremendous effort of will. Even then, there was something strung very tight inside Sister Dolores, something that never relaxed.

Yet she was exquisitely, unobtrusively kind. She watched the younger sisters struggle to learn the ways of poverty, chastity and obedience, tried to help them through days that could grow bleak that long first winter. No task was too small for her. She was quick to kiss the floor when she'd broken silence, a penance Claire detested. She jumped to anticipate the smallest wish of their superior. In mid-winter she volunteered to carry garbage to the pigs, half a mile up the snowcovered road, a task everyone avoided. Always, she took the dirtiest jobs. This beautiful young novice bent her considerable intelligence to mining possibilities for humility in a life that offered a bottomless lode.

She was bent on becoming a saint.

The audience this morning is composed of about fifty women, all ages, shapes, sizes, sitting on a graduated platform. The visiting guests sit in a row on a small stage facing their audience. Laura LeMonde, holding a microphone in one hand and her notes in the other, fairly leaps among the audience. She seems to have had an enormous surge of adrenalin now that the camera's eye is focussed on her. It's hard to believe she just finished another hour of this with the same audience.

She waves her notes as she talks. Her guests had a few seconds before the show after Laura left the room. Three married women, one nun, all familiar with the patriarchy, one way or another. They've seen the pitch she plans to make and resolved, quietly, to deflate it. Maybe something serious will emerge. It's clear they're all intelligent women who have grown past some forms of bitterness. They are wary.

Laura works them quickly through the factual part. How long were they in? Why did they leave? Rachel: "I ceased believing in the structures of the life." Claire: "A tragic fire was the ultimate catalyst. It brought home to me that I had only one life." Judith: "I was too young. I was impressionable and infatuated. My idea had little to do with the reality." Laura doesn't linger over Sister Clothilde.

Now she's on to the juicier question. "I want to ask you what we all wonder. How could you . . . I mean . . . " — here she waves her sheaf of papers and turns to the audience for confirmation — "I'm sure many in the audience have this same question. It just isn't NATURAL to live without . . . sex. Is it? I mean why would you choose that? What's the point? You can teach, you can help the poor, you can do all sorts of things, but you don't have to go without . . . "

Ah, THE question.

For a fleeting instant Claire wishes she dared address the audience directly: *How many of you are married? How many of you long for a man? How many of you have tried it and found it wanting? How many of you really hunger for intimacy? Are you lonely? Do you feel valued? Are these real questions for you? Is there anyone you really trust?*

It isn't until later, on the flight back home, that she thinks she should have said, "Is it natural to live without God? Or without belief in something larger than oneself?"

But under the glare of blinding lights, faced by a hungry audience, prodded by a canny hostess and flanked by other guests, limited by the time allotted for commercials, one can't find these thoughts. The audience watches, the camera swivels, and the hostess paces herself and you, aims to finish each segment on a tantalizing question that will keep that larger audience out there glued to the tube.

What on earth *is* natural?

Sister Dolores taught in high school. An excellent teacher. Her major as an undergraduate had been English literature, her minor Latin. After the novitiate and her first profession, she was sent on to graduate school at Catholic University. It so happened that the septuagenarian classics teacher at the college would soon have to leave teaching. It was decreed, therefore, that Sister Dolores would undertake the study of Greek and Latin. Perhaps the reasoning went that she already had a start with the Latin.

Claire remembers seeing her bent over her Greek grammar, propping it up by the ironing board when she had work in the laundry, silently mouthing vocabulary as they walked back and forth to campus, straining always to look happy. It was a burden, no doubt about it. Languages did not come easy to her. But it would be hard to assess the weight of her burden in those days. They were all straining.

Even then, Claire knew that the assignment to learn Greek and Latin would have done her in. It would have meant the Boobyhatch or out the nearest window. Which would have won? She was never put to that test. Evidently her superiors had sized up the limits of her potential for virtue.

Sister Dolores, however, persevered and conquered. She went on to teach Latin for a year or two at one of the Order's academies. This was the late fifties, before questions of relevance and social usefulness became an issue for high school students. Her students liked her, even though she taught Latin. She was perhaps a trifle too bright, just a bit too resolute in her joyousness. Still, she was better than some of the lemons they'd experienced in their earlier years of Catholic education.

Eventually, she was sent to teach at the college. She brought to her classes there the same competence and enthusiasm. The years were passing. She was thirty-four. She'd been a professed Agnetine for almost ten years.

At the college, she and Sister Claire met again, now as teachers. During the school year following that summer of the hymen fiasco, Sister Claire began to suspect that all was not right with Sister Dolores.

Scruples. A loss of a sense of proportion. A tendency to see sin or fault in the most infinitesimal slip. A need to be constantly reassured.

She scrupled to use a tampon.

She scrupled to rupture the hymen.

She wanted to remain intact.

That, perhaps, was the first clue. There is no remaining intact. Broken is the norm, healing the wonder.

Such thoughts would come only years later to Claire Richardson.

The Laura LeMonde Show is still on segment three. Laura LeMonde has pranced up the steps in the midst of the audience. She turns to face her guests, camera swinging with her. "Can one of you explain this to me?" she asks, a challenge in her voice. She has not been satisfied with their explanations. "I mean, I can see wanting to do social work. I can see helping the poor. I can see teaching. But . . . I just can't see why you'd have to be living like that. Celibate! Explain!"

One by one they take her on.

"You completely overlook one part of this life," says Rachel quietly. "We lived in community. We had sisters."

"The point was," says Claire, suppressing her own sense of irony, "that as well as teaching, or social work, or nursing, or whatever the work of the Order was, our life together was to bear witness to Christian charity. To represent the reality of Christ in this world."

Laura looks puzzled and a bit anxious.

"Why," says Sister Clothilde, "would you insist it's unnatural? How can we decide for anyone else what that is? And by the way, I'd just like to say that you keep ignoring me. As if I'm the one who's unnatural on this platform. I resent that."

Laura is taken aback. Or appears to be.

"But, but," she insists, looking to her audience for agreement, "I still say it just isn't natural. I mean you were all normal women. That's clear. Why then . . . why no men?"

Later, as the family sat together watching the video, Claire's husband would say drily, "You should have said to her *what makes you think life with a man is normal?*"

"I mean, didn't you ever want to be married?" Laura goes on. "Or at least — at least share your life with someone? Now you, Sister . . . uh . . . Clothilde," Laura glances at her notes, "it says here that you regret never having married."

"No! I never said that! I don't know where you got it but your information is wrong!" Sister Clothilde is outraged. Her tone is convincing, winning. She leans forward, addresses not Laura but the audience. "I don't believe lacking a husband is the greatest loss," she says. "There are loads of miserable marriages. We all know that. I don't deny religious life has its loneliness. Of course there have been times when I might have liked a partner with whom to share things. But I have my community. They are my family. And I've taught hundreds of children over the years. They are my family. My life is given to God."

Laura tears her prompt papers in half, tosses them in the air.

"Well," she says, looking at the audience with a laugh, "I've been misinformed!"

Four years ago, Claire got a phone call. It broke into her universe of marriage, wifehood, motherhood. A voice from the past.

She had no French classes that day. She was ironing, an occupation she found meditative, as she listened to Bob Kerr's early afternoon music show on CBC radio.

"Is this Claire Richardson?"

She knew the voice instantly. Sister Dolores.

"Where ARE you?"

"In Toronto. I'm on my honeymoon. I wondered if we could come and see you. Just overnight. We have to be in the Maritimes for a couple of days."

Anna at that time was twelve. She'd just had her first period and they'd shopped for a bra a few months before. She was feeling grown up, shy and evasive about it. They'd had fun over the bra shopping and Claire was pleased at her daughter's matter-of-fact acceptance of her menses. Some things, at least, were no longer such a Big Deal.

"Come," she said to former Sister Dolores, delighted. "Stay as long as you want"

It had been over twenty-two years since she'd seen or heard from Sister Dolores.

So it was that Fran Cullinan, formerly Fran O'Neill, formerly Sister Dolores, arrived at the Richardson home on an early December evening. Fortunately, the predicted snow had held off. She and her husband Mike landed in Moncton, rented a car, and planned to drive on the next day to Halifax. As luck would have it, since Jim was in Ottawa, there was no one to share the impact of the visit with afterward. Except Anna, and somehow she seemed too young.

They arrived shortly before eleven o'clock. The children were already in bed. Mike was a tall, extraordinarily thin man with a pockmarked face and a scraggly sandy-colored moustache. His handshake was limp. *Dead fish*, thought Claire, as she tried to make him feel at home. She wanted to like him.

They accepted one drink, a Scotch, chatted for a few minutes in the living room.

"You're just here for a couple of days?"

"Getting some information on software markets in Canada," said Mike. "I have a little company in New Hampshire. We're looking to expand our markets."

"Mike knows everything about computers," said Fran, eyeing him with pride.

"You should talk to my older son," said Claire.

He didn't pick her up on it.

"What're you doing?" she asked Fran.

"For now, I'm going to help Mike with his company."

"She'll be a big help," said Mike. "She's a technological whiz."Fran had a strange puffy look. Before, as Claire remembered well, she'd been slim, almost skinny. Her cheeks looked bloated now, stretched and shiny. She smiled less. When Claire hugged her at the door, Fran's body had felt stiff, reserved. Still, her eyes were bright, she had the same breathless intensity to her voice, and she seemed capable of enthusiasm. She wore a stunning suede suit and a deep green coat with a high stand-up fur collar.

After half an hour of small talk, Mike yawned meaningfully and looked at Fran. "Well, I guess . . . "

His bride stood up instantly.

"I've put you in our room," said Claire, leading them down the hall together. "If you need anything, just yell."

She longed to corner Fran, ask her directly: *How are you? What happened?* There was no opportunity. Nor had there been any indication that Fran wanted that. Besides, why push it? Maybe the last thing wanted, needed, was a question, the regurgitation of a story, a part of a story. Some things were better left buried.

Next morning, Claire took Anna and Jerry to school. She came home, made blueberry muffins, and waited.

Ten o'clock.

No sound.

Eleven o'clock.

No sound.

She ate a muffin and drank a cup of coffee.

Twelve o'clock.

No sound.

She cooked herself an egg.

Twelve-thirty.

At last, the shower was running.

Her last view of Sister Dolores had been at midnight from a third-floor window in the girls' residence at the college. Sister Claire watched, on that early spring night, as two white-coated attendants carried a body out of the main convent across the street, wrapped in a blanket and strapped to a board. The face was exposed, but she could barely make it out as she leaned on the window sill in Sister Dolores' room. Just a few moments before, she'd climbed the stairs in the dormitory to talk to Sister Dolores who was always in her room at midnight. She found the door unlocked, the room empty. No sign of her. Sister Claire opened the closet: Sunday habit, shoes, nightgown, bathrobe all hanging neatly, side by side. The headdress and everyday habit were gone. She looked at the desk: *Dear Reverend Mother* . . . A letter started, unfinished, left lying there.

Disturbed, she had gone over to the window, looked out. An ambulance was parked in front of the main convent, where Reverend Mother and the older nuns lived. Claire jerked open the window. The sweet smell of lilacs hung in the night air. Above the convent a full moon shone, tinging the slate roof with silver light. The air against her cheeks as she stood there watching felt gently warm, like a loving hand.

The ambulance moved down the street. No siren sounded.

This was the climax. There had been a narrative, but Claire knew only bits and pieces, not enough to make a satisfying story. This last piece — the ambulance, the darkness, the body on the stretcher, the white coated attendants, the figure of Sister Marianne, community infirmarian, standing in the doorway of the convent with another nun (Reverend Mother?) and finally, the ambulance taking off down the street — had an ominous feel to it. Claire went back downstairs to her own room with a shadow on her heart. She wouldn't know for sure what had happened until the next morning, when she read the note on the refectory bulletin board: *Please pray for Sister Dolores. She is in the hospital.*

In the hospital. One never knew what that meant. What *kind* of hospital?

They had taught at the same college for three years. They had studied together in graduate school for one year. They had shared time in the novitiate. There were gaps, years unshared. Yet crucial times in the cauldron of formation they had gone through, survived, together. They were not intimate friends. They were sisters. And Sister Dolores had always been kind and generous, sensitive to the needs of others. She was a person who kept a promise, came through.

After that first summer at Elk River, her problem had become more and more evident, though no one in community spoke of it.

Day after day, in most of the free hours of the day, she was to be found sitting outside the superior's office, waiting. This was a busy community of eighty nuns, many engaged in teaching at the college. No one had time to sit by the hour outside the superior's office. Only Sister Dolores. She was there before class in the morning. At midday she could be seen there, sometimes with a book on her lap. After school hours, if she was not busy advising a student activity, she sat there. Sometimes she was saying her rosary, other times simply sitting. And in the evening, after night prayer, before she returned to the girls' dormitory, she could be found there.

Obviously, she was troubled.

"Now," says Laura LeMonde, "I understand that in many convents there were aberrations . . . lesbianism, alcoholism, whatever . . . "

WHY is she calling lesbianism an aberration? thinks Claire.

"Would you care to comment on that, Judith? Was that your experience?"

Judith is smart. "I would say," she begins, "that there were proportionately no more aberrations inside the convent than outside. There will always be cases where one seeks compensation . . . through drink, whatever. It could be a lonely life." She adds, "Even though it was a community, or was supposed to be a community."

Claire feels disinclined to comment. The camera facing them has taken on strange, ominous weight. If she speaks, she'll say too much.

Let me tell you about a nun who stood by the clothesline and wouldn't dare use a tampon, she'll say. She watches Laura Le-Monde prance about the audience. *Let me tell you how she was carried out one night to the mental hospital, how they put her through shock treatments, how she returned hollowed out, how I never saw her afterward until she appeared at my house one December evening twenty-two years later . . . Let me tell you what I felt, what I saw.*

You want aberrations? I'll give you aberrations.

Frances and her new husband never came to breakfast. Around two o'clock that afternoon they arrived in the kitchen, a bit sheepish. Hungry. Ready for whatever Claire could concoct for them.

They were in a hurry. Fran was, perhaps, embarrassed. It was hard to tell. She still carried traces of the old resolute smile. Still the same shell — protectiveness? self-doubt? virtue? scrupulosity? — that one could never really break through. And perhaps, anyway, that wouldn't have been a good thing. There had been enough breaking. That was clear.

Claire offered them grilled cheese sandwiches, a salad, fancy cookies from a tin. She asked no questions. If Fran wanted to talk, she'd find a way.

Tell me, she wanted to ask. *How is it? Are you okay? How is marriage? Are you afraid? Does he treat you well? Is he a boor? A bore? Were you a fool?*

She said none of this.

She was a perfect hostess.

There are stories we never tell.

I don't mind lying to her, said Anna's note to her friend. *I only mind that I can't share. That she never tells me any stories like other mothers do.*

Why don't we tell them? What keeps us back, makes us hold them in? Is it the fear that there's no one to hear?

Laura LeMonde is untroubled by such a scruple.

Look at her now as, into the last segment of her show, she cruises through the audience with her microphone, looking for raised hands. "Come now," she says. "Some of you must have questions. I want a question, a comment. Ah, here's one!"

A thin woman in a yellow coat. Loose mousey hair falls about her thin face. She brushes it out of her eyes as she speaks into the mike Laura holds before her like a chalice to catch the golden question.

"I'd just like to say to you all," says the woman, her voice shaking, "that I'm in awe of you. I think we all are. You've done something with your lives. You took a risk, made a commitment. And most of us, in the rush of everyday, don't ever do that — "

Claire feels like vomiting. She leans forward to interrupt.

"I want to answer you," she says loudly, distinctly. "Why do you insist on making us *different*? Can't you see there's more that joins us than separates us?" The woman is listening, shaking her head. "We've put ourselves together today to be on TV, we're up here separated from you, but really, underneath it all, we have the same problems as you. We just had a certain chance and a certain kind of conditioning. Three of us chose to leave that life. One of us remained in. But we're still women, all of us, we're still more like you than different. We're still human beings."

The woman is stubborn in her point of view.

"No," she says. "You've done something."

"My younger sister," says Rachel quietly, "has two small children. When I visit her, I see what an opportunity I had, in one sense. I had the time to reflect, to consider my life, to *look* at it. That's a real luxury. Most women, especially those who have a family and are also working at a job outside their homes, simply don't have time."

The woman is nodding. "That's it," she agrees. "But you took the opportunity. You *did something.*"

One afternoon in the February before Sister Dolores was taken away, a few months before Claire left the Order forever, they met in one of the classroom buildings. Sister Dolores was coming out of class. She looked haggard. She stopped Sister Claire, muttered something to her.

"Pardon?"

Even here, away from the convent, Sister Dolores was using the silence tone, a tone usually reserved for after Great Silence or within the convent walls. Sister Claire was struck by a look of desperation in her sister's eyes.

"I said, could — could I see you for a few moments?"

"Sure. Where?"

They looked about.

"Maybe down the hall in the faculty office room?"

This was a large room for the use of younger faculty, with ten desks spaced equidistant from each other. It was Friday afternoon. No one would be there.

They went down the corridor, pushed open the heavy door. Empty.

They went to a far corner and sat down. Or Sister Claire did. Sister Dolores remained standing.

"What's up?"

"It's just that . . . well, she's refusing to see me."

Sister Dolores looked around nervously, anxious that she might be overheard.

"She?"

"Reverend Mother."

Sister Claire saw Sister Dolores's left eye begin to quiver. Would she start to cry?

"Sit down," she said, pointing to the chair beside the desk. "She can't refuse to see you. Superiors are required to see any subject who asks to see them. How do you know she refuses?"

She was, of course, well aware of the hourly vigils Sister Dolores kept by Reverend Mother's closed doors. One could only guess what went on between the two of them. This was a matter too intimate, too private, to probe. Superiors were bound to hold their subjects' confidences as sacred.

"I write her a note and she doesn't answer," said Sister Dolores, finally relenting and placing herself on the edge of the chair by the desk. "I knock on the door and she doesn't answer. I waited for four hours yesterday. She never opened her door. I just don't know what to do." Her hands rested on her black lap. The cuticle was bitten raw.

Claire could think of nothing to say, nothing to do. Blank. She did not trust this superior. She couldn't say that. First of all, it would not be comprehended. Second of all, why inflict her own doubts on another? Pain and bafflement were writ too large on Sister Dolores's fair features.

"Maybe she's just busy."

Lame. They both knew it.

"But . . . but . . . you don't understand," sobbed Sister Dolores. "I have to see her. The voices tell me — "

"Voices?" asked Sister Claire quietly. This was definitely out of her depth.

Sister Dolores nodded. Tears were running down her cheeks,

falling onto her plastic guimpe. Sister Claire fished in her deep pocket for a handkerchief as she listened. "Yes. Voices. They tell me when I'm doing wrong. They tell me to see Reverend Mother. That she is the only one who can guide me. She is my superior. She is the voice of God in my life. This is the only way I'll grow perfect in obedience."

Sister Claire looked at her watch. Matins would begin in five minutes. She handed the handkerchief to Sister Dolores.

"Look," she said. "We've got to go to chapel. Clean up. You're a mess."

Sister Dolores tried a brave smile and began to wipe her face.

Sister Claire felt inadequate. A betrayer. No friend at all. Here was a need she could never meet. If she said what she really thought it would be destructive. There was no way she could make a genuinely helpful remark. The only thing to do, it seemed to her, was nothing.

"We've got to go," she said. "But listen, if I can ever *do* anything, even just listen, I will," she added, as the two of them stood.

The door swung open. A small bearded man in jeans and a sweatshirt entered. Mr. Stenson, the art teacher. "Oops, sorry."

"That's okay," said Sister Claire quickly. "We're just leaving."

"Seen Harry around?" asked Mr. Stenson.

"No, we haven't."

"Thanks. Sorry to disturb." With a quick last look, Mr. Stenson was gone.

And so were they — over to chapel for Matins, supper, recreation.

A few days later the midnight meetings began.

Incredible as it now seems, the dormitory had a nightly curfew then. Lights were to go out by eleven o'clock. Sister Claire could remember when, back in her days as a college student, curfew had been even earlier. A master switch was pulled at ten o'clock. Gone the days of those extremes, thank God. Time marches on. In these days, the early sixties, students would be roaming around until midnight or after, disdaining curfew. They did try to be quiet, however.

Sister Claire and Sister Dolores were both "Corridor Mothers," nuns who lived in the dorms with the girls as advisors, overseers, surrogate mothers. They stayed up late preparing classes every night. The desperate plea of Sister Dolores, her reference to "voices," her hour-long vigils, her evident distress of spirit, haunted Sister Claire. After midnight, impelled by a sense of impending disaster she couldn't name, she'd often climb the stairs to Sister Dolores' third floor room.

In her black bathrobe, ready for bed, her head covered with her nightveil, Sister Claire crept up the worn stone steps quietly, hoping not to meet students. Her slippers made no sound and she wore no rosary beads, so she travelled stealthily. A gentle knock on the door.

Sister Dolores would be at her small desk studying, perhaps, or writing a long note to Reverend Mother. Sometimes she was already in bed.

"How'd it go today?"

Sister Claire knew her coming might pose a conscience problem for Sister Dolores. Technically, in Great Silence time, one was to speak only necessary words. What was "necessary"? Clearly, Sister Dolores, whose whole being these days projected a certain hopelessness, needed help. Someone to hear her. That, at least. Week by week she grew thinner. She was visibly nervous. A few girls had questioned Sister Claire about her, wondering if Sister Dolores were sick. Her face had grown so thin her headdress hung loose against her cheeks.

Yes, having a visitor at midnight might trouble her conscience. What wouldn't? Clearly, Sister Dolores was past the power to choose her own poison.

"I'm okay," she might say. Or, as on one night Claire particularly remembers, she might burst out crying. More and more, she was given to crying late at night. "She still won't see me," she'd sob. "She says she has no time to see me. She's ordered me to stay away. How can I stay away if she is to tell me what is obedience? How can I know the right thing to do?"

The situation seemed crazy to Sister Claire. Yet, looked at from one angle, quite understandable. Sister Dolores had never been one to compromise. She took things to extremes, even in the novitiate. Always, though, to her own pain. She had absorbed to the finest jot and tittle the lessons of humility and obedience. She was ruined. No doubt a secular analyst would have a fancy name, perhaps even a cure for her condition. The term scruples, however, seemed accurate enough. A deadly disease of the spirit.

The stakes were high. Sister Claire sensed that. That's why she climbed the stairs at midnight so often. Yet she couldn't see just what to do. It seemed impossible to say: "This obsession is nuts. You need to free yourself of it."

Because she couldn't. That was clear.

So Sister Claire would stay with her, hear her out for half an hour, an hour, and wonder just where it would end.

Until the midnight of the ambulance, the body strapped to a board, the white-coated attendants, the shining silvering moon . . .

That was all Claire knew.

"You've done something with your life," said the woman in the audience. Admiration filled her voice. "You've *done something*."

There came one more scene — brief, troubling, electrifying — a week after Sister Dolores disappeared.

After dinner at noon the nuns would file through the long parlor into chapel to recite their *Miserere* before recreation. Not all of them could stay for recreation, of course. During the week many had duties elsewhere on campus. Most, however, could manage time for the brief chapel visit.

Sister Claire, as one of the younger nuns, was near the end of the line that day as they were filing toward chapel.

As she entered the long parlor, a sedately appointed room where, on reunion week-end, alumnae were treated to high tea by the nuns, she felt a tap on her arm and heard a whisper: "Sister Claire."

She looked up.

And stepped out of the line to face her superior.

Reverend Mother's face was almost purple. Her eyes — a bright penetrating blue — burned with anger. She didn't touch Sister Claire. She stood there with her hands hidden in her black sleeves, almost hissing as she spoke.

"Sister," she said in a low voice, struggling for control, "I want the truth."

Ah, the implication of it.

Sister Claire flinched inwardly. "Yes, Reverend Mother."

"When did you call Sister Dolores's mother?"

Blank. Utter blank.

"I didn't, Reverend Mother. I don't know what you're talking about."

"Don't lie to me, Sister. I want to know when you called Mrs. O'Neill."

"I did not call Sister Dolores's mother, Reverend Mother."

If she stood there another instant she'd say too much. What was the point? Clearly she wouldn't be believed. Sister Claire turned on her heel, away from that contorted face, started to leave, then wheeled back for a moment to face her superior. "I'm only sorry, Reverend Mother, that I never even thought of doing it."

As Reverend Mother opened her mouth to reply, Sister Claire wheeled away again and headed through the long parlor toward chapel.

She was furious.

Furious with Reverend Mother. Furious with Sister Dolores. Furious with herself. Because it had never once occurred to her to do that. Because obviously someone else had had the wits, the good sense. Thank God! Someone else had found a way to bring to light the hidden condition Sister Claire had seen and felt for months, but found no way to deal with. Someone else had taken action. Such a simple action. So obvious, if you thought about it.

And so necessary. No doubt about that.

But she, Sister Claire, for all her well-intended listening and praying, for all her supposed smarts, for all her wariness and calculation, had never once thought of calling Sister Dolores's mother.

Oh, there were stories afterward: How Mrs. O'Neill was enraged that the family had never been notified until Sister Dolores was hospitalized, diagnosed, already under treatment — but what did they expect? She'd left their life, put that world behind her. How the family made trouble for Reverend Mother — but how much trouble could they really make? Sister Dolores had merely sought a way to obey. Someone to obey. How Sister Dolores, returned from the hospital some eight months later, a shell of her former self (what exactly did that mean?), had been sent to do bookkeeping in an academy far away from the college.

By that time, Claire herself had terminated her connection with that life, that place, that set of questions.

Four weeks later, the promised video of the *Laura LeMonde Show* arrives. They're all in the living room viewing it: Jim, Anna, Jerry, Claire. Jim has made a fire in the fireplace and the room feels cozy as the logs crackle and he fiddles with the TV to get a perfect picture. Anna is on the chesterfield beside Claire, nestled in beneath an afghan. Jerry, sitting crosslegged on the floor in front of them, is stuffing his face with fresh popcorn. "Gotta have stuff to eat for the show," he said. Chomp chomp.

"Laura LeMonde is a pretty ditsy specimen," says Jim, adjusting the light on the picture. She's already into segment three. "Think she could tolerate a serious thought?"

"Anyone with her legs," says Anna, "wouldn't need a serious thought."

Anna wears a T-shirt tonight that should be in the ragbag. The eighties look. When she appeared at breakfast with it on, having silently rescued it from the Sally Ann bag, Claire concentrated on swallowing her coffee. All things are passing.

Anna leans forward, takes a handful of popcorn, crams it into her mouth.

Tonight Claire sees, more clearly than ever, that the whole Laura LeMonde thing was a mistake. Her idealism run amok again. As if this dumb show could reveal anything. Accomplish anything. But it's over. On tape forever. And little damage done. Certainly no good.

She feels her daughter's body, warm and solid, beside her on the chesterfield. They haven't said much to each other since her return from Toronto. Anna appears to be in a pretty good mood tonight. Maybe the popcorn, maybe just being here, in the warm room, with them, no pressures on her. Who knows?

Her T-shirt has a jagged gash near the right shoulder.

As she slips out from under the afghan again to lean forward, stretch her arm over Jerry's shoulder and scoop up another handful of popcorn, Claire catches a glimpse of purple and yellow through the gash.

It all comes back: Sister Dolores, the tampon, the hot day, the refusal to break the hymen. The board, the attendants, the desperation, the surrender of self.

Suddenly she thinks, *I'll tell her. Tomorrow. I'll tell Anna about Sister Dolores and the hymen. The whole damn story. Surely something of it can be communicated. I'll tell her how absurd I thought it was. I'll tell her about Dolores being carried out to an ambulance in the dead of night. I'll even tell her about the voices. . . . I'll tell her about the young men with the binoculars. About trying to figure out how to use a tampon. About the innocence of Mother Josefa. I'll tell her everything.*

Maybe she won't understand a word of it. Maybe she'll even laugh.

But I'll tell her. I'll give it a try. Take my time and spread it all out before her.

If she laughs, what of it?

Something may sink in.

Who am I to know?

PRINTED IN CANADA